The DURIAN PACT

Praise for The Durian Pact

. . .

'A timely read by one of Westminster's great insiders which vividly conjures up the fears and nightmares of our political class.'
James Heale, Political Correspondent, *The Spectator*

. . .

'Westminster veteran Christopher Howarth sets his unparalleled inside knowledge of a Conservative Party leadership campaign against an escalating global crisis in this entertaining, imaginative and rip-roaring read.'
Christopher Hope, Political Editor, GB News

. . .

'Christopher has been at the epicentre of Westminster politics for over fifteen years; his book merges fact with fiction. Frighteningly believable.'
Sam Coates, Deputy Political Editor, Sky News

. . .

'Christopher Howarth knows his stuff, and from the inside. He uses his first-hand experience to devastating effect.'
Michael Dobbs, author of *The House of Cards*

. . .

• • •

'A fast-paced, cracking good read that immerses the reader in the Machiavellian and murky world of party and Westminster politics (so well understood by the author) entangled with plausible real world events.'
Admiral Lord West of Spithead, former Royal Navy Commander and Security Minister

• • •

'A compelling read and so true to life that it is hard to tell where the novel ends and reality begins.'
Rt. Hon. Sir Jacob Rees-Mogg, former Leader of the House of Commons

• • •

'A great read. Takes you straight into the heart of Westminster. Believable and often far too recognisable; keeps you gripped to the end.'
David Maddox, Political Editor, *The Independent*

• • •

The
DURIAN PACT
When Two Worlds Go To War

Christopher Howarth

Published by Affable Media Ltd
Hampshire

All rights reserved. No part of this publication may be reproduced, stored in a retrieval system or transmitted, in any form or by any means, electronic, mechanical, photocopying, recording or otherwise, without prior permission in writing from the publisher.

© Christopher Howarth, 2024

The moral right of Christopher Howarth to be identified as the author and compiler of this work has been asserted.

ISBN 978-1-916846-15-9

Design by Vivian Head

Printed by Short Run Press, Exeter, UK

> The plot, names, characters and incidents portrayed in this book are all fictitious. No identification with actual persons (living or deceased), places, buildings, and products is intended or should be inferred.

Preface

It was 2028 and the Chinese Communist Party's 100th anniversary celebrations are a distant memory. Crippled by debt, a banking crisis and harvest failure, its economy has hit the buffers, a rising mass of unemployed men in the cities creating a political tinder box. In Beijing, powerful forces within the Central Military Commission think they have an answer – the long-planned invasion of Taiwan, the reunification of the motherland. But not everyone in the Chinese military agrees.

In the UK an untested Prime Minister is tackling an intractable problem – a new, ruthless and well-funded Scottish Nationalist leader who will stop at nothing to achieve independence. Her leadership is on the rocks and the political sharks are circling, key among them the former minister Tom Rosenfield, who seems to be the coming man with his record of opposition to Scottish Nationalism and warnings of Chinese expansionism.

In Singapore Mei Ling, one of China's Ministry of State Security's best agents, has been assigned a top-secret mission on which the future of the Chinese Communist Party depends, in her possession files that could shake the UK political establishment to its foundations.

Taking time off from a febrile Westminster, the newly elected Richard Reynolds MP is looking forward to a trip to Singapore to observe the UK's contribution to the Durian Pact, a military exercise involving five countries. Little does he know, but he is about to be plunged into the middle of one of the most dangerous political crises of modern times. Scared, alone and not knowing whom to trust, Richard is forced to navigate the colliding worlds of the South China Sea and Westminster politics. The Durian pact – a relic of Britain's colonial defence – is about to acquire a new and frightening relevance.

UK

- Ashton, Michael MP Chief Whip
- Bell, Sir Andrew, Admiral, Chief of the Defence Staff
- Braithwaite, Nicholas MP former Defence Minister
- Broadhurst, Jeremy 'trade official', MI6 operative
- Craig, Sir Iain Permanent Secretary, FCDO
- Edwards, Mark Prime Minister
- Fisher, John, Commodore, Commander of the HMS Prince of Wales Task Force
- Howard, Sir Bill MP Chair of 'Union' group of MPs
- Lacy, Robert MP Cabinet Minister
- Lord Strachan Scotland Office Minister
- MacIntyre, Malcolm MP SNP leader
- McLean, Sir Richard MP Chairman of the 1922 Committee
- McVey, John Tory Donor/entrepreneur
- Murray, Alistair MP Secretary of State for Scotland
- Reynolds, Richard MP FCDO
- Rosenfield, Tommy MP Cabinet Minister
- Sitwell, Angela MP International Development Minister
- Summers, Caroline MP Prime Minister

USA

- Aldridge, Bart State Department China Desk
- Gracey, Tom CIA London
- McColl, Jack of Singer & McColl LLP

China/Singapore

- Cai Qi, Mayor of Beijing
- Chen Wenquing, Minister of State Security
- He Weidong, General, Commander of Eastern Command, People's Liberation Army (PLA)

- Hu Zhijian, General Commander of the PLA's 73rd Group Army
- Mei Ling, a Chinese Ministry of State Security agent
- Tan Geng, Second in command, Ministry of State Security
- Melville, Victoria UK High Commissioner to Singapore

Australia
- Lloyd, Edward, Vice-Admiral, Chief of (Royal Australian) Navy
- McDonald, Bob MP for Cairns and member of the Australian Foreign Affairs committee
- Smith, His Excellency Robert Australian High Commissioner
- Spencer, John, General, Chief of the (Australian) Defence Force

Companies:
- Environ, a Chinese multinational technology company
- Greenslade Limited, a British investment company
- Hibernium Wafer, a Scottish based semi-conductor manufacturer
- Salisbury Partners, a British polling and public affairs company

1. Singapore, 15 February 1942

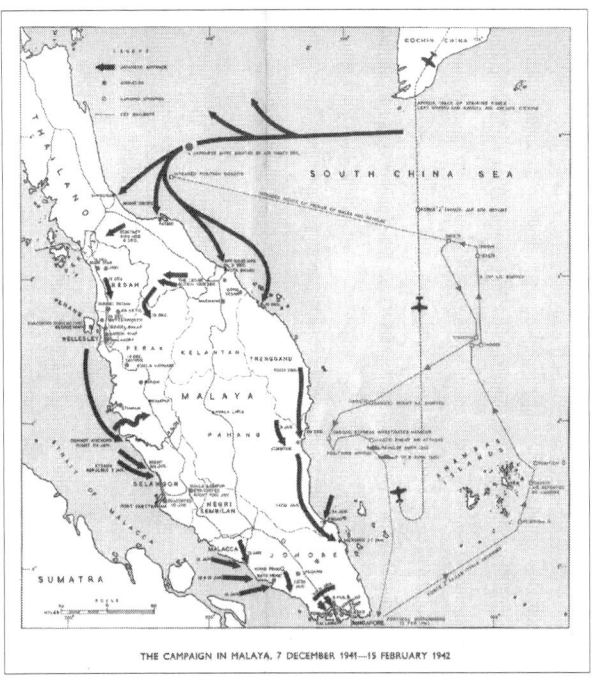

THE CAMPAIGN IN MALAYA, 7 DECEMBER 1941—15 FEBRUARY 1942

9.30 a.m., 15 February 1942, Headquarters Malaya Command, Operations Bunker, Fort Canning, Singapore

Lieutenant-General Arthur Percival, General Officer Commanding Malaya, read out the telegram he had received from his superior, Field Marshal Wavell, Commander-in-Chief, India:

> *So long as you are in position to inflict losses and damage to the enemy and your troops are physically capable of doing so you must fight on… When you are fully satisfied that this no longer possible I give you discretion to cease resistance…*

In the dim, flickering electric light of the windowless room, thirty feet below Fort Canning, the mixture of exhaustion, depression and helplessness was overwhelming. None of the eleven senior officers around the table had slept much for the last few days. None had had any real rest since 4 a.m. on 8 December 1941, when, only hours after their attack on Pearl Harbor, seventeen Mitsubishi G3M Japanese planes flying from Japanese-occupied Indochina had bombed Singapore. The same day the Japanese had landed on the east coast of Malaya and come up against a disorganised and ill-prepared British defence.

The British had had a plan – the Singapore Strategy – to defend Malaya from an increasingly aggressive Japan in the 1930s. The plan involved the building of a naval base in Singapore and, in time of war, the transfer of the massive Mediterranean fleet to the east. A good plan on paper, it had been rendered useless by the collapse of France, the removal of the French Navy, and the Italian entry into the war in Europe, rendering the Mediterranean a hostile theatre. There would be no massive fleet sailing to Singapore's defence. When a hastily assembled 'Force Z' did sail into Singapore on 2 December 1941, it was underwhelming, comprising two battle ships – HMS *Prince of Wales* and HMS *Repulse* – four destroyers and no aircraft carriers. This force had sailed through the straits and up the east coast of Malaya to intercept the expected Japanese landings, but, with no aircover, had been bombed by Japanese aircraft, the two capital ships sinking with the loss of 840 hands.

It had only taken the next two months for the Japanese to defeat the British Army in Malaya, and despite fierce resistance by Australian, British and Indian troops, the last Allied soldiers in Malay – the Argyll and Sutherland Highlanders – crossed the causeway onto Singapore island on 31 January 1942 before the sappers blew it up, severing the connection to the mainland. Britain's Gibraltar of the East was now surrounded and vulnerable.

Winston Churchill had understood the importance of Singapore, but somehow its defence had always come second to other priorities. Churchill had told Wavell that Singapore should fight to the last man, but the Prime Minister was in another bunker on another continent.

Eleven officers sat around a map of the island fortress of Singapore; it was diamond-shaped, the southern coast facing the Malacca Straits, the vital lifeline connecting British India to the colonies to the East, Hong Kong and trade with China. A momentary silence overcame them save only for the distant whirr of a generator, reminding them that the stale air was perfumed by the acrid taste of diesel fumes.

Lieutenant-General Arthur Ernest Percival had arrived in Singapore as General Officer Commanding (GOC) Malaya the previous year, fresh from organising the defences of the south coast of Britain from German attack. He was fifty-five years old, tall and angular, with a moustache that accentuated a slightly oversized mouth. But a caricature British general he was not. Physically brave, he had survived the first day of the Battle of the Somme and still craved active duty. But more importantly he had spent much of the previous decade in Malaya surveying British defences and warning a disinterested War Office of the dangers of a Japanese attack, not from the sea but by land down the Malay Peninsula from the undefended north.

Percival broke the silence and began to set out the situation.

Days earlier on 8 February the Japanese had managed to cross the Johor Strait onto the island. Since then the situation had deteriorated. Fierce resistance by the Australian 8th Division along the shoreline had momentarily looked as if it would hold the Japanese back, but their advance had proved relentless.

Percival methodically set out the situation. They had no airpower, no ships, they were low on ammunition and now, with the capture of the reservoir in the centre of the island, there was little water for their troops or the civilians in the city. Any hope of reinforcements from across the Bay of Bengal had vanished.

'Gentlemen, we have two options: we mount a counter-attack to retake control of the water supply at Bukit Timah, continue the fight and wait for reinforcements. Secondly, we can seek what terms we can from General Yamashita.'

Percival looked around the room. He saw sullen faces, horror and exhaustion.

One officer broke the silence. 'If a counter-attack has a chance we should try it. We cannot surrender Singapore; it's unthinkable. We have over 100,000 men here. The Japanese aren't invincible, we must be able to push them back.'

A second joined in. 'We may well have overestimated the number of Japanese, and they've been on the march for two months: they must be as low on supplies as we are. I say we give it a go. The orders from Wavell seem to me to be clear – fight as long as we can still "inflict losses".'

An RAF office spoke up next. 'All well and good, but we have no planes! If we did retake the reservoir, what next? There'll be no reinforcements: India and Burma are a million miles away and the Japanese control the waters. We'd need to retake the airfields to even give us a chance. I'm sorry, but we're out of options.'

Then a senior Royal Navy officer spoke. 'They've already sunk one of our most modern battleships. We need aircraft carriers, but they're tied up in Europe and even if we had them here, resupply ships would need command of the skies. I don't see how we can continue to fight with any chance of success.'

The air was stagnant: the recycling system that was supposed to refresh the room had packed up some time earlier and the mood of the officers was worse. None of them had ever imagined they'd be asked to take part in one of the most humiliating surrenders in their country's history.

Percival let the meeting run for a little over fifteen minutes; the room was dividing into two camps, one reluctantly accepting the inevitable, but a few still holding out. 'I'm grateful for your thoughts,' he said. 'We've fought bravely but continuing the fight would only needlessly endanger our soldiers' lives and those of the civilians. I will seek terms with the Japanese general.' He looked around the table. 'Are we all agreed?' There was silence from the officers who'd been arguing for a counter-attack.

'Well, we're unanimous. That makes it easier.'

He gestured to an orderly. 'Take down the following message for C-in-C India: "Owing to losses from enemy action, water, petrol, food and ammunition are practically finished. Unable therefore to continue the fight any longer. All ranks have done their best and are grateful for your help."

'Now – the matter of organising a party to go and speak to General Yamashita.'

The officers broke up, some remaining in the bunker

complex, others heading out to rejoin their soldiers. Major Buchan of the Gordon Highlanders, a senior staff officer to General Percival, headed along the corridor to a room from where he'd been organising the defence of Singapore. The latest in a long line of professional soldiers from Aberdeenshire, he was racked with guilt: surrender was not something he imagined he would ever experience.

Like Perceval, his father had survived the Somme. What would he think of his son surrendering the same battalion to the Japanese? How would he explain it when he got home? Would he ever get home? What would happen to them now? Major Buchan started to survey the contents of his command room. The filed messages and codes which would all now need to be destroyed.

Outside in the sunlight and the warm tropical air, the sound of distant gunfire and the crump of artillery was coming from all directions. Major Buchan could now hear it reverberating down into the bunker complex. Perhaps, he thought to himself, there was no other option.

2. Prime Minister Edwards

Whitehall, 18 May 2028

It was an unusually hot Thursday afternoon shortly before Parliament went into recess for the May Whitsun holiday, and as was traditional on such occasions, the air-conditioning system had broken. The pending holidays, the heat and the sweltering offices had subdued the cut and thrust of politics. After months of infighting, Prime Minister Edwards' Government was tired and MPs wanted to go back to their constituencies for a rest. Journalists were preparing for their holidays – filing stories for their 'silly season'. Parliament was emptying out. But in Dover House, something was beginning to stir.

Richard Reynolds, a junior minister in the Scottish Office, looked over to Alistair Murray, the Secretary of State for Scotland, and observed: 'As I've often said with Edwards we're always at least ten years away from a leadership contest… Or just ten hours – well it now looks like it really is ten hours.'

The day had started quite uneventfully, speculation circulating on social media that a tabloid paper was going to report that the Prime Minister had had an affair with Arabella Armstrong, a controversial socialite, businesswoman and political lobbyist, not the first blonde thirty-something he'd been linked with. These stories usually caused a frisson of excitement before they, like the early mist hit by the morning sun, quickly dissipated.

But by lunchtime some details had begun to emerge, photos of a party attended by the two of them. They weren't the best quality and the room where the drinks reception had taken place was dark, but they bore the unmistakable image of the Prime Minister. He had a glass of champagne in his right hand, his left arm around Arabella's slim waist. Despite his black tie he looked slightly dishevelled, while Arabella, always a master of her own image, wore a striking black cocktail dress.

They were obviously enjoying themselves and one of the pictures had caught a glance between the pair which seemed to betray the fact this was more than just a chance acquaintance.

Richard had flicked through the pictures on his phone on his way into work. As he saw it, the problem was not necessarily the content, for as inappropriate as they looked, the pictures themselves weren't particularly damning. Yes, she was pretty and yes the Prime Minister looked as if he was behaving like a teenager, but on their own they weren't dynamite. But it was only lunchtime: these were a mere taster to help the tabloid newspaper sell their next day's edition. He knew there'd be more to come.

Richard typed Arabella Armstrong into a search engine on his phone. He couldn't remember meeting her, but the name rang a bell. The results showed she was a partner at a political consultancy and had formerly worked for the Conservative Party. Not wholly unexpected. Her lobbying company was mostly known for its lavish spending at party conferences, sponsoring some of the better drinks receptions, and there were already unproven rumours of her relationship with the Prime Minister.

By the time the Tube train was pulling in to Westminster Richard had decided there was nothing particularly exceptional about the photos, but he did have one lingering question: why was she at a donors' soirée? She didn't appear to be a tycoon with her own money to waste on political donations so it must be other people's money that made her interesting: her clients' money. Perhaps there was more to this than just a tabloid story of an affair. The UK had by and large come to disregard politicians' sex lives, but money – anything to do with money – that would be far more damning.

Richard headed for his office. With the recess coming he intended to finish off some correspondence before going over to the Scotland Office.

'What do you make of the Edwards photos?' he asked of his assistant Tom.

'Doesn't look good to me,' Tom answered, adding, 'They look genuine, and there are witnesses.' They agreed that the Prime Minister had really dug a hole for himself this time.

'It's not as if this is the first time, but it *is* the first time since he promised a new start a few months ago,' said Tom.

'Quite,' replied Richard, 'very in character. Do we know anything about her?'

'Not much, I know someone who works for her, met her once at the Party Conference, she used to work in CCHQ some years ago, then as an adviser to Robert Lacy when he was first a minister.'

'Any other news I should know about?' asked Richard.

'More shootings in China, Hong Kong seems to be calm today, so nothing particularly new. There may be an Urgent Question[1] on it later, then it's just Northern Ireland Questions and the adjournment; oh and a request to speak on the Union from that new think-tank. I'll write something.'

---

[1] An 'Urgent Question' is an emergency Parliamentary debate held on short notice.

'Great', said Richard. 'Could you call the Scottish Office and tell them I'll be over to see Alistair after lunch; I think we'll need to take stock.'

Although Richard had only been an MP for three years, the last year had been perhaps more eventful than many MPs' whole careers. Since his appointment as a Parliamentary Under-Secretary of State – a junior minister – in the Scotland Office he'd been jumping from fighting one fire to another. It now looked as if the rollercoaster was about to lurch in an entirely new direction.

He had enjoyed the last year. Steering through controversial legislation had made him something of a lightning rod for the ire of the Scottish Nationalists and he had defended his boss from numerous political attacks. It had been a long year.

Until this morning the growing threat from Scottish Nationalism had kept the occupants of Dover House busy, but now only one thing was consuming Westminster – could the Prime Minister survive?

• • • •

Once at Dover House Richard knocked on the Secretary of State's door and went in. Alistair looked up from his desk and Richard took up his usual perch at the window overlooking Whitehall. Alistair remained behind his desk pretending to read some letters, but was equally transfixed by the drama unfolding on his television; his PPS[2] Peter Miller and Lord Strachan, their department's spokesman in the Lords, were also already ensconced in armchairs.

---

[2] A Parliamentary Private Secretary (PPS) is an MP who acts as an unpaid assistant to a minister.

Richard's mind wandered. Like half of Westminster, he'd been preparing for a break: a trip to his holiday home in Scotland, some walking, perhaps some fishing… But he was beginning to realise this was unlikely to happen any time soon.

He suspected the newspaper had by now put its meatier allegations directly to the Prime Minister for comment – a necessary step insisted upon by the paper's lawyers to mitigate any legal action. Number 10, Richard thought, would now know what was coming, but whether they were concerned or not was anybody's guess.

The four of them had been through a lot together, and had come to trust each other as a tight group fighting those seeking to weaken Scotland's place in the UK. They'd had run-ins with nearly everybody, not only the Nationalists but opponents within the Conservative Party, those who were either indifferent to Scotland's place in the UK or who believed that capitulation to Nationalist desires would buy them off. Chief amongst these was Robert Lacy.

While they chatted about the declining chances of a summer holiday, they pretended to discuss departmental business, sharing updates from social media, listing Arabella's connections to previous scandals.

By 4 p.m. they were all firmly glued to the television screen as the news came in. The line from the Labour Party was simple. While dancing around the libel laws, they were keen to point out that there were 'numerous issues the country had to deal with and the Prime Minister appeared to be "distracted" by other matters'; 'Questions needed to be asked about Conservative party funding'; 'Who knew about this matter, was the Prime Minister being lobbied?'

Tommy Rosenfield MP then came onto the screen, a long-term enemy of the Prime Minister and, in his own mind a 'thwarted genius, cruelly denied promotion,' he could hardly hold back his glee at Edwards' misfortune, his smug, puffy face oozing with faux moral outrage.

This wasn't a surprise to anyone: Rosenfield was one of a select band of MPs who never wavered in their belief in the overwhelming superiority of their own distinctly mediocre ability. Elected as a Conservative MP in 2015, he'd previously served in the army, although his uniform had remained carefully pressed and it was uncertain whether he'd ever actually left headquarters. Nevertheless, this was still enough to impress the selection executive of the West Berkshire Conservative Association.

However, despite or perhaps because of his high opinion of his own talents, ministerial office had initially eluded him. Through stints at the Foreign Affairs Committee and the Public Administration Committee, he'd made a name for himself within the Party. The 2019 election was to prove his breakthrough. Realising that the votes of new MPs would be critical, he set about cultivating the new intake from the minute they arrived in Westminster and he managed to secure the chairmanship of the Public Administration Committee. A small soapbox in the grand scheme of things, but just high enough to broadcast his views, starting with his resentment at not being given a ministerial job by the PM.

'Oh, that swine Rosenfield again!' exclaimed Alistair. 'He's really going for it. He seems very certain of the details. Perhaps someone's tipped him off.'

The BBC rolling news continued to show broadcasters standing outside Number 10, struggling for something to say. The irritating buzz of a news helicopter could be heard overhead, a tell-tale sign, a political story was about to break. The clip of Rosenfield wielding his stubby knife kept being re-run.

Lord Strachan, a jovial man in his mid-sixties, muttered, 'Rosenfield, so predictable. Why are your biggest enemies always within your own Party?' The silence spoke – they all agreed.

The television feed then suddenly cut away from the commentator to the familiar image of the front of 10 Downing Street. The phalanx of cameras and press across the road was growing, the correspondents excitedly explaining to their viewers that they'd been told to expect an imminent statement by the Prime Minister.

Richard turned up the volume. Alistair Murray, who'd been chatting to an adviser on the phone, went quiet as they all looked at the screen.

The door to Number 10 opened and a couple of staff members placed a lectern in the middle of the street directly in front of the bank of cameras. The quick-thinking Sky correspondent immediately told his audience, 'Now, if you look at the emblem on the lectern, it isn't the official Number 10 insignia but the tree logo of the Conservative Party – this means this will be a Party announcement. I think that can only mean one thing.'

After an awkward few moments, the famous black door started to open inwards and the Prime Minister walked out alone and headed straight to the lectern.

'Thank you for coming. Well, you've all seen the news concerning the new investigation into Environ Technologies. I'm confident I'll be cleared of any wrongdoing, but in the last few hours I've come to accept that this matter has become a distraction from the vital work the Government is undertaking at this crucial time.'

Richard Reynolds heard himself saying, 'He's resigning. Well, I didn't expect that so quickly.'

The PM continued. 'I have today met with the Chairman of the Conservative 1922 Committee to request that he accepts my resignation as leader of the Conservative Party and to start the process of selecting a new leader as soon as possible. In the meantime, I will remain as Prime Minister and Government will continue as normal. Now if you'll excuse me, I have important engagements to attend to.'

And with that the Prime Minister turned and walked back to Number 10, waving to the press corps, who were baying 'Prime Minister! Prime Minister!'

• • • •

Alistair switched off the sound, leaving the room in silence.

'So that's that then. The idiot – didn't we warn him until we were blue in the face? What was he thinking, inviting her to a donors' drinks party when half of Fleet Street were just desperate to get a pic of them together? And now what? We all suffer because of his stupidity. Well, it's always been like that, one moment pure genius, the next pure idiocy. I guess we should give him credit for the last election, not many could have pulled that off, but deary me…'

Richard joined in, 'Was I the last one to know about this affair? And I seem to have missed something else. What's this Environ company?'

Alistair looked up in surprise: 'Richard, I usually come to you for gossip! Yes of course, she was the worst-kept secret in Cabinet, and we know how bad that can be! There's been a complicated arrangement in the Number 10 flat for months. I'm not particularly surprised – difficult to tell who was using whom. I guess we'll find out eventually. But why he had to invite her to one of those donor meetings, mixing money and, well... it was always going to be a problem. Anyway, it wasn't even a good party!'

'You were there?' said Richard.

'Yes, Cabinet ministers were told to attend. Fundraising – those elections leaflets don't print themselves you know. I spent most of it talking to some dreary infrastructure fund boss about toll roads. Thought it best not to say anything before it all came out, but yes, I saw it all, not very becoming of a Prime Minister: he was drunk and wouldn't leave. After all our work defending him, he does this.'

'Did you see who took the photo?' added Peter Miller, who had remained subdued throughout.

'Not really, it was an odd guest list. Some of the usual donor names were there. I didn't speak to anyone from the Environ crowd; it's a Chinese company I believe, with a UK arm. Anyway, I was one of the first to leave. Lord Strachan: you stayed on I think, did you not?'

Lord Strachan replied: 'I don't know why they were taken but the photos are real enough. Edwards was hardly being subtle; he seemed quite smitten with her. I assume Environ was paying her for some indirect access to the Prime Minister, to lobby him. I doubt he gave it much thought. Money wasted for them I should think.'

Richard replied, 'Yes, I think the Prime Minister's motives were quite clear; hers, perhaps less so.'

He was left to his thoughts. Why had the Prime Minister

decided to pack it in? It was a bit messy for sure, but he could have brazened it out: he'd survived several times before. Perhaps he'd just had enough. But that was all in the past now. What did it mean for the Government, the country, the party and, indeed, himself?

• • • •

Since his university days Richard had been fascinated by politics: working out what would come next at any particular juncture had become second nature and he had gained something of a reputation for his predictions among his colleagues. But this whole episode had taken him by surprise. What was more, there was no obvious successor and when it came to a contest the Party was as deeply split as ever between the 'wets', who fittingly watered any policy down to homeopathic lengths, and the traditional 'right' with which Richard identified. The Party had split along these lines on Brexit and was doing so again on Scotland. What would happen now was unclear to him.

There's never a good time to change Prime Ministers, but Richard knew the next leader would inherit a series of particularly intractable problems, most pressing of which was securing Scotland's place in the United Kingdom. Richard was partly Scottish and although he'd lived in England nearly all his life, the fight against Scottish independence had been one of the first political campaigns he'd been involved in.

But who should they aim for as a replacement? Someone who understood the importance of the Union? Someone who had a fighting chance to win an election? Someone who was competent? Even if their preferred candidate actually existed, there was a potential rival who was competent in all the wrong ways. Focus on stopping him, Richard thought, and then hopefully an acceptable candidate would come through the middle.

The Secretary of State was looking pensive. He exclaimed to Richard: 'Well what now? That's all just bloody brilliant! He causes seven circles of chaos then just says I'm off, no warning. Leaving us poor souls high and dry!'

Richard answered, 'Yes, but what are we supposed to do? He never trusted anyone enough to allow a successor to emerge. The Cabinet, excepting yourself of course, is full of second-raters. None of them are remotely capable of winning an election. To put it bluntly, we're stuffed. But apart from that, it's all going great guns. I have a holiday planned, it's nice weather…'

While Miller and Lord Strachan chortled in agreement, Alistair said, 'Richard, if you were asked to pick a leadership candidate, who would you back?'

'Excepting yourself of course?'

'Ha! No need to say that, you know. I'm as tainted as he is.'

Richard continued: 'Well, let's think. Us MPs must produce two candidates and then the membership gets the final choice. That's the theory anyway. Now the membership – what is it – 150,000? That'll tend to favour our wing of the Party.'

Lord Strachan interjected: 'So we get a Grand National of candidates, but most will fall at the first fence.

'Yes, that's what usually happens,' Richard continued. 'Failing us finding our own candidate who can go on and win, we can at least try and stop someone truly dreadful getting into the final two.'

Alastair smiled at that. 'Yes, I said it was bad, but remember, if we have problems finding someone we like, then so do our opponents, the wets or whatever they call themselves these days.'

'Yes, they might be too clever for their own good,' added Strachan. 'But the one to stop is Robert Lacy: Machiavellian, as we well know, disastrously weak on the Union, distrusted by the voters and MPs alike, but he is clever and can come across as quite convincing. He might try again, but I guess he'll settle for being a king-maker.'

Richard chipped in. 'Lacy must be stopped.'

Alistair looked quizzically at him. 'Richard, I know your views on Lacy,' said Alistair. 'Why should we be so concerned about him?'

Richard continued, 'I don't trust him, the people he employs, the effortless policy pirouettes he makes when he sees an advantage for himself. He has no principles. Then there was that matter of the Party-funding inquiry in Scotland – very odd. Oh, and didn't Arabella work for him some years ago when he was at DEFRA?

'But it's not even that, Lacy's a potential threat in the way the others of his ilk aren't. If he were to get into the final two along with a 'wet' candidate – say Caroline Summers – then he tacks to the right with the members and is probably home and dry and Prime Minister in a few weeks. And we know he'd be a disastrous PM. So, this is a race for second, not first place We have to stop him getting into the final two, and that means denying him the centre-right MP votes and ensuring there's a left-wing candidate.'

Alistair had been listening with a grin on his face. He'd gamed this exact scenario himself many times but it was gratifying to hear it from someone else he trusted. 'Yes, I think that's it. Caroline Summers will probably emerge as the centre and left candidate. But I don't think she could win if there's a convincing candidate from the right.'

Lord Strachan was beginning to catch up. 'So, we need someone from the right who can gain enough MPs and then has a fighting chance against Ms Summers… Go on Richard, you make everything sound so easy.'

Richard continued, 'Oh this won't be easy, but I'm thinking of a certain female Cabinet minister, usually on our side, needs a bit of work on presentation but she is personable and could pull it off. I suggest Alistair calls her, sounds her out. If she's tempted, we'll need to form a team and get working.'

Alistair added, 'We also need one or two Party veterans to launch her campaign, and sooner rather than later.' He looked over to Lord Strachan in the depths of his red leather armchair. 'I know who can help, but we need to reel them in. M'lord, could you let us use your house in Lord North Street for a dinner?'

'Of course. Yes, I was thinking along the same lines; let me know a date. It's all yours, and I'll lock up the wine cellar.'

• • • •

At the other end of Whitehall, in the Department for Culture, Media and Sport, Angela Sitwell, the Secretary of State, had just finished digesting the implications of the Prime Minister's shock resignation when her phone rang.

'Angela, it's Alistair here. What are your thoughts on what's next?'

'Well, I hadn't given it much thought until now; unlike some we could mention I was totally loyal to the end.'

'Well, you know I'm not one to beat around the bush. If you're planning to stand, then I'd like to help you. I think you have a strong chance of winning.'

Angela responded coyly. She'd been thinking of this moment for months, years even, quietly positioning herself in case the opportunity arrived: a few careful speeches to the Party faithful, attention to her image, quietly cultivating the younger MPs.

'That's very kind of you Alistair, but I haven't made any decision yet.'

Alistair went in for the kill. 'Yes, but I think you can make it to the end. The candidate from the left will probably be Caroline Summers; if there's no clear candidate from our side, from the right, it leaves it open for Lacy. I've been talking to a few MPs and we all think that you could stop him. The members will vote for you over Summers… Think about it. But not for too long, please!'

Alistair sat back in his chair, quietly pleased with himself, and turned around to Richard. 'She'll do it. I could sense the excitement in her voice. So, we have a campaign on our hands…'

3. Washington

Washington DC, 18 May

Bart Aldridge, the head of the US State Department's China desk, had just called one of his brightest analysts, Joe Wright, into his third-floor office in the Harry S. Truman building in central Washington DC.

'Joe, have you seen the Senate Committee request?'

'Yes, got to love the timing, what with the turmoil in China.'

'What do you think the Secretary will make of it? I assume she's seen it?'

'Well, the request was copied to half the building!'

Bart was deep in thought. This was going to be a long week. He hated giving evidence to Senate Committees and the timing of this one couldn't be worse. With Chinese politics in flux the last thing he needed was a group of simplistic politicians stirring things up. But that came with the territory.

'Okay Joe, start preparing. I think we know what they'll ask about: the shootings in Fujian, our assessment of their likelihood of attacking Taiwan, and US preparations for it.'

• • • •

It was mid-morning but it had already been many hours since Bart had come into the building and the black coffee he was drinking in his glass-walled office wasn't really helping. For years his berth on the China desk had been fairly uneventful, a tranquil backwater compared to the Middle East and Afghanistan, but this was now changing rapidly. And today he'd woken to the news that the Chinese People's Liberation Army had fired on major protests in Fujian Province in the south of China. Suddenly he was on the receiving end of Presidential requests for information he didn't really have. And now a Senate Committee….

The Harry S. Truman building was the biggest in a run of official buildings marching off down to the River Potomac. The area was still known as 'foggy bottom' on account of the fog that could roll in from the nearby river: not, as some wags would have it, the quality of the intelligence provided by the State, but for now the summer's sweltering heat and humidity was more of a concern.

Bart had specialised in US–China policy for the majority of his youthful fifty-three years. Brought up in South Carolina, he'd never moved far, graduating from the University of Virginia and never quite losing his southern drawl despite a tour of Afghanistan with the US Army followed by a transfer to the Defense Language Institute at Monterey, California, where he'd opted to learn Mandarin. From then on his life had revolved around China.

He was competent and had an ability to negotiate various changes in policy over a number of years. When he'd started, US China policy had been relatively uncontroversial, second fiddle to Russia and then the Middle East, but that had changed: now everyone was an expert on China. Except the President of course, who seemed more concerned about the economy and attacking the Republicans. Anything that might upset the economy, the free flow of trade or, worse still, involve more military spending was unwelcome news to her.

Bart knew his subject as well as any official in Washington, and certainly better than any of the politicians who were likely to question him. He'd have no problem with the plodding questions the Senate Foreign Affairs Committee were likely to ask him, but they might not like his answers. They weren't the most dynamic group of politicians but Bart knew that even they must have spotted the huge red warning light flashing over China. A warning to which Bart had no answer. That left him in a dilemma.

He read through the email from the committee again. They were looking for reassurance, to know that everything was in hand, that there was no danger of destabilisation or disruption to trade. The US economy was beginning to splutter and the mid-term elections were coming up and there was no appetite for any noises emanating from the western Pacific. But this was too big and too immediate a problem.

'Joe, what should we tell them?'

'Perhaps break it to them gently that they've ignored this problem, refused to make the tough calls, for too many years. And now here we are.'

Bart looked up from his coffee.

'Very helpful, but if we do go public and admit we've been caught short by events, might that not encourage China? But if we tell the Committee there's no problem, that we can continue trading with China, let them believe the Chinese dragon's all bark and no bite?'

Joe looked thoughtful, his chin in his hand. His background was in economics, but the seriousness of the situation wasn't lost on him. 'Easy for me to say as I'm not the one having to go up there,' he said, 'but I think we should give them the blunt analysis.'

'Thanks Joe, we'd better start preparing.' With that, Joe left and Bart rang the assistant to the Secretary to warn her of what he was going to say.

• • • •

The day came around soon enough, an afternoon session on the Hill. Bart had two analysts with him and several files containing information on everything from Chinese agricultural yields to naval construction.

The Senate Committee room was vast, with a thick dark-blue carpet, white walls and pilasters. A large semicircle of desks pointed towards where Bart was seated, flanked by two other State Department officials and a Department of Defense general. Behind them were the two analysts and members of the public, making for quite a theatrical setting. Bart poured a glass of water to calm his nerves, but when that didn't work, he looked around at the assembled senators.

The Chairman was first to speak, a Republican from Colorado, an imposing character with a booming, direct voice equal to his outsized frame. 'Mr Aldridge, what is your estimation of the chances that China might attack Taiwan?'

'Senator Hurford, that is a complex question. I will try and give you as full…'

'A simple answer would be a great help.'

'This is not a simple issue, but I would say there's a genuine chance that China may attempt to invade Taiwan. With the current political situation there, the risk appetite of those in charge may have increased.'

And then it all started. Question after question came in.

'Thank you, Mr Aldridge. What is your assessment of how the recently publicised tensions in the Chinese economy will affect its foreign policy?'

Bart thought about this and answered carefully.

'Chinese statistics are largely a work of fiction and getting a true picture is very difficult, but our analysis, based on satellite data of crops and emissions, is that China is now in a state of acute crisis. Recent lack of rainfall in the south and west has led to scarcity of food and rising prices. The debt issue is beginning to bite and unemployment is starting to rise. The banking system is particularly fragile and any shock might cause it to collapse completely. But that said, this is an authoritarian state, and the Chinese Communist Party doesn't have to respond directly to public pressure in the same way we would.

'As to foreign policy, there will be those in China who see salvation in confrontation – specifically the riches of Taiwan. There are perhaps parallels with the years leading up to the Second World War. By 1939 Germany was on the brink of bankruptcy, with military spending amounting to nearly a quarter of their economy – a level they couldn't sustain. They decided that war was a way of avoiding economic and political collapse, the point being that Germany knew that 1939 was their moment of peak advantage, but with the UK and France rearming, that couldn't last.'

The senator jabbed a finger at this 'You're not accusing China of being in the same league as Nazi Germany, are you?'

'No, but I do believe we might be seeing something similar there. This is speculation. The financial and agricultural crises mean that a war today has perhaps a better chance of success than a war tomorrow. That is a concern.'

Bart could feel himself moving into dangerous territory and was relieved when he was eventually cut off. But the next topic was no easier.

'Thank you, Mr Aldridge, can we move on to the Department's analysis of the Chinese leadership?'

Bart paused, carefully choosing his words. 'President Xi is a rational man, but he is an authoritarian and a true believer in the Communist Party. He is also personally associated with the 'unity' of China ideology, by which I mean including Taiwan. In our opinion he's a stable personality, he may make a rational calculation based on his desire to maintain CCP rule. He's been brought up in the Party and cannot be seen to oversee the end of Party rule. He would also like to be remembered as the leader who reunited China, but his rule would be imperilled if he failed.

'So, what does he do? We've seen from Fujian how ruthless the CCP can be, but force alone won't sustain the regime. Xi can continue on the current course, or gamble on a successful invasion of Taiwan, gain internal legitimacy that way and harness the island's considerable resources. He'll make some sort of decision soon; any delay and his opportunity will slip away.'

The Senator for Colorado who was chairing the proceedings looked agitated. This was not the routine committee hearing he'd been expecting. 'Thank you, Mr Aldridge. The next question is for General Tucker. Surely an invasion of Taiwan across the straits is impossible?'

'Thank you Senator,' said Tucker. 'It would indeed be a major undertaking. China has been expanding its navy, but we don't think it's there just yet in terms of amphibious ships or airpower to guarantee a high chance of success; but the moment when it might be is foreseeable.'

'How about US assets in the region?' asked the senator. 'Are there enough to act as a deterrent?'

Tucker tried not to show any emotion. In his last few years in the Western Pacific Command he'd argued again and again for more involvement but had met a wall of resistance in Washington, the last humiliation being the cancellation of a planned freedom of navigation transit of the Taiwan Straits for fear of upsetting China, with the President herself ordering USS *Gerald Ford* to change course to bypass the contested area. Proposals for reinforcements, new missiles and planned US deployments in the region had all been quashed and the Chinese had become increasingly dismissive of US influence in the area.

He fought back a wry smile and answered: 'Senator, the Chinese have been building up their military for two decades now, while we've remained static. We'll inevitably be at a disadvantage, at least in the short term, if China were to further destabilise the region. We have no continuous naval carrier presence in the area and our bases at Okinawa and Guam are potentially vulnerable. We're not the deterrent and stabilising presence we were ten years ago.'

'General, has anything changed in the Chinese stance in the last few months, in terms of the forces at their disposal?' asked a senator from New Jersey.

'We've seen some unusual troop movements, perhaps linked to the ongoing disturbances. Their medium and long-range missile programmes remain a cause for concern, as do recent reinforcements of their illegal island bases in the South China Sea.'

'I see. General, lastly, I'd like to ask you about the recent Australia, UK, USA submarine pact. How useful is that?'

'Well, AUKUS is significant and it may unsettle the Chinese leadership. China is hemmed in by the island chain from Indonesia to the Philippines, Taiwan to Japan, and there are very few openings for Chinese trade to the "blue water" beyond. If our submarines can patrol these sea lanes, China might have cause to consider what would happen in the event of hostilities against Taiwan.'

The session over, Bart and the two officials quickly left the building. He noticed a number of reporters had been gathering outside the room, a sign his answers had been a bit too interesting.

Back in his office he was told the Secretary would like to see him immediately. Well, that was quick. He must have gone too far in his uncomfortable truths, but they could hardly fire him for that.

• • • •

The Secretary of State's offices were on the top floor of the State Department building, commanding views over the Federal Reserve and the Washington Monument obelisk, up the Mall to the Capitol. Bart had been up here numerous times, but this time he felt as if he were being summoned to see the school principal.

Secretary Christie was sitting behind her desk with a senior official.

'I expect you know what this is about, Mr Aldridge?'

Bart wasn't expecting such a blunt approach, but there was none of the animosity he had anticipated.

'Did you have to mention the 1930s? Still, you're not wrong.' Both relieved and surprised, Bart realised he wasn't in trouble after all. Christie continued. 'No, this isn't about that. Have you seen the recent National Security Agency read-out on the Taiwan Straits? They make very ugly reading. Not the usual PLA provocation but a fully planned exercise with landings, the *Fujian* aircraft carrier and, most concerning, signs of planning for the requisition of civilian ships and hospitals. And the stockpiling of fuel in south coast ports. We've really been caught in the open here. We don't have a carrier group anywhere near or even ready.'

Bart listened as a visibly concerned Christie continued. 'We, I mean you, need to talk to the Taiwanese urgently and get a full appreciation of the situation before it gets out of hand. I suggest you get out there as soon as you can. We need to know what we can do at short notice to prevent a full-scale invasion.'

4. Taipei

Taipei, Capital of the Republic of China – Taiwan, 24 May

The theatre lights shifted their focus to the stage, leaving the audience in darkness. The room went quiet and, after a dramatic pause, the soon-to-be-former Prime Minister Edwards appeared next to the Prime Minister of Taiwan and began to address the Taiwan Chamber of Commerce.

Taipei wasn't the obvious choice for Edwards' first appearance in public since the hasty announcement of his departure, but despite strong opposition from the UK Foreign Office, they'd been happy to organise it at short notice.

'It's a great pleasure to be here in Taiwan,' he announced, 'a free and democratic Taiwan that has a lot to teach us in the West.'

Edwards built on a theme of democracy, of freedom, the impressive economic growth that freedom and the rule of law had brought to Taiwan in the seventy plus years since it had de facto separated from China. He made the case for Taiwan as a democratic ally, stressing the importance of its dominance of high-end semiconductors to Western industry. At this point Edwards pulled the pin out of the rhetorical hand grenade he'd been fumbling with ever since his departure from office and threw it into the unsuspecting audience.

'This is why Taiwan will always be independent. It cannot be allowed to go the way of Hong Kong, its freedoms stifled, the outlook of its people closed shut by Beijing. Freedom is not merely a Western preserve but is present in all societies and is the right of all people on this planet. This is why we've developed closer defence ties with our friends and allies in this region, this is why we've maintained our naval presence in the South China Sea when others didn't. The West should and I believe will fight for Taiwan, for democracy not just in the South China Sea and Taiwan Straits but in the entire Asia-Pacific region. For let us consider the alternative. One where democracy does not prevail in Taiwan, one where an assertive China wins, where Russian wins, where China and its technology of repression dominates the developing world and, increasingly, in the West. That is the stuff of nightmares.'

His voice went suddenly quiet, as if he were taking the audience into his confidence. 'I can't say too much about it, but Chinese money and influence reaches some very surprising places. Well known, very senior personalities are in the pay of China, doing their work: I have a whole binder-full of evidence. But I won't go into that now.'

The grenade had by now gone off and there was no going back. Edwards moved onto more mundane matters, but the UK media wasn't interested in Taiwanese investment. A British reporter had chosen his one allotted question well. 'Prime Minister, 'would you care to name any of these "senior personalities"? Are they politicians or officials? Are they still serving?'

Edwards forced back a wry smile. 'Oh, did I say that? I probably shouldn't have. I'll refer you to the Official Secrets Act and the thirty-year rule,' he said, before moving on to a Taiwanese journalist.

Back in London the Prime Minister's comments were exacerbated by a 'source close to Edwards' claiming that he'd received from the security services a 'binder-full of personalities who'd received illicit funding from China'.

The media now did exactly what Edwards wanted them to do: speculate. But this speculation was not confined to the media: the Cabinet Secretary immediately summoned the heads of the intelligence services demanding to know if this list existed and, if so, who was on it.

• • • •

While Edwards knew that his speech would have a major impact on UK politics, he would have been surprised and perhaps delighted when the shockwave hit and reverberated on three separate continents.

Eighty miles away from Taiwan there was a very different China: the People's Republic. While on the surface the two countries looked very similar, in China the state was ever present, controlling what people said, what they thought. The Prime Minister's speech was not reported there, and neither was the financial crisis, the food shortage, and now the economic chaos caused by the Taiwanese suspension of the sale of their newest, most advanced semiconductors to China.

While Edwards spoke of Taiwanese democracy, in the city of Fuzhou another protest, based on a heady mix of unemployment, inflation and local corruption, was being met by troops of the People's Liberation Army. Students from Fujian University had surrounded the city's government buildings and had in turn been surrounded by a ring of armoured personnel carriers, with troops and security officials gradually arresting and carrying the students off to prison. This protest would soon be over, but the resentment would last.

Watching the crowd from a safe distance was General He Weidong, the commander of the PLA's Eastern Theatre, whose troops had been requested to end the protests. This was not a task he relished: he had a son and daughter both at university in Beijing and, looking out at the students, his mind wandered to his own family. Still, the protesters were a danger to China and the Party, and he had his instructions.

As a senior and trusted officer in command of the troops facing Taiwan, he'd received a transcript of Edwards' speech. It had shocked him. Not only had a Western leader, albeit a disgraced one, visited Taiwan, but they'd spoken of independence and had not been contradicted by the Taipei Government.

'This will infuriate Beijing' he'd said to a trusted junior officer. 'Let me guess – further exercises in the straits? One day we're dealing with our own students, then it's Taipei. Who's more terrifying, I wonder?!'

• • • •

Two thousand miles to the west, HMS *Vampire*, a new Type-26 general purpose frigate, was making its way to Chittagong in Bangladesh as part of a defence diplomacy tour that had already taken in Oman, Kenya and Sri Lanka.

Captain Barker, on his first command, was about to take a harbour pilot on board when the ship received a message from London: 'Reports that a Chinese flagged vessel *Han Hang Zhi* departing from Myanmar has been hijacked in the Andaman Sea grid 13 15 17 N, 96 43 14 E, proceed to grid and await further orders.'

Barker thought for a moment before ordering the grid to be added to the navigational system. It was over 200 nautical miles away and would take the best part of a day. He gave the order to alter course and notified London.

To Captain Barker this was an exciting departure, and potentially a chance to demonstrate his ship's capabilities. He allowed the ship to settle into its new course and then addressed the crew and organised anti-piracy drills.

Vampire was within a few miles of the stricken ship early the next morning. Visible in the distance with the sun setting behind them, it looked like an old cruise liner; smoke seemed to be rising from the bridge. Captain Barker notified London that they would attempt to contact the crew and give aid if possible.

At that moment the ship's radar picked up two aircraft heading from Myanmar airspace to the east directly towards the ship. Shortly after, two dots appeared on the horizon. The two fighter jets overshot the *Vampire* and circled around.

'Chinese J-22s – stealth fighters!' a bridge officer exclaimed.

'What are they doing out here?' asked Barker.

'Looking after their ship, I assume, but they don't seem very friendly!'

'Yes, send a message to Northwood;[3] tell them we're disengaging from the *Han Hang Zhi*.'

Suddenly a white tower of water erupted about 500 yards in front of the ship, a bomb dropped from one of the Chinese planes.

'Sound the alarm!' Captain Barker yelled; seconds later a siren shrieked across the ship's tannoy system.

'Action stations, action stations. Condition Zulu.'

With that, Captain Barker ordered the ship to turn to port away from the *Han Hang Zhi* at full speed. The vessel rocked at the sudden surge of speed and the noise of its engines increased.

---

[3] The UK's military operations HQ.

In London, the messages from *Vampire* had been received with increasing alarm. In the wake of official Chinese protests at Edwards' speech, Chinese state media had begun to threaten retaliation against Britain, openly discussing the possibility of firing missiles at any ships that entered the South China Sea. Realising too late that the presence of *Vampire* close to a Chinese vessel was a moment of real danger, defence officials' panic had only somewhat dampened with time as the ship put some distance between itself and the Chinese vessel.

The next day the Chinese Ambassador was summoned to the Foreign Office, but the move was pre-empted by a statement from Beijing:

'Yesterday a Chinese-flagged merchant vessel was attacked by pirates operating from the islands of Myanmar and subsequently threatened by a British Royal Navy ship in the Andaman Sea. The PLA air force responded with the help of the Republic of Myanmar to protect the vessel. The PLA navy will now send a naval force to protect our shipping in the Andaman Sea.'

• • • •

Two police cars were parked at the constituency home of Prime Minister Edwards, a fine manor house surrounded by a high stone wall and rolling Gloucestershire countryside. The policemen themselves were in the downstairs kitchen enjoying a cup of tea when their small talk was cut short by an almighty crash at the other end of the house.

The more senior of the two jumped up and shouted, 'Bloody hell, what was that?!' before adding, 'You guard the front door, I'll investigate,' before running towards the noise.

He opened the door into a room at the far end of the house and immediately saw that a window at the far end was open. The blow that knocked him unconscious was later discovered to be from a two-foot-long metal baton. But he knew nothing of this.

The other policeman fared less well: confronting a man in the hall, he suffered a blow to the head before being tied up. It was two hours before back-up arrived.

It was unclear if anything had been stolen and potential links with Edwards' speech in Taiwan hours earlier were never investigated. The break-in was classified as secret and placed under the thirty-year rule.

5. Angela Sitwell Stands

House of Commons, Westminster Monday 5 June

An MP wishing to exit the Chamber has a few options; one is to walk to the side of the Speaker's chair and into the long Victorian Gothic corridor beyond, with high ceilings, tired green carpets and little natural light. Turn to the right and the corridor eventually leads to the Members' tea room, where MPs swap gossip between votes.

Head straight on and another booklined corridor takes you down to the Shadow Cabinet Room and a staircase leading to an exit near the bottom of Big Ben.

On your way down, if you looked to your left, you'd see the Prime Minister's suite of parliamentary offices, all designed by Augustus Pugin in high Victorian style during rebuilding after the 1834 fire.

Nearby, in a slightly less opulent office, sat Angela Sitwell, Secretary of State for Digital, Media and Culture. And a short distance away, in Alistair Murray's office, her fate was being decided. After attending Scottish Questions, Richard walked in to see Alistair deep in conversation with one of his ministerial advisers.

The office was dark, its wallpaper a Pugin-designed floral pattern of crimson and gold.

'Good, come in, sit down' said Alistair, looking up briefly from where he sat engrossed in a multi-coloured print-out of an Excel spreadsheet.

Richard looked over Alistair's shoulder to see a list of MPs, some highlighted in different colours.

'This, Richard, is the start of our campaign. We have a few definites, and here in green, the possibles. We need to get that up to a respectable number by the end of the day to build some momentum.'

There were 330 Conservative MPs in total, but they had only a small core-group of friends they could count on.

'Very impressive, Alistair,'

'Well, Excel lists won't win us any support, but hopefully we won't miss anyone. I have Sir Bill and Greg signed up. Hopefully Angela's junior ministers will follow her, out of loyalty if nothing else. Not a bad start, but we need, say, ten to go public and kick things off.' So, what's best: do you want to call your contacts or hit the tea rooms?'

Richard pondered. 'I'll try to pin down the ones I know we can persuade first, then perhaps a tour of the tea rooms if our candidate is free?'

Alistair nodded. 'This isn't all of it of course. If we're successful here we'll need a national campaign, funds, supporters. This'll be a busy few weeks.'

'We also need to find out the rules of the contest,' Richard added.

'Very true. I'll get on to Sir Richard.'

Sir Richard McLean was the Chairman of the 1922 Committee, a powerful backbench MP who acted as shop steward for the Party's MPs, and, most importantly, organised the leadership contests.

'What should I ask? The dates, numbers of proposers, deadlines, hustings?'

'That seems about it,' said Richard. 'But aren't we missing something else?'

'What?' said Alistair, looking up.

'Our candidate. Are we sure she's up for it? We should get her over here,' said Richard.

'Yes of course. So caught up in it all I nearly forgot. I'll go over there now, see how she is, and if she has her ministers on side by now.'

'Good, well I'll be off. Shall we meet back at say 2 p.m. and swap notes?'

'Yes, and I'll bring our candidate!'

With that, Richard departed and headed off down the corridor towards his office.

Alistair picked up his phone.

They needed more MP pledges, but even more urgently than that they needed Lord Strachan, veteran fund raiser from previous campaigns.

'George? Alistair here, how are you? I have a plan you might be interested in...'

Lord Strachan was in the kitchen of his London house. 'Alistair, how lovely to hear from you. What a to-do all this is; yes, I listened intently to Richard's little seminar. I concur. I think we've found our woman.'

'Great! Well George, coming straight to the point, we definitely have our ten MPs to back Angela Sitwell. "Sitwell to stand" as it were.'

'Very good, we should use that!'

'I know Angela – presentable, not a great intellect, not many in politics have one, but not stupid either, generally sound on the Union.'

'Yes, I can see why you like her. Now I presume you'd like some help?'

'Yes, I was thinking of a dinner, say tomorrow; yourself, a potential donor or two, Angela – obviously – myself and one or two supporters. We'll kick some ideas around to get things moving?'

'Yes, I'll see who I can rustle up.'

• • • •

Richard entered Alistair's office at 2 p.m. to see Angela at the head of the table and Lord Strachan halfway down, as well as the two junior ministers from Angela's department and their PPSs. A good sign, he thought. We'll soon have our ten.

Lord Strachan had a mischievous look on his face; he was obviously enjoying his role.

Alistair was keen to appoint Lord Strachan as an unofficial campaign treasurer. As well as being a minister, he was a 'Tory donor', not one of the richest but he'd made a modest fortune in property in the 1990s. More importantly, however, he acted as the shop steward for the real tycoons. He loved to be involved and was happy to wield the influence of funds held by people with less time on their hands than himself. He also owned a charming Georgian town house in Lord North Street that was ideal for intimate political dinners and drinks. Besides he was a fount of gossip, and gossip was at a premium.

Alistair opened the informal discussion. 'Thanks for coming at short notice. I'm glad we're all agreed that the Party needs a new direction, and Angela's the one to give it.

The MPs banged the table, half in jest and half out of habit.

'What we need over the next few days is MPs, numbers, but also, we need to set out the basics of our campaign. Why Angela? etc. This will be tough going.'

Richard caught a gap and thought he would throw in his two pence. 'My starter for ten. We need to continue with the mandate from the General Election. We're the strong Conservative team and we also have the benefit of not being the other candidates!'

'Yes, that's the basic message,' said Alistair.

Angela smiled and looked at Alistair. 'That will do nicely. The manifesto candidate with a mandate.'

6. The Contender

**Houses of Parliament, Westminster, London,
Tuesday 6 June**

'Have you spoken to Mark (as Prime Minister Edwards was known to his friends)?' Richard asked Alistair in a quiet moment as they left the Commons Chamber after a division.

'Yes, I rang him at the weekend.'

'How is he?'

'He's in a very bad place to be honest, everything's crashed down on him at once, his marriage included. He doesn't know what to think.'

'Did you ask him about Arabella and Environ?'

'He claims to know nothing about that, and I believe him. He accepts the business with Arabella wasn't exactly a good look, but he feels somehow there were forces out to get him; he can't put a finger on it, but he's mystified.'

'Poor thing' said Richard, 'I guess he may have a point: the press were so quick to bite on the story and he left so soon. Strange really, our press, they're like a herd easily led from one trough to the next. I suppose this story was just too good.'

'There was one other thing', said Alistair. 'He's very upset about the break-in. The policeman was more seriously hurt than is known. And it could have been a member of his family.'

Alistair and Richard were in one of the long-panelled corridors that ran around the chamber and had come to a halt hear the library. Alistair gestured Richard towards a quiet corner.

'There was another element to it. The file, the one he

mentioned in the Taiwan speech – it does exist, or rather it did exist – it was stolen from the house, it was in a safe. That hasn't been reported.'

'My God!' explained Richard. 'Do you know whose names were on it?'

'The problem is, the fool didn't take any copies; he knows the names but without the actual file there's no proof.'

'Can't the next Prime Minister make enquiries?'

'From whom? Edwards specifically asked for this list from the intelligence services. I'm amazed they gave him anything, but it's over now and they won't want to start it all over again. The whole thing stinks. I wouldn't be surprised if the whole series of events leading to his resignation was a set-up and somehow linked to this list he requested. We need to keep digging, there's more to this. And a British Prime Minister has been chucked out in very dubious circumstances.

'Agreed, but who's behind it?' asked Richard. 'One leadership contender springs to mind. I don't suppose Arabella would spill the beans?'

'Claims to know nothing. I believe she's as shocked as Edwards,' said Alistair. 'I have a very uneasy feeling there are people out there capable of doing in a Prime Minister, and we don't know who they are.'

• • • •

Robert Lacy claimed to be a descendant of the medieval Norman de Lacy family, but in reality, he was born Robert Levene in south-east London, but had decided to shed his roots and change his name in his first year at Oxford University. While his accent was not quite the same as the public school boys he'd wished to associate with, it was no longer the accent of his youth. Like much of his image, it was at once real but glaringly fake, a real Londoner talking with a London accent of his own creation. But it worked, because he was generally considered authentic and a 'good communicator'. Clever and at ease with the media he'd become a household name – a regular participant in political panel debates on the BBC, well known by the public, respected even, if not exactly liked.

He was perhaps more quick-witted than wise; his enthusiasm for a clever line had made him lazy about his policies, but that hadn't held back his rise through the Party ranks. Although his reputation as a safe pair of hands was not entirely deserved, he was a serious candidate to be leader of the Conservative Party.

For months, as the vultures circled the wagons of the Edwards caravan, the thought of Prime Minister Lacy had been a constant horror for Alistair and Richard, forcing them to defend the ailing Prime Minister long after many others had deserted him; it was driving them now to ensure Angela Sitwell became Prime Minister instead.

Lacy and his team had been planning for months, ensconced in a loaned office in a tower overlooking the Thames on Millbank. Within a day of Edwards' fall Lacy had a website up and running with a slick video featuring stirring music by Purcell, the White Cliffs of Dover and exhortations to public service. His team were working on polling figures that asked just the right questions – 'Who do you consider the most experienced?', 'Who is the most competent?' These would be dutifully run in *The Sunday Times* – their political correspondent having long been cultivated by Lacy.

The news that Angela was standing was picked up by one of Lacy's media team.'

'That'll be good for a laugh.'

Lacy did not laugh; this had taken him by surprise. He'd expected opposition, of course he had, but he thought he'd be up against a centrist – probably Caroline Summers. But the Tory Right agreeing a candidate?

He regained his composure. 'Interesting. Very interesting, I think I know who's behind her. We need to watch them like a hawk. James, see what you can find on her, there must be something we can add to the *Times* story?' He gestured to his political adviser.

Lacy loathed and feared Alistair Murray and Richard and they returned the favour.

Despite his misgivings, Richard had actually got on quite well with Lacy when he'd first entered Parliament. Lacy had already been a MP for a few years and taken several of the new MPs under his wing and had helped support him when he'd wanted to ask questions in the Chamber. It was a some years later that Richard's view of him changed, in the form of a phone call which Richard had listened in on between Stewart Leggett, a Conservative MSP, and Alistair. Leggett had initially seemed very guarded but gradually his concerns had begun to flow out.

'I've been working on a Scottish Parliamentary inquiry into campaign funding – mainly to address concerns over possible overseas funding in Scottish elections – but it's equally relevant to any new referendum on Scottish independence. What we found is rather puzzling, disturbing even. It relates to a string of companies linked to the Nationalists.'

Richard had listened in fascination as Leggett set out how he thought money declared as legitimate donations to the SNP's accounts from a string of Scottish companies had actually come from elsewhere.

It was the elsewhere that had intrigued him; the suspicion was that one donor company had ultimately received money from Environ Technology, a Chinese telecoms company that had been in and out of the papers for its deep pockets and appetite for acquiring British technology companies.

Leggett had continued: 'Our inquiry was going quite well, but just as we were making some progress on the origins of the money – we'd heard evidence from a former UK director of Environ – the Scottish Parliament called a halt to it; the chairman said no more evidence was required and a dry, rather dull report was produced. You remember it, I'm sure.'

'Indeed, whitewash in Holyrood,' said Alistair wryly.

'What you don't know is that we'd been told to send the findings to London, to the Scottish Office. They then supposedly took over the investigation at a higher level with the Met Police, but we never heard another word.'

Following the call, Alistair had asked the Permanent Secretary in the Scottish Office for some of the documents and organised one of his advisers to put a paper trail together, sending the results to a Scottish journalist he'd known since university. Their combined investigations had met with moderate success, but there'd been no killer document and, after the allegations had briefly hung around in the Scottish media, they'd died away.

Alistair had discovered later that the then Secretary of State for Scotland had requested the whole enquiry to be quietly terminated.

The Scottish Government evidently had no interest in pursuing the funding of their own Party, but why would a

Conservative minister seek to terminate the enquiry? That Cabinet Minister had been a certain Robert Lacy...

Alistair had never really trusted Lacy again. Had he been involved with these companies in some way? But why? Money? It made little sense. And now Environ was in the press again, linked to the downfall of Prime Minister Edwards.

So this was who Angela Sitwell was standing against – the star of the Conservative Party, but a potentially tainted and untrustworthy star. But more importantly Lacy disagreed with them on the central question of the hour – the future of the Union. Lacy wanted to devolve even more powers, in Richard's view hollowing out the UK government to an extent that it would barely function.

But Lacy didn't have it all his own way. He had no natural area of support, the candidate neither of the Left nor the Right, with no big names to bolster his position.

There were three candidates: the Right had Angela Sitwell, the Left had Caroline Summers, and then there was Robert Lacy. This was a high-stakes game – the future Prime Minister and the direction of Government.

7. Lord North Street

Westminster, London, Thursday 8 June

Lord North Street had been home to various politicians over the years, Harold Wilson and Jonathan Aitken among others. Lord Strachan found the short walk from Parliament ideal for political entertaining, drinks parties that could spill out into the small garden at the rear or, more often, small dinner parties where he'd play host in return for being part of some important political event. Tonight's dinner was going to be one to remember.

Alistair and Richard met earlier for a drink at The Marquess of Granby, a well-known watering hole for political types. They had much to discuss: how to get Angela's campaign off the ground but also what to do if they won. They sat down in a quiet corner and looked around to make sure no journalists were hanging around.

'Alastair,' said Richard, looking over the pints of bitter he'd just bought, 'when I was at school in Hong Kong, I never thought I'd one day play a hand in deciding who the next Prime Minister would be. I mean, all that time we spend on the mundane side of politics, that's all forgotten, but the odd moment like this… Angela could become Prime Minister, we could make a difference…'

Alistair smiled, sipped his beer and replied: 'I wouldn't get too carried away. The odds are stacked against us, but even if we fail, we can still make an impact. The next Prime Minister has to be able to hold the country together. And I have to tell you I do not trust many of the other candidates. I suspect you share my concerns over Lacy; if we can stop him, we'll have done the country a good turn.

'Now drink up! We don't want to keep his lordship waiting.'

They set off across Smith Square, past the old Conservative Party office where a victorious Margaret Thatcher had once appeared at the window, before arriving at Lord Strachan's door where they were ushered through to the drawing room. Angela and the other guests hadn't yet arrived.

Lord Strachan explained what he'd planned. 'We'll have Alan Black, the hedge fund manager, and Lord Edenbridge, and John McVey you know, of course.'

John McVey was an entrepreneur, a long-time supporter of the Conservatives and a friend of Richard's. Richard was glad he was there; he trusted his abilities; they'd both been a part of the Edwards' campaign a few years back. Now in his mid-seventies McVey had a string of businesses successes to his name, but more importantly he was well-versed in fundraising and knew a wide range of other businessmen whom they could collectively draw on.

When Angela had arrived with her adviser, they exchanged a few pleasantries and then went through to dinner. Lord Strachan was serving duck with sautéed potatoes and some of his renowned choice of red wine, this time a robust Merlot.

Alistair allowed Angela to have the first word. 'Thank you all for coming. This is an exciting time, so let me run through two key areas I'm sure you're keen to discuss. Firstly, I believe I can win this contest, with the support of MPs such as Alistair and Richard here. I'm best placed to appeal to the party membership at large.

'Secondly, as Prime Minister I will govern with a clear vision, keeping the UK as one and delivering for our voters, be it on tax, immigration or revitalising the regions that put their trust in us in 2019 and have stuck with us since.

'I should also mention the alternatives. There'll likely be a candidate from the Left – probably Caroline Summers. If we can galvanise the core of the Conservative Party, we can prevent votes going to someone from the centre – I think we can assume that someone would be Robert Lacy. So that's the choice. Support me and we can win; support me and Lacy cannot win.'

The party broke up into light conversation as they ate, Strachan updating Angela on his recent trip to Washington to meet various US Republican senators, concerns over the situation in China and what it might mean for Hong Kong.

Between courses Alistair took the opportunity to break in. 'I'll speak candidly. I think we're in a very dangerous position as a country and as a Party. I mean of course the Union. Scotland is again in a bad way politically; the Nationalists are still in control and it may only be a matter of time before the next independence referendum. We need to change the dynamic and show that the UK is relevant and means something in Scotland. We've made a start, but this current leadership crisis will be seized on by the Nationalists. We need a new leader who's happy to take on the Union issue. That's why I support Angela.'

John McVey interjected. 'If I may cut to the chase on this, I am very concerned about the possibility of Lacy getting into the final two. He may well win against Summers. Frankly, I don't trust him as far as I could throw him. I had some dealings with him once, years ago, when I sat on the board of a think-tank with him. Some strange goings on. I could never put my finger on it. But I always suspected there was something or someone else standing behind him.

'He was keen on employing this academic for our work on "Britain in the World" – remember it? Funding came in for the project, via his contacts, I should have asked more questions but didn't; there always seemed to be another purpose behind it all.

'Anyway, it's his views on the Union that really concern me, though. He was always a fan of devolution, the more the merrier until there's nothing left to devolve. He started it all rolling when he was Secretary of State for Scotland. If he got his hands on power the Nationalists would have a field day.'

Richard added, 'Something similar came up. Nothing concrete, but again very odd. It looked like the SNP were going to be exposed on funding, then suddenly he clamped down on it all. But putting that on one side, let's look at his record. On the Union, it'll be a one-way road to de facto separation.'

The dinner continued in an unstructured manner. Angela was gently quizzed by the hedge fund managers on her plans for the economy, energy supply, North Sea oil, foreign relations and the size of the armed forces.

After some time, Alistair tapped his glass and silence fell.

'Thank you all for coming. This is an exciting time for politics and it's a great privilege to be here at the beginning of a new chapter for the Conservative Party and hopefully for all of Britain. Angela has my full support and I hope she has yours as well. We have a lot to do over the next few days and weeks but it'll be worth it. With a new leader of Angela's calibre, we can achieve great things.'

After shouts of 'Hear, hear!' and the banging of fists on the table, the assembled guests continued their meal until the party eventually drained away into the early summer evening.

8. The Campaign

House of Commons, Westminster, Tuesday 12 June

Chairman of the 1922 Committee Sir Richard McLean was a traditional Conservative from a rural seat in the Midlands, his time as an army officer instilling in him a quiet sense of loyalty. Not one for the limelight, he preferred to work in the background, exuding the calm demeanour of someone who was 'steady under fire'. On this particular day he needed to be: the resignation of the Prime Minister as leader of the Conservative Party placed him in the centre ground.

McLean walked into a packed Committee Room 11 in the House of Commons to set out how the leadership contest would run, joining the officers of the 1922 executive in the middle of a table at the head of the room.

'Colleagues, it is my duty as Chairman of the 1922 Committee to oversee the election of a new leader of the Conservative Party. Each candidate requires a proposer and a seconder. All nominations are to be sent to me by Thursday. The first ballot will be next Wednesday in this room, from 9 a.m. until 1 p.m. If there are three candidates, the two with the most votes will go forward to the ballot of members. If there are more than three, we will hold further ballots. This is a difficult time for our Party and the leadership question needs resolving as soon as possible, but we also need to have an open contest. I am not an archbishop and it is therefore not my business to arrange a coronation!'

Nervous laughter broke out. The thought of a protracted leadership contest filled most with dread, but there was no obvious candidate who could unite the Party.

With that, McLean departed, the packed room erupting into hundreds of separate conversations, mostly concerning who was backing whom.

• • • •

Following the meeting Angela's team made their way to her office, where a campaign plan was forming.

'Right. This is where we are', Alistair said to the assembled MPs. 'Tomorrow's our big launch, against a backdrop with the words "Building a United Kingdom". Richard has been working with Angela on the speech. The key theme is uniting the UK, and Angela can deliver strong leadership in a changing world.'

The following day Angela, flanked by Alistair and Richard, addressed the assembled media from a panel they had assembled in the Georgian library of an institute on Whitehall.

'When I was growing up in rural Lancashire, if I'd told friends I'd be here one day explaining why I'm standing as leader of the Conservative Party and Prime Minister, they'd have thought I was mad; mad because where I come from, politics was something others did; mad because it wasn't exactly a Conservative area, and mad because back then I was more interested in climbing mountains… but here we are.

'But it's my sad duty to tell you that something we've taken for granted all our lives – our identity, solid and timeless – is in danger: the United Kingdom. If we fail to act now to avert danger, to stop the drift to inevitable separation… But all is not lost, we can renew our Union…'

The MPs in the room, initially nervous as to whether their

candidate could perform, soon relaxed and by the time it came to questions, the media were no longer expecting to knock her off balance and the next day's newspapers were universally positive.

The first vote came around very fast. Foremost amongst the other contenders was Robert Lacy, his slick campaign videos proclaiming him to be the 'experienced choice'. Caroline Summers' campaign slogan was 'The time for steady Government': uninspiring, but cleverly targeted at those MPs unnerved by weeks of political turmoil. Five other candidates, including Tommy Rosenfield, had little chance of winning, but perhaps hoped for a promise of office in return for supporting one of the leading candidates further down the line.

Thursday came around and McLean, enjoying his unexpected role in the limelight, began to announce the results as if he were the compère of the Oscars. The first five names were immediately ruled out with little fanfare.

Three remained: Robert Lacy, Caroline Summers and Angela Sitwell, and the defeated candidates were now hot property.

'Which way will Rosenfield and his cronies jump?' pondered Richard.

'Whoever offers them something?' said Angela, smiling.

'I suspect they'll go with Lacy, he and Rosenfield are of a type!'

Over the weekend, Angela's campaign worked around the clock calling the supporters of the five defeated candidates, the waverers and the undecided, all in the knowledge that Lacy and Summers were doing exactly the same thing.

• • • •

The following Tuesday McLean again assembled in Committee Room 11. He announced he would read out the final three in reverse order. The tension mounted and the room went quiet. Caroline Summers, as always, showed no emotion. Lacy looked tense but confident, and then there was Angela, smiling and looking around the room.

McLean then read out the third-placed candidate: 'Mr Robert Lacy.'

The room erupted and it was impossible to hear the actual results. Lacy's face deflated like a balloon and Angela's smile increased in intensity. MPs came over to congratulate her.

The BBC declared the result 'a big upset; Mr Lacy the seasoned old hand is out of the contest, leaving Caroline Summers and the new challenger Angela Sitwell.'

The MPs then began to disperse, apart from a lingering crowd of well-wishers and new-found friends surrounding Angela.

Standing a short distance away, Richard heard Angela rattle off some lines: 'Honoured to go forward... Look forward to putting my case to the Membership... thank my supporters for their trust...'

After everything had died down Richard went over to her. 'Congratulations Angela, you did it... only the small matter of winning over the Membership now... But I really think you can.'

'Did you ever doubt me, Richard?' said Angela playfully.

'Well, frankly yes! Beating Lacy like that will go down as one of the political upsets of the century. He'll be livid; we'll need to be very careful, you know what he's like.'

'Yes, no doubt he'll try to bite me on the ankles. I will try to mend fences with him though, assure him I acknowledge and value his talents, that we need a broad church...'

'Probably a good idea, but I don't trust him, as you know.'

'No doubt he'll be fully signed up with Caroline Summers by now,' said Angela. 'Promised a Cabinet seat in return for doing her work. We need to be on our guard.'

9. Sitwell Falls

Kennington, London, Thursday 14 June

Angela Sitwell lived in a modest but expensive house in Kennington, south London. Every morning she went for a run and despite now being one of the only two candidates to be Prime Minister, she felt no need to change her routine.

She'd made it down to the end of her street before an enterprising journalist shouted a question at her: 'Have you anything to say about your shares in Environ Limited?'

Angela ran on. She had a dim recollection of the name but couldn't recall where from. Having completed her circuit of the block she went back into her house and turned on the breakfast TV news. Only half concentrating, she glanced at the banner on the bottom of the screen.

> 'BREAKING NEWS: Leadership contender Angela Sitwell in Cash-for-Influence sting?'

She sat down as if she'd just been passed a heavy weight. This did not look good. Had any lobbyist ever offered her money? Not that she could remember: she disliked them and kept her distance. In fact, she'd barely earned anything other than her salary in years, other than a mere pittance for a few articles. Still watching the screen, she reached for her phone and called Alistair.

'Have you seen the news? I have no idea what this is about.'

Alistair responded: 'It looks like it's from that blog site "Ground Zero" run by that nasty piece of work Rory O'Connell.

They apparently do stings now as well. They're saying they'll publish something later. Any strange conversations recently? People claiming to be lobbyists? Foreign governments?'

'No, I'm very careful who I talk to. I don't talk to lobbyists and I certainly haven't been offered cash for anything.'

Alistair said, 'I think we should bide our time for now. I'll put in a call or two and try and find out what this is about.'

Alistair then rang Richard.

'I assume you've seen the news? Angela genuinely has no idea what this is about. Can you see if you can find anything out? I'll try a few contacts, try to find out if O'Connell's touting it to the mainstream papers.'

Richard set to work, calling a few journalists and asking what they'd been told. It seemed the story had come from somewhere else before hitting the 'Ground Zero' blog, and was apparently related to a family member, not Angela herself.

Richard told Alistair. 'There's a tape recording of a family member apparently.'

'Oh, thanks, do you think it's serious?'

'Not sure, but I guess the tape'll come out sooner or later. You'd better have a talk with Angela. She must be in a right state not knowing what's going on.'

Alistair phoned Angela. 'I've done some calling around. I know a little bit more.'

She responded quietly. 'It's okay Alistair; the swine rang me just now and put their allegations to me. They involve my husband. It's beastly of them to go after him, but there you are, that's politics I guess.'

'I'm so sorry; what have they done?'

'Well, seemingly they found out that my husband isn't a very well man. He went off the rails a few years back and is still recovering. Drink, drugs, mid-life crisis. It's been a real heartache. So someone must have found out and offered him money for access to me if I become Prime Minister. The idiot apparently chatted away for hours. God knows what he may have said.

'O'Connell asked – well, that's too polite – threatened me really with various things: Are we still together? Did I know he accepted cash for arranging meetings? How long have I known that he was a drug addict? Really unpleasant stuff, I'm afraid.'

Alistair was trying to take it all in. Did it affect their leadership bid, and if so what could be done to draw a line under it? Play the victim? Dutiful wife coping with a troubled husband? It would be complicated. The public would certainly take a view on an occupant of Number 10 being a drug addict.

Angela said, 'I'm so sorry Alistair, I should have told you, but I thought we could continue like this until he recovered, but that seems impossible now. I think I should withdraw from the contest. This can only get worse.'

Alistair thought for a moment. Could they sue? Obtain an injunction? Make a virtue out of it, a moral tale? Difficult.

Yes, he concluded, this *was* a problem.

'I hate to say it, but you may be right. I can't predict what effect a leadership campaign would have on you and your family, but this is an unforgiving environment and some of the media can be awful.'

Angela replied, 'I am so sorry.'

'No need to apologise, it's not your fault. It was fun while it lasted *and* we've already achieved one of our goals: stopping Lacy becoming Prime Minister.'

The next day Angela walked out of her house to a mob of cameras and journalists on her doorstep.

'Thank you for coming. As you know I have been the subject of a vicious smear against my husband, who's currently undergoing treatment. This has been a great distraction from my campaign and all those supporting my vision of a United Kingdom. I thank them all for their work.

'However, on reflection, I will be contacting Sir Richard McLean to let him know I'll be withdrawing from the contest. I would therefore like to congratulate Caroline Summers.'

And with that, she thanked the press for coming and went back up the stairs into her house.

• • • •

Caroline Summers was in her office in Westminster watching the announcement.

Sir Richard McLean rang shortly afterwards.

The next thing anyone knew was that she was in a car driving down the Mall towards Buckingham Palace, with a BBC correspondent explaining that she was to be invited to form a government by the King.

After a short twenty minutes' audience it was back to Number 10, where a hastily assembled podium was waiting for her.

Caroline Summers wore a blue jacket and looked somewhat agitated. The sound of jeering from a large crowd beyond the gates on Whitehall added to a slightly tense atmosphere.

'His Majesty has asked that I form an administration and I have accepted' she paused before adding 'I will work day in and day out to deliver for the British people She then stumbled and the press opposite immediately started to shout out questions at her: 'What are your priorities. Prime Minister?'

Caught in the glare monetarily she seemed unsure what to do, but composing herself, she turned and headed for the famous black door.

• • • •

Richard had been watching this all unfurl with Alistair at the Scottish office, mostly in silence, but with the occasional barbed comment aimed at people they could see forming outside Downing Street, the advisers she was planning to take with her.

'Well, that's it. I guess we'll be getting our marching orders soon enough?' said Richard.

'Yes,' replied Alistair. 'With her views on the Union, I can't see how she can keep us here. We tend to upset all the right – I mean wrong – people. They'll want a smooth talker, someone who goes with the flow. Dreadful, but there it is.'

'We might be moved, I guess.'

Alistair shrugged his shoulders. 'Well, as far as I know we remain in post until we're told otherwise. It'll be sackings first, appointments later. I don't have a huge amount in the office, but I heard once that a reshuffled minister's items are moved to his new department while his meeting with the PM is still going on!'

• • • •

The following afternoon Richard received a phone call from the Whips' Office: 'Can you be in Number 10 at 3 p.m. to meet the Prime Minister?'

Having navigated the crowd of onlookers outside, he tried

to look confident as he walked up alone to the door of Number 10, the assembled press no doubt bashing out a commentary that he was either due for a promotion or a demotion; more likely, he thought, they were trying to work out who he was.

'Now Richard,' said the new Prime Minister. 'I've always thought you had a very good appreciation of the UK's place in the world. I would like you to join the Government as Parliamentary Under-Secretary in the Foreign Office. Your responsibilities will be Asia, the Far East in particular, China of course. Will you accept?'

'Yes, Prime Minister, I would be most honoured.'

'This has been a difficult few months for the Party and country. It's time we all worked together to try and make the country work. You'll be working with Tommy Rosenfield, who's agreed to serve as Foreign Secretary with an additional role as 'Minister for the Union'. He assures me this will cause no difficulties.'

'I would be delighted to serve you and the Foreign Secretary.'

Richard's heart sank as he tried to hide his annoyance: one minute he was appointed to one of the most interesting roles in Government, the next he was told he'd be working with Tommy Rosenfield, a narcissist who he really didn't like.

Caroline Summers then asked him what he thought his focus would be.

'I've obviously been more involved with the Union and Scotland over the past year, Prime Minister, but as you know I have some knowledge of the Far East. I worked for a bank in Singapore for a time. There's much to be done to improve relations there. With the increasing threat from China and Russia, they're suddenly in the middle of it again.'

'Again?'

'Oh, in a broad historical sense; Singapore was threatened by an expansionist Japan in 1940 and is now part of the Western bloc, a democracy with… well, what you could call rather unpredictable neighbours.'

'Very diplomatic.'

'Prime Minister, may I ask whether your notes on me mentioned my grandfather by any chance?'

'They did. I had no idea, sad story. It makes sense why you're interested in that region; it can't have been easy for him after that ordeal.'

Richard said, 'I remember him when I was young. He hardly ever spoke about it but I asked him shortly before he died and he told me the whole story. The fall of Singapore cast a shadow over so many families' lives, both those who died and those who survived. When I lived there, I once had a look at the spot where they were all held – the infamous Changi Prison. There are a lot of ghosts around there. My grandmother told me once what he looked like when he returned to Scotland. He was like a ghost: the body recovered but the mind, well, not so fast. Still, Singapore's a very different place today. I look forward to visiting if there's an opportunity.'

'I hope so Richard, and I'm glad to have you on board.'

As he got up and headed towards the door, Summers gestured to him to stop. 'One more thing. There is another, rather delicate responsibility I'd like to entrust you with. The matter of my predecessor and this lobbyist. You'll be fully briefed. I trust you'll keep me updated.'

Later, walking along Whitehall, Richard cast his mind back to Edwards' last days as PM; it now seemed a world away, but really wasn't. An Investigation? What could they have been up to?

••••

The next day Richard entered the Foreign Office to take up his new position. Once through security he was met by Permanent Secretary Sir Iain Craig, the senior civil servant in charge of the department, who escorted him to his new office.

Reaching the top of a grand staircase, they headed for the Foreign Secretary's office. The room was vast, decorated in an ornate Victorian style, its windows looking out onto St James's Park and Horse Guards.

Rosenfield, who was seated in an armchair to one side of a large fireplace, stood briefly and beckoned Richard over to a chair opposite. Richard assumed Rosenfield knew of his efforts to prevent his rise up the party and prevent his ally Lacy becoming Prime Minister. Would he bear a grudge? Perhaps. But he was too clever to show it. He always polite, overly polite, even with those he was trying to ruin. And so it was this time. He oozed unctuous faux bonhomie.

'I was so pleased to hear that you'd accepted the position; it'll be a great benefit to have your talents in the department. We have much work to do. The Asia brief is an interesting one. I understand you have some knowledge of the area.'

Richard told him of his Singapore connection.

'That should come in useful as we rebuild our presence in the region. The geo-political tilt since the Russian invasion of Ukraine is real. China is now asserting itself and we need to reassure our historic friends that they have alternatives to the gold being doled out from Beijing.'

'I agree, we've taken things for granted for too long.'

Rosenfield replied, his mind clearly elsewhere. 'One other thing, Richard. I'll also be very busy working on the Union.

This may mean you'll have to act on your own initiative; that's fine, as I trust your instincts. You seem to be ideal for the job.'

Richard left the office and was met outside by Sir Iain Craig, who'd evidently been hanging around waiting to catch Richard on the way out. When they were safely out of earshot, he confided in Richard in little more than a whisper, 'You are aware of your other… responsibilities?'

Richard responded in an equally secretive tone. 'Yes, a sensitive matter, but one that needs investigating.'

'Indeed, one that involves Chinese influence,' said Craig. 'I'll organise a briefing for you on it with the SIS officer responsible; there are several other parliamentary inquiries into it, but that's a separate matter. It's best you get up to speed. And one other thing to bear in mind: you should keep this to yourself. Only you and me and some of our friends across the river are aware of this.'

This was intriguing: perhaps there was a genuine reason he'd been placed in the Foreign Office after all?

10. President Xi of China

Zhongnanhai, Beijing, June

The collapse of the Commercial Bank of Fujian in the summer of 2025 went largely unreported in China and unnoticed elsewhere, but two years later it was seen as the trigger for the great Chinese Banking Crisis and resulting recession. Banks stopped lending, companies went bust and the ever-powerful construction sector hit the buffers. By 2026 unemployment had soared to 15 per cent. The Communist Party's hold on power had been shaken to the core.

But then things got worse. Low rainfall led to a serious failure in the rice harvest in the South, contributing to already raging inflation.

The world's largest economy was in crisis, but a newly assertive China still seemed unopposed globally. The People's Liberation Army navy's control of the South China Sea went largely uncontested and its ships ranged from Africa to the Americas, docking at Chinese-owned and operated ports. Be it technology, media or space flight, China seemed unstoppable, but President Xi knew this was illusory. The economy would steady itself in time, but it was the withdrawal of the United States from areas of Chinese interest that gave his country the aura of a superpower.

• • • •

It was six years since Major-General Chris Donahue, the last United States soldier in Afghanistan, walked up into a C-17 transport plane and departed from Kabul. It was only two years since the United States warship USS *Ronald Reagan* had turned away from entering the Straits of Taiwan after encountering a squadron of Chinese FC-31 stealth fighters, conceding, in the eyes of the world, US naval supremacy in the area to China.

President Kamala Harris had been in the position for less than a year but had already let it be known that following the 2025 election race riots, her priorities were domestic. She promptly cut the US Navy and recalled troops from Japan and Korea. Gone were the days of a confident United States, armed with its own brand of muscular liberalism. The world, and particularly China, had noticed.

The space where the US feared to go was now filled by China. Chinese money flowed through international discourse as never before.

But as President Harris sought to insulate the United States from the world, the world had not lost interest in the United States.

For President Xi the United States was for now a secondary consideration. The very survival of the Party was entrusted to him. How would history judge him if he were to be the last Communist leader of China?

The Party had relied on economic growth and competence for its legitimacy. In the absence of that, a new unifying force was needed, and in some places that was only a few clapped miles away from mainland China – Taiwan. He could be the leader that finally completed the unification of China and made it a truly global power.

Ever since his readoption by the quinquennial 20th People's Congress in 2022, President Xi Jinping had known his time was limited. He had to stand down in January 2029, only a few months away. The rules could of course be changed, but other insurmountable problems could not. In his seventies, with troubles mounting up for his country, he was a man in a hurry.

He had his successor lined up: Cai Qi, the Mayor of Beijing – but there were other, more pro-Western figures who might stand a chance. And if they succeeded, then what? He had many enemies, those he'd put on trial for corruption and those who'd lost their fortunes in the recent economic collapse. Might he suffer the same fate, stripped of his wealth and property?

And things were only going to get worse, with an ageing population, a sea of debt and now the food crisis. It was only a matter of time before his weaknesses were exposed.

Yes, Xi was a man in a hurry. He had to secure the Party and his legacy, and he thought he knew how.

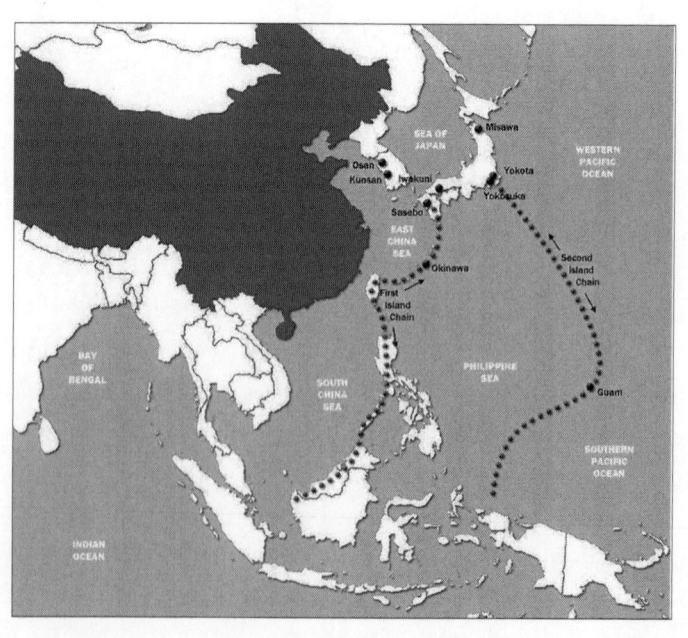

Xi was in his offices in Zhongnanhai, the former imperial garden adjacent to the Forbidden City. He had just returned from a visit to Nanjing to inspect the Eastern Theatre, the military command most closely involved with plans for operations against Taiwan. But word of his visit had got out and by the time he arrived at the base, a large and angry crowd had assembled.

He'd never seen anything like this before; 20,000 people shouting his name and that of a local Party official on trial for corruption.

What happened next was still unclear, but the local security forces, panicked by having Xi in the middle of a protest, had tried to disperse the crowd. People had died. Many people had died over the last few months, but what else could the Party do?

But what he'd heard from the Eastern Command had rekindled his interest. A successful invasion of Taiwan was possible. He'd seen the equipment and the calculations: they had air superiority, enough landing ships and dock capacity. Taiwan was a risk, no doubt, but a reasonable one.

Having finished skimming through a pile of paperwork handed to him by an assistant, he rang his senior secretary. 'Call Chen Wenqing. I want to see him this afternoon. Tell him I want an update on the United States political situation, and that of Taipei.'

Chen Wenqing was the head of the Ministry of State Security, responsible for both domestic counter-intelligence and foreign intelligence-gathering operations.

The two men knew each other reasonably well. Xi asked, 'In your assessment how would the United States react to Operation Hǎishī?' This was the name they'd chosen for the prospective invasion of Taiwan.

'Our belief is that the United States at present would not directly react to an invasion of Taiwan,' said Chen, 'if it was achieved quickly and with minimal impact on other United States interests. Our intelligence sources believe that the United States would impose sanctions and reinforce key allies, but they'd stop short of direct military aid to Taipei.'

President Xi digested this; he had many questions. 'What form would the sanctions take and how would they be enforced?'

'Based on those imposed on Russia in 2022, financial sanctions would be imposed on Chinese companies, particularly on those directly associated with the invasion. There would also be sanctions on key materials – oil in particular.'

President Xi: 'How badly would that affect us?'

Chen continued: 'Well, as you know, we import 90 per cent of our oil, mainly, from the Middle East and Angola. There's also Venezuela, and Russia has diverted some oil to us by pipeline, but only small amounts so far. The real question is how the United States enforces the sanctions. You see, the vast majority of our oil must transit the Straits of Malacca. If the USA decided to block them, we'd run out in as little as three months.'

'How likely is that, in your opinion?'

'At present we're unaware of any US planning for that scenario. Singapore and Malaysia have no US treaty obligations and a blockade of the straits without their cooperation would, we believe, be impossible.'

President Xi remembered something similar from history. Faced with the threat of Japanese aggression, the Americans had imposed oil sanctions, forcing them into a choice between suing for peace or seeking alternative sources of oil through military expansion. This wasn't an option for China: there weren't enough Asian suppliers to replace those lost if the United States choked off supplies from the Middle East. China, it was clear to him, would need to fiercely maintain its access to the open sea and the freedom to import oil from the Middle East.

'Mr Chen, that is a very helpful summary. We seem to have more work to do. I will be issuing further instructions in the next few days.'

Xi turned to his military adviser, who had been listening in on the conversation. 'The Straits of Malacca: they could be the key to success. Come up with some suggestions that I can put to the Central Military Commission.'

Xi had never imagined he'd be preparing for a war. China was not an imperialist power like those he'd been taught to loathe when he was younger. But this was different. Taiwan was China. And furthermore, China was not Russia: it was the largest economy in the world, and its wishes should be respected.

Besides, did he have any other option? This was a troubled time for China. A war might be just what was needed to unify the people.

But for the invasion to succeed, the United States must stay out of it. A US warship in the invasion lanes, intelligence sharing or resupply would tip the balance in favour of Taiwan. A Chinese failure would be a severe shock for the Party. Would Xi or the Party survive it? Having seen the crowds earlier, he doubted it.

II. Operation Sleeping Dragon

Zhongnanhai, Beijing, June

'Now let's get to Operation Sleeping Dragon,' exclaimed President Xi to Chen.

'Yes, Comrade President. We've had some noticeable successes of late. We've been concentrating on the United States, Australia and the United Kingdom. Germany and France are less of a concern with regard to Taipei and Chinese unification.'

Chen now had President Xi's full attention. He loved hearing about China's success extending its influence over greedy and feckless Western politicians. His contempt for them and the ease with which they fell for their plans was a matter of great amusement to both of them.

'The United Kingdom is now showing some promise, Comrade President. There's the politician we discussed previously. His greed is bottomless and he's been providing our Embassy in London with some useful information. We've upgraded our team to get the most out of this contact.'

President Xi's eyes lit up. This was great fun.

'We've also been working on some special projects in case of hostilities. The United Kingdom is not as "United" as it once was, and this has provided us with some options. We believe we can seriously impact the United Kingdom's role in the world and its desire to cooperate with us. We've also sent one of our best agents to London to make contact with our key asset. This has proved particularly fruitful.'

President Xi laughed; he knew exactly what this meant.

Chen continued, 'I've briefed General He Weidong of Southern Command on the international political situation and what is being done to neutralise the threats from out of the South China Sea theatre. This has improved his commanders' morale.'

With that, Xi concluded the meeting.

12. Vauxhall

MI6 Headquarters, London, 18 June

Richard had never been inside the Ziggurat before, the building on the River Thames in Vauxhall that was the headquarters of MI6. He admitted to himself a certain childish excitement at seeing the home of James Bond and the infamous M. While that was obviously a fantasy, the truth was often stranger than fiction

He was prepared for disappointment. His experiences of the Civil Service had always left him distinctly unimpressed, management driven by Human Resources dictates and process, where having the right fashionable views and values was praised above imagination and competence. He'd made a name for himself calling such behaviours out, and he suspected the Civil Service only dealt with him on sufferance.

These thoughts circled in his mind as his Foreign Office car pulled up outside. Richard was shown straight in and escorted to the Director's office overlooking the Thames.

The Director of MI6 was about fifty years old and of slight build; to Richard he gave the impression of someone who'd seen little sunlight in his long career. The human equivalent of a veal calf, an image not helped by his plain white shirt and dark suit. He was middle aged and of middling appearance; in fact, virtually everything about him seemed to be middling.

'Thank you for coming, Minister. I believe the Secretary of State has already explained the purpose of this meeting. Our concern, to be blunt, is Chinese influence, which has grown enormously in the last few years. We have people here in the UK helping the Chinese.'

Richard took this in. Was he talking about the scandal concerning the previous Prime Minister? Was there a Chinese connection?

'Many Chinese who study here enter our key industries, or sometimes join the Civil Service. They're then put under various forms of pressure to leak our technologies and information to supplement what the Chinese acquire via their extensive hacking. There has been a marked increase recently in attempts to gain access to all levels of politics. This is fiendishly difficult to spot.'

Richard ventured a thought: 'The Chinese-sponsored research institutes?'

'Not just them. It's everywhere. It's not so much ideological, but they use blackmail or bribery, and the currency they pay in isn't always cash. There's also the growing phenomenon of the Chinese buying UK companies and using them to source technology. There are protections for some industries, but they don't really work.'

'Yes, I've read about similar issues in the USA,' said Richard. 'What have they done about it?'

The Director smiled. 'Oh the less said the better about that. President Harris doesn't want to scare the horses, or, in this case, the dragons. They are officially at least aware of the issue, but nothing will get them to take it seriously for now, I'm afraid.'

Richard was rather taken aback by the candour. 'That's rather disturbing. Surely the Republicans can ask questions, even if the administration's not prepared to?'

'But that's all they can do: ask questions. Anyway...' the

Director said abruptly, clearly wanting to move on. 'To the main reason for your visit here – these companies in Scotland. I believe you have some knowledge of this?'

Richard woke up at this: how much did the Director know? He decided he'd keep what little he knew to himself, nodding sagely and ventured that it was 'Very troubling.'

'Yes, we've been working on the Environ case for some time, and it's one of the most complex and sensitive investigations we've undertaken in years – although you know all about that.'

'Indeed', said Richard knowingly. Although he did not in truth know much, he hoped that by implying that he did, he might get to understand why he'd been invited to this meeting.

The Director continued: 'It's a highly sensitive matter, not least due to the former Prime Minister's involvement and the Scottish dimension. It's a minefield, but proceed we must.'

The Director placed a file on the desk between them. 'This is what we know about Environ so far. You'll see from the company structure diagram that it's based mainly in China; it's involved in the low-value assembly of mobile phones, and more recently some work on mobile antennae.

'They have subsidiaries in a number of countries, including the UK, where they've bought one of the few semi-conductor manufacturers based here. As we know, they now want to buy one of our mobile networks. They're effectively an arm of the Chinese state and are expanding rapidly. They've made some forays into the public sphere, including sport sponsorship. And as we now know, they've dabbled in lobbying.

'There are a few well-known figures sitting on their UK and Europe board, including a former civil servant connected to this place, I have to admit. But we don't think the board does much other than lending an air of legitimacy and independence to what is in effect a Chinese state enterprise.'

Richard interjected, 'What exactly has this to do with the former Prime Minister?'

'You'll know all about the Arabella Armstrong affair. I won't share all the details with you, but it's clear she was being paid by Environ. What we don't know is what they received in return.

'As for the companies in Scotland, they now own Hibernium Wafer, a semi-conductor manufacturer who've supported the Nationalists in the past. Beyond that we know very little. The technology's available elsewhere, so why spend all this money in the UK? What do they expect to gain from a string of largely loss-making technology companies?'

The Director looked at Richard with a conspiratorial air.

'It might be worth you visiting Environ headquarters in Beijing. They're in the process of acquiring yet more British technology companies and may be after reassurance that the new Prime Minister won't try to block them. You'll be accompanied by Jeremy Broadhurst, one of our trade officials. I doubt the Chinese will spill the beans, but it might throw up some leads.'

13. Caroline Summers

Prime Minister's Office, House of Commons, London, 19 June

Late one Tuesday, having decided to beat the herd to a vote on local planning reform, Richard was heading up the back stairs towards the Chamber. The division bells were now reverberating around the building as he passed the Prime Minister's office. Caroline Summers emerged, also on her way to vote.

'Good evening, Richard, I'm glad I caught you. I wondered if I could have a word with you about something.' Noticing the look of concern on Richard's face, she continued, 'Don't worry, you haven't done anything wrong! My office will contact you tomorrow.'

The next evening Richard was shown into Summers' office in the Commons by one of her team. Her private secretary took notes during their meeting, but said nothing.

'Richard, thank you for coming. I thought it best to meet you here rather than in Downing Street.

'Things have moved on a bit since you met those nice people in Vauxhall. There are possible links between Arabella, the SNP case and what happened to Angela Sitwell. Environ being the common denominator is perhaps a coincidence, but that does seem unlikely. As a strong supporter of Angela and with your in-depth knowledge of Scotland, I think you'd be in a good place to deal with this sensitively. The services do not wish to be accused of getting involved in politics.

'You'll continue to work with the Director if need be,

but report directly to me on anything you might discover. Hopefully nothing, but you can never be too sure. I also don't want to wake up in the morning to see a national security issue splashed all over the papers.

'Oh, and I understand the Director will be organising a trip to Beijing for you, with an official from UK Trade – perhaps you can stop off in Singapore on the way?'

'Thank you, Prime Minister, I would enjoy that. I'll talk to the Department.'

14. Scotland

Bute House, Edinburgh, 25 June

Caroline Summers had been most Conservative MPs' second choice to be Prime Minister and remained so. In private, most admitted she was indeed second rate, not awful but with none of the star quality of her predecessor. She had been a perfectly competent Cabinet minister but with remarkably little in the way of memorable achievements to show for it. She had risen to Home Secretary in Edwards' first Government, when mere survival had been a feat in itself.

Richard had always found her well-briefed and across the detail, a solid, diligent and public-spirited woman, but to his mind unimaginative and deeply dull. In the inevitable silences in their conversations, he couldn't help feeling judged, and their chats always seemed to have the air of a public meeting.

On the question of how to respond to the Nationalist threat in Scotland, she had the benefit of having no known viewpoint. And a description of her predecessor John Major could equally apply to her: 'risen without trace' and unencumbered by many original ideas.

She owed her position to the support of the Left of the Party, the 'reform' wing, who'd been unable to come up with a suitable candidate of their own. She also had the support of the middle of the Party, those like Tommy Rosenfield who saw an opportunity for advancement under her regime. Many of them were indeed now sitting around the Cabinet table. However, she did not have the support of the traditional 'Right,' the former pro-Brexit group now transformed into what some had begun to call 'muscular Unionists', committed to holding the UK together and forcefully pushing back against the Nationalists in Scotland and Northern Ireland.

When it came to Scotland, Summers was an empty vessel, one that would soon be tossed about by a political storm. The first sign of this coming tempest was the May Scottish elections. Malcolm MacIntyre, the new leader of the SNP, had waged a good campaign, or more accurately the main opposition parties had performed incredibly poorly.

A re-energised nationalism, a depressed and divided Unionist cause and the chaos of Prime Minister Edwards' departure had emboldened MacIntyre to agitate for independence: more powers now, a new referendum on Scottish independence later.

This left Caroline Summers in a quandary. Should she negotiate with MacIntyre, or simply say 'No' and risk accusations of refusing to engage with the elected Scottish Government? True to form, while Summers had no fixed view, the two camps in her Party were already well defined, both sides now on very bad terms and only communicating via articles in Conservative-leaning newspapers. It was becoming clear that this issue had the potential to define her time in office, for good or ill.

In the inevitable reshuffle the day after she arrived, Alistair Murray had, as he'd expected, been dismissed as Secretary of State for Scotland, and then been forced to watch as, later that day, Robert Lacy, an advocate of a softer line on Nationalism, walked up Downing Street to take his old job with the support of Rosenfield.

While this of itself did not herald a new approach, it was obvious by her second week in office that Summers had no clear policy towards Scotland. An early meeting with the new Scottish First Minister proved a disaster. Arriving at Bute House in Edinburgh she was met by a crowd of pro-independence protesters arranged by the SNP, and then had to endure a patronising welcome on the steps of MacIntyre's official residence.

The day got even worse. After an uneventful private chat about independence and 'working together', MacIntyre had used the ensuing joint press conference to launch a series of attacks on a clearly shocked Caroline Summers, against the backdrop of a Saltire and Union flag display deliberately chosen by the Scottish Government to give the impression that this was a foreign visit

'I thank the UK Prime Minister for coming to Scotland but I had expected concrete proposals for transferring the powers that Scotland needs to help build jobs and prosperity. Despite my repeated questions, however, she has come with nothing. We're always glad to see her here, but she really should be better prepared next time.'

The trip had been a disaster and Summers had since then been keener than ever to delegate work on tackling Scottish independence to her ever-eager-to-help Secretary of State, Robert Lacy.

It was a course of action that was soon to lead to the innocuous-sounding, but ultimately fateful White Paper *Modernising the Governance of Scotland. A New Union*. Billed as a plan to settle once and for all the constitutional status of Scotland within the UK, it was in fact a blueprint for the wholesale transfer of power, money and responsibility to the Scottish Executive.

15. To China and Back

Beijing, 26 June

Arriving in Beijing at 10.20 p.m. the following Monday, Richard was met as arranged by an embassy official on the other side of passport control. It was then a hellish forty-minute drive through the Beijing traffic to the British Embassy, a large compound two miles to the east of Tiananmen Square.

It was now very late and after a brief meeting with the Ambassador, Jessica Winchester, Richard headed to his room to retire for the night. Jeremy Broadhurst, the UK trade official joined Richard Winchester for breakfast the following morning, an unassuming man with a faint northern accent who exuded calm professionalism. They ran through the day's programme: a meeting at the Ministry of Foreign Affairs followed by some trade engagements with selected Chinese companies.

Ambassador Winchester was clearly bright and keen to demonstrate her knowledge of Chinese politics. In her mid-fifties and a veteran of several postings in the Far East, she was clearly enjoying her current posting, her anecdotes regarding previous ministers' interactions with Chinese officials all carefully reeled off to illustrate key mistakes to avoid. She set out the main structures of power in Beijing from President Xi downwards.

'Minister, I don't need to remind you that China is an old civilisation and one that is harder to understand for an outsider than most. You have some advantages, but things have moved fast and recent events have, if anything, made our task even more complex.

'Firstly, we have Xi, the great emperor. It's fair to say he's become more autocratic as time has passed, mainly in response to internal pressures, the debt and financial crisis and Covid etc. The deal's always been that the Party provides rising prosperity and jobs in return for a limit on political rights, but weak growth and high unemployment has been disaster for them. So how did Xi respond to these pressures? Well, he clamped down even more tightly: more restrictions and control, more power centralised in the Presidency.

'As for other players, we have Chen Wenquing at the Ministry of State Security; he's powerful, but not seen as a potential successor to Xi. Quite moderate as they go. But he has a hard-line deputy called Tan Geng, and Xi plays them off against each other. We've also tried to establish relations with Cai Qi, the Mayor of Beijing; he's a Politburo member and a genuine contender to be Xi's heir.'

Richard stepped in. 'Ambassador, we've seen the shootings in Fujian. Who do *you* think's behind them? How do we mention it without destroying the purpose of our visit?'

Yes, we're due to meet Vice Foreign Minister Qin Yi. I expect he'll be polite, but he won't say very much, just receive and deliver messages. You can deliver our messages urging restraint in Fujian, Hong Kong and Taiwan, and mention the folly of their cooperation with Russia. I suggest you start with some positives: the need to cooperate in fighting crime and corruption. Then politely move to the messages. They'll be noted, and mostly ignored.'

Richard replied carefully, with a wry smile, 'It sounds like you're telling me there's little point to this meeting?'

'No, I wouldn't put it like that. It's always worth talking, but don't hold out any hope we'll win them round. I get on with Yi reasonably well, but I'm still the British Ambassador and that comes with hundreds of years of history.'

• • • •

The Ministry of Foreign Affairs of the People's Republic of China was a modern, ugly hulk of a building about a mile and a half from Tiananmen Square. Richard, Winchester and Broadhurst were met by an official who took them up to a meeting room where two tables faced each other, decked with Chinese and British flags. Vice Foreign Minister Yi shook Richard's hand and beckoned him to sit opposite. Despite the presence of an interpreter, it was soon clear that Yi understood and spoke at least some English, answering some questions directly. After exchanging pleasantries, the stilted conversation moved to trotting out platitudes about the need to build a better UK–China relationship. It was hard going for both sides.

After half an hour, Richard noticed Winchester trying to attract his attention and managed to slip in an 'innocent' question 'Minister, as a sign of the cooperation between our two countries in terms of technology and investment, we'll also be visiting Environ headquarters here in Beijing to discuss its investments in the UK.'

Yi's grip on the conversation faltered for a second as he took this in; he spoke a few words of Chinese to the interpreter. Quite clearly, he hadn't expected Environ to come up, and had no prepared answer. The interpreter said, 'Yes, the Minister is aware of your visit. He trusts that it will be fruitful.'

It soon became clear from the stuttering conversation that Yi intended to bring the meeting to an end. Richard's opportunity to express his concerns about the current situation had passed. 'Oh well', he thought to himself, 'it wouldn't have made any difference anyway.'

• • • •

Back at the Embassy the three of them met in the drawing room.

'What did you make of that, Minister?' Winchester asked.

'Much as you predicted, until the last question about Environ. His reaction was interesting; my Mandarin's not very good, but I think he said something like "Why are they asking about that, we should end the meeting."'

'Yes, he wanted to pull the plug," said Broadhurst. 'Quite why, I'll leave to you two.'

Both Richard and Winchester knew that Broadhurst was actually from the Secret Intelligence Service branch of the Foreign Office, but they played along with his cover.

'Our Environ visit will be most intriguing,' Broadhurst continued. 'Yi knew about it, which is interesting in itself.'

• • • •

Environ's headquarters was a fifty-storey aquamarine-coloured glass structure in central Beijing, close to the China Commercial Centre. It was designed to impress, with a huge glass atrium and a glass pod that lifted them up through the floors. Richard was glad when they arrived and were taken through to see the Chairman.

Li Quiang was a smart, middle-aged man, his English excellent and American-accented from his time studying at a US business school. He had been well briefed on the visit.

'Mr Reynolds, I'm glad you've had time to visit Beijing so soon after your promotion.'

Slightly surprised at the openness of the conversation in contrast to their earlier meeting, Richard responded in kind. 'I'm glad to be here. The UK puts great store in its renewed links with China and so, given the links between your company and the UK, it seemed only polite to visit you while we were here.'

Li continued, 'We're planning to increase our investments in the coming months, and are keen to ensure that no barriers are put in our way.'

There followed an interesting hour, with Richard and Broadhurst asking about the sponsorship of a science faculty at Glasgow University and the recent purchase of Hibernium Wafer, and what they could do to attract more investment. Having agreed to follow up on various initiatives, the meeting broke up.

Back at the Embassy Broadhurst said to Richard, 'It's more what was left unsaid that interests me. When I asked about profitability and tax rates, he didn't seem to have a clue. Their UK investments are loss-making, but the finances are a bit of a mystery. It's not a conventional company, that's for sure.'

Richard answered, 'Interesting. If they're not financial investments but more of an expression of the Chinese state, and given the technology's available elsewhere, what are they trying to achieve?'

· · · ·

The flight from Beijing touched down in Singapore early in the morning and Richard felt the warm, moist tropical air hit him in the face as he walked down the gangway. It had been some years since he'd been in Singapore, but the enveloping heat felt welcoming, as if he were back home.

Arriving at Eden Hall in the centre of Singapore near the botanical gardens, Richard and Broadhurst were briefed by High Commissioner Victoria Melville on the next day's visits, before going out into the city for dinner. She was in his mid-forties and had been in the post for two years, long enough to know the ropes, but by no means an expert on the island state

Singapore had indeed changed since Richard had lived there, but it still felt familiar. They were driven down to the Singapore River, close to where it joins the Marina Bay lagoon before emptying out into the Singapore Straits.

It was a small area of low-rise restaurants and bars lining a terrace above the river, popular with expats and city workers. The High Commissioner chose a traditional Chinese restaurant looking over the river towards a Victorian colonial building that now housed the impressive Singapore Museum. Richard was taken back to his twenties and thirties, to many after-work dinners and drinks where the expat British, US and Australian banking community mingled with Singaporeans and chatted about the week's work.

'You must remember this area well from your time in Singapore, Richard?' Melville asked.

'Yes, the restaurants have changed but it's got the same feel, just as I remember it.'

'Of course it's a bit of a sham really,' she said. It looks like it's been here for years, but in reality, these are mostly Western restaurants. But still, it's a nice place to have a drink.

'Tell me, Victoria,' said Richard. 'Is Singaporean politics as stable and tightly run as I remember from fifteen years ago?'

'Yes, by and large,' Melville replied. 'But we have a novelty now – opposition MPs – not many, but enough to have their own Leader of the Opposition.'

'They might live to regret that,' joked Richard.

'But by and large it's still quite a tight ship. They take security very seriously and so politics is democratic, but only up to a point. They'd probably be appalled by Westminster politics!'

'Yes, I can empathise,' joked Richard.

'A recent trend is, of course, concern about China, which I presume is part of your reason for coming here.'

'Partly, but it's not a bad stop-off on the way back from Beijing.'

Richard went on to explain his appointment and the new UK Prime Minister's focus on Asia and China. The High Commissioner then set out the itinerary for the next day.

'We have a few things planned. The meeting with the National Security Minister is of course the most important, but there's also a reception for UK expats.'

Broadhurst smiled at this and suggested he should come along to the security meeting, as there were some 'trade' angles that might come up.

The next day, on their arrival at the Internal Security Department, a large 1950s stone building surrounded by a security fence, Minister Chew Yong was there to meet them, and they headed up to a meeting room on the second floor.

'Perhaps you could explain what you'd like to discuss,' said Chew Yong.

Richard kicked off. 'In a word, China. How do you see China using its influence in the region, what are its aims? Is there anything we can learn?'

Chew Yong briefly considered. 'I assumed as much. There's a lot in that question! Well, let me make a start. We've always lived with China. Most of us immigrated here from China's southern provinces before the Cultural Revolution. So, we know China, we speak various Chinese dialects.

'As you know, the Chinese Communists tried to take over here in the fifties and sixties. They failed, but we've had to be careful ever since. But things have changed recently. President Xi has adopted a much more aggressive policy in the area. We don't claim any the South China Sea, but our neighbours have had to contend with Chinese expansionism. Chinese nationals here pose some security concerns but they also have genuine shipping and commercial interests. The difficulty is distinguishing between the two.'

'Any sign of encroachments into the media and politics?' asked Richard.

'Nothing serious so far. We're perhaps more concerned about our neighbours. We're a small and open state; if they align with China, it becomes much more difficult for us. But we guard our independence and our old friendships.

'As you know, we host the UK, US, Australian and New Zealand navies. We have Australian troops here and cooperate with our friends in Malaysia. You should visit the naval bases if you haven't already.'

Richard had once visited the former British Royal Navy base while trying to track down where his grandfather had been imprisoned by the Japanese. Once covering 26 square miles, with the largest dry dock in the world and enough fuel to power the Royal Navy for six months, it had shrunk to a small but useful Royal Navy logistics set-up.

'I went there once looking into some family history,' said Richard. 'I'll try have a proper look round next time I'm here. Perhaps when some ships are in port!'

'Yes, a good idea. Your family was in the Navy in Singapore?'

Richard tried to change the topic. 'Something like that. In the war.'

Sensing Richard's hesitancy, Chew Yong continued. 'A fascinating area, the docks, we get visitors all the time. Some cause us more trouble than others. In a month or so we'll even have a Chinese vessel, stopping off while transiting to the Indian Ocean.'

Richard, sensing the conversation was drying up, steered the topic to one of the reasons for the visit. 'Oh! One other thing you might be able to help us with. We have some interest in a Chinese company called Environ. I noticed it has quite a big presence in Singapore; I saw some signs on the way in from the airport.'

Chew Yong suddenly looked interested. 'Yes, I know of the company, what's your interest? I can ask our people to share with you whatever we can find out.'

The three of them continued to chat. Richard was quietly pleased with himself: this had been a useful visit.

• • • •

Richard was late arriving at his office in the Foreign Office the next day, still tired from the overnight flight. Drinking a cup of coffee at his desk, he caught up on the past week's international news. The Chinese riots showed no signs of abating and the financial situation there was beginning to look even more precarious. At one point the Chinese Government had halted all trading on the Hong Kong and Shanghai Stock Exchanges after the rumour of another bank failure had sent them into a tailspin. They managed to shore it up, but everyone was wondering for how long.

Richard turned to domestic issues and read that the Prime

Minister's long-awaited report on Scottish Governance, overseen by Robert Lacy, was finally due to be released the following week. A sense of foreboding came over him and he messaged his former boss Alistair, asking him if he'd heard anything about it.

Richard hadn't put much thought into Scotland for the last few months, but knew the problem hadn't gone away. Every night there seemed to be a new opportunity for MacIntyre to be on the airwaves castigating the UK government – the 'English Government' in his terminology – be it spending, oil exploration, fishing, education, even rejoining the EU. In some ways he was glad it was no longer his responsibility, but he still cared. He was after all partly Scottish, and had kept his links with Scotland through his holiday home in the Cairngorms.

Alistair phoned him back. 'It's very bad, I'm afraid. It recommends a full-scale transfer of powers across the whole spectrum. Reinforcing the failures of the past. And, of course, the SNP will just use it as a starting point. For goodness' sake, why's she doing this? Can't they just say no and close it down? Lacy is a nightmare.'

'What can we do?' said Richard. 'Do you want to meet? We could see what others are thinking?'

· · · ·

Later in the day Richard found himself in Alistair's large office on the second floor of the historic part of the Houses of Parliament, overlooking the Thames.

'This is like old times Richard – Scotland and the travails of keeping our Kingdom together' he said as soon as Richard entered.

'Yes, although this time the enemy seems to be within the

tent. That'll be our epitaph if we're not careful! Anyway, good to see you again.'

'Now, it's not officially out yet, but one of my former officials has sent me a copy – have a perusal. I won't prejudice you on them any more than I have already.'

Richard took a copy from the coffee table that stood amidst a cluster of armchairs to one side of the room. He sat down and started to read. First off he noticed the branding: Union flags and many images of the Secretary of State. A bad sign: if this was to be painful medicine for the Nationalists they'd have gone with saltires and given it a Scottish name, he thought.

He started with the section on defence: the right for Scotland to have its own command structure within the British Army, with its own regiments. How would that even work, Richard thought?

'So, what do you think?' asked Alistair.

'Good Lord, it's as bad as it could be, a virtual dismemberment of the country. How can you have one state with two immigration schemes, visas, effectively two trade policies? The defence plans are bonkers. It even says that Scotland should have the ability to rejoin the EU and hold constitutional referendums! It's de facto independence for Scotland, wrapped up in a Union flag with an irritating picture of Lacy staring out at us for good measure.'

'The thing is, Richard, the minute this is published all hell will break loose. MacIntyre's no fool, this will provide him with all the momentum he needs on the slippery slope to independence. This must be stopped.'

Wearily, Richard stopped flicking though the document. 'I agree entirely, but I have little say on this. We need to get to the PM and make sure she stops this madness. Can you rustle up some MPs to feed back their concerns?'

'Yes. I haven't been idle. We're holding a meeting of some MPs later, where I'll explain everything. We can't make this public though, I'm not in Government. We need a group of ministers to go to the PM and tell her this is a resignation issue. We have a group forming, but I hope it doesn't come to that. What do you think?'

'I come up for a cup of coffee, and instead get offered the opportunity to resign?! Joking of course, but I am enjoying the Foreign Office and I have some useful work to do there, But I agree with you – this is existential. I'll contact the PM's PPS and demand a meeting with Her Eminence.'

'Good,' replied Alistair. 'You're not alone; hopefully this'll turn out for the best, but as you know, she doesn't really understand these issues.

'And many others, it seems,' replied Richard.

• • • •

The next day Richard was waiting in the Number 10 foyer for his allotted meeting with the Prime Minister. It seemed he was not alone: a Cabinet Minister had just gone in before him, presumably for the same reason. After the minister left, Richard was ushered through into the PM's study where she was sitting on a sofa. She gestured him to sit opposite. 'I believe you wanted to see me about something urgent.'

'Yes, Prime Minister, as you know I'm greatly honoured to serve in your government. I enjoy the Foreign Office and think we have a great programme for Government. However, I am also partly Scottish, and beyond my loyalty to the Party and the Government, I am loyal to the unity of our state. I'm very concerned that these proposals will threaten that. If they were pushed through, I'm afraid that I would feel it my duty to resign from the Government to fight them from the back benches.'

Summers looked surprised: Richard had come to the point rather quicker than she'd been expecting. For a moment she looked at him as though he were mad. Then, glancing down at her papers, she said, 'I understand your concerns, I really do, but I believe you misunderstand the situation we find ourselves in. We are in an incredibly delicate position in Scotland and if we ignore the First Minister's mandate, there'll be an immediate referendum, which I fear we would lose. This is the only way I can see to keep the UK together.'

Richard interjected forcefully. 'But Prime Minister, it would be kept together in name only. What is the UK without a single shared policy? If we concede this principle, we'll have a virtually independent Scotland with a leader seeking to cut the final tie that binds our great country together. I ask you, please think again. I cannot put my name to this.'

The Prime Minister went on. 'Myself and Robert Lacy have been through this over and over Richard, and I'm afraid there's no other alternative.'

After a pause, Richard chose his next words carefully. He had expected a longer discussion, to be fobbed off with the promise of further talks, but for once the Prime Minister had been decisive.

'Well in that case I have no alternative. I will have to resign from the Government.'

There was nothing else to say. Richard looked again at Summers, who sat there impassively. He showed himself out, striding past an aide who'd been waiting outside.

Once out of Downing Street, Richard called Alistair. 'I've

done it, I've resigned.'

'I am sorry for you, but you're in good company. Three Cabinet ministers will be making an announcement shortly – you can join them if you like over on College Green. I'll see you there.'

College Green is a small area where the press can conduct impromptu interviews against the backdrop of the Victoria Tower. Richard headed for a huddle of journalists and MPs. The Secretary of State for Defence was speaking.

'That is why I have today tendered my resignation as Secretary of State for Defence.'

A journalist then shouted out: 'Mr Braithwaite, what do you make of the Prime Minister's statement a moment ago that if she has lost the confidence of her Party, then she'll put her proposals for Scottish devolution to the people in a General Election?'

That came as a shock to Richard. There was no danger of a no confidence vote, but perhaps Summers hoped to win more seats, catch the opposition off guard? Maybe Lacy had convinced her it was a chance to destroy Richard's side of the party for good and then force his Scotland policy through?

But by the evening it had been confirmed: the Prime Minister had indeed gone to the King to request an election to settle the matter of her Bill.

• • • •

The next day everything in Westminster was turned upside down. MPs were preparing to pack up their offices and decamp to their constituencies before they were locked out of Parliament when it was dissolved at the end of the week. Across Whitehall all work ground to a halt, while civil servants held furtive meetings behind the backs of their ministers on preparing for a possible change of Government.

Richard's seat had never been particularly safe: he'd won it for the first time ever from the Labour Party yet despite the problems with Scotland, the Conservative vote was holding up in the opinion polls and he had a reasonable reputation for getting things done locally. He was therefore quietly confident, but you could never take things for granted. There were leaflets and posters to be printed and election addresses to compose; in fact, he had everything to do and very little time.

16. Re-election

Silksworth Sports Hall, Sunderland, 27 July

It was 12.30 a.m. and Richard was in a state of mild anxiety. His election campaign had gone well and he remained quietly confident he would remain an MP. However, the count in his Sunderland West constituency had been slower than normal, suggesting the result must be close. This left him in the awkward position of having to mill about the sports hall where the counting was taking place, making small talk with local councillors and trying to seem upbeat, when talk was the last thing on his mind.

Back in the days of huge Labour majorities the constituency had prided itself on having the fastest count in the country. Richard thought it was perhaps the speed of the count that guaranteed the large Labour victories, but he kept that to himself. Well, that was the past; this was a Conservative constituency now and the count was considerably slower. The delay at least meant that he would not be the first Conservative MP to be defeated live on election night, which was always a risk.

The snap General Election had caught everyone offside, not least Richard who had only six weeks to get a campaign together in his decidedly marginal constituency. Still, he'd managed to put up a good fight. The leaflets were printed and delivered, despite the winter nights closing in.

He padded around the sports hall checking up on the tables of council employees counting the ballot papers, his initial confidence draining away to be replaced by increasing anxiety. His agent, a retired Glaswegian teacher, wasn't helping his mood, fretting over every incident of potential fraud and regurgitating everything he thought they could have done better.

Nothing would have made much difference. He knew that the council workers, mostly Labour Party supporters, wanted to see the back of him, but there were only so many complaints he could make to the Returning Officer, and a few cases of ballot papers shuffled into the wrong piles wouldn't tip it one way or another.

When he had first won the seat in 2019 it was something of a surprise to himself, but even more so to the Conservative Party. If they had known it was a 'winnable seat', he would never have been chosen as the candidate.

Richard was under no illusions as to the ephemeral nature of his role as MP. He was first elected in the heady days of Brexit. Sunderland had voted to Leave. The referendum result was widely seen as a one-off victory for the Conservatives, but the idea that the Conservative vote would evaporate when 'normal politics' resumed had proved false. Edwards had won the following General Election and the former PM's useful work in Sunderland had enabled Richard to made a name for himself locally and he was now a regular feature in the local media. His re-election in 2024 was to him far more remarkable and something he was quietly very proud of. He was now faintly amused to observe that the Party had now gone from believing the constituency was unwinnable to expecting him to be re-elected.

This time things were different again. Edwards' resignation had changed the dynamic. Caroline Summers had been something of a drag anchor on Richard's campaign in Sunderland.

She was the chalk to the Edwards cheese. The product of a Conservative Party drive for more women in top roles, she'd risen rapidly to ministerial level. Earnest, untalented, with little sense of humour and few original ideas, she seemed to exude disapproval of the Sunderland voters. Richard had failed to strike up a conversation with her on the few occasions he'd met her, and thankfully, due to his resignation, he'd been spared a prime ministerial visit during the election campaign.

And what a dreadful election campaign it had been. Edwards had been a lucky Prime Minister, and had probably seen the acrimony over Scotland coming before 'retiring' to his writings and royalties. So it was left to Summers to walk straight into a political crisis she had little notion of how to deal with – the rising threat of Scottish Nationalism under Malcolm MacIntyre.

This election was billed as a chance for Scotland to reject separatism and to give Summers the mandate she needed to negotiate a new settlement and force it through the House of Commons, but nobody had thought to ask why the rest of the UK would vote for a Conservative Party pledged to waste their hard-earned money on placating the truculent Scots. So the campaign had inevitably descended into an auction in Scotland, an auction the Conservatives could not win. All this was met with reactions ranging from ambivalence to outright annoyance south of the border, and indeed in Richard's own constituency.

Furthermore, the election campaign had lacked focus right from the start. What were they asking the electorate for? A mandate to overcome Conservative opposition to a Conservative Government?

Despite this, Richard had reason to feel confident. He'd run a reasonable local campaign and his Labour opponent, a militant far-left trade union activist, was as close to unelectable as you could get. He could see her at the other end of the sports hall with her agent and a group of local Labour councillors in deep discussion. Noticing they looked downcast, Richard fought back a wry smile.

Not long now he thought. What would he do if he lost? Go back into business? Perhaps he could work for a consultancy that had interests in the Far East? Or perhaps a think-tank?

He looked around the hall: the activity on the desks had subsided and the ballots were assembled in piles.

He spotted the Returning Officer walking over to him. 'We're ready Mr Reynolds, if you could make your way over to the stage.'

Richard walked over slowly; the candidates were forming a huddle around the Returning Officer to hear the results before they were made public. They then went up to assemble on the stage.

'The results are as follows: Green 431, Liberal Democrat 1,532, Independent 210, Labour 17,658…' There was a half-hearted cheer – the number was lower than they'd expected. 'Richard Reynolds, Conservative 18,342.' The remaining results were inaudible, drowned out by a mixture of boos and cheers.

Richard's anxiety was replaced by a certain glee when he saw a look of pure hatred on the face of his Labour opponent, of an intensity only those deeply imbued in the Labour Left could generate when in the proximity of a Tory. He'd pulled it off again. Remarkable, he thought.

Richard walked to the podium. 'This is a great night for

the Conservatives and the Prime Minister and a great night for Sunderland,' he said. 'I will continue to work tirelessly to ensure more investment comes to the city…'

But was it a good night for the Conservatives and, more importantly, for the United Kingdom? Was Summers up to dealing with the wily MacIntyre? Failure meant the end of the UK. This was high stakes stuff.

Walking off the podium, Richard checked his phone to see what was going on elsewhere. Better than he expected, it seemed – they were holding on to seats – but the big majority Summers felt she needed and deserved was evidently not materialising. And then there was Scotland. He phoned Robert Clarke, a neighbouring MP who'd also been re-elected earlier in the evening.

'Well good evening, Robert, how's it looking?

'I think we might just make it. Your result certainly stirred things up. Labour thought they'd won it! But have you seen Scotland, not good, not good at all. It looks like we've lost every seat, Labour and the Liberals likewise. This will make things very difficult.'

Richard digested this news; it was what they'd all feared. They'd run a dreadful campaign in Scotland, but that wasn't the whole story. Malcolm MacIntyre was a nasty piece of work, but he was highly effective, adept at turning everything into an independence issue, and he'd now managed to silence nearly all opposing voices.

If you did business in Scotland or worked in the media you had to toe the line. The Scots budget and the SNP's powers of employment patronage meant that pro-Union figures had all but ceased to exist. Scotland had become MacIntyre's private domain, and echo chamber where even the BBC had given up reporting national stories. The Union had many supporters and many sound arguments, but nobody to articulate them in public. Even when they did, the legion of SNP foot soldiers would muddy the waters. Nobody knew what to believe.

'Well, not much we can do about it tonight. Are you heading to London tomorrow? Catch up then?' said Richard.

'Yes, that'd be good,' Clarke replied. 'Oh, by the way Richard, before I go, did you see Tommy Rosenfield on earlier? As smug and overbearing as always – reading between the lines he seemed to criticise the Prime Minister. What's he up to I wonder?'

Richard took a large intake of breath to calm himself, Rosenfield's very name was enough to dissipate any positive feelings remaining from the election result.

'Yes, I did. You know I don't like him, even less so since he's started scheming with Lacy. I have no doubt he's up to no good. I'll try and find out.'

· · · ·

Richard's first encounter with Rosenfield had been in Afghanistan, at what should have been a safe distance. Rosenfield had served there with the Intelligence Corps, but had rarely ventured out of Camp Bastion in Helmand Province. Richard was a second lieutenant in an infantry unit, responsible during his six months there for conducting patrols, sometimes by vehicle, sometimes on foot. Often, they'd be accompanied by Afghan National Army (ANA) soldiers who they were there to mentor and train.

Rosenfield's job had been to vet the ANA recruits and report on their morale. Sadly, this had gone tragically wrong when one of Richard's patrols had come under fire in a village, where, it transpired, some of his ANA soldiers came from. One Scots soldier was seriously wounded before they managed to fall back.

The debrief revealed that the village was a known centre of Taliban activity, and it should have been Rosenfield's job to make Richard aware of this. He felt as if he'd been led into a trap.

More recently, during Richard's short spell as a minister in the Scotland Department, Rosenfeld had used his committee to hamper their work on the funding of political parties, making life as difficult as possible for him by, for example, insisting on an evidence session while Richard was supposed to be abroad, or cancelling a committee session at short notice and, when it finally went ahead, aiming scathing language a little too directly at him.

So what was Rosenfield up to? Probably, as per usual, promoting himself, scheming and covering up his incompetence and greed by ingratiating himself with those in power. As time went on, the chances of him causing real damage increased.

• • • •

Safely back home Richard turned on the television to catch some more of the results coming in. It had been a surprisingly good night for the Conservatives: Labour had clearly lost but had not yet conceded defeat. A slightly improved Conservative majority, so no need for the Northern Irish Unionists, yet not large enough to give Summers a free hand in her promised negotiations on Scotland.

The BBC then switched to a count in Scotland. Malcolm MacIntyre, who was contesting a Westminster seat, was giving his victory speech: 'This is a great result for Scotland and something the English Tory Government cannot ignore. We have a clear mandate for an independent, non-aligned Scotland. If the Prime Minister does not grant us a referendum, we will hold one ourselves.'

Well, there it was: a clear provocation, an illegal referendum with its ensuing chaos while the world looked on. And that curious wording 'non-aligned' – like something out of the Cold War – probably a negotiation play, a threat to leave NATO and to remove the RAF and Royal Navy bases from Scottish territory. A truly dreadful situation, made worse by an unknown and untested Prime Minister. He dialled Duncan Turnbull, a now-former MP for the Borders who'd lost his seat that night

'Very sorry to see the result. Dreadful. Guess you stood no chance. What happened?'

Duncan replied, clearly exhausted. 'Well, partly Summers' campaign. Our message almost encouraged people to vote for the SNP, but as you know, they've monopolised the media up here. They've exploited it very cleverly.

'But there's something new. There's always been bitterness, but never quite at this level. The SNP were organised and well-funded, whereas the little assistance we had soon vanished: helpers were warned off, posters disappeared within hours etc. What's to be done?'

'Hopefully we can learn from this,' said Richard. 'The legislation we've planned can't come fast enough. Let's have a proper chat about it in London.'

Richard struggled to get off to sleep, feeling the weight of responsibility for what might happen next.

17. The People's Liberation Amy

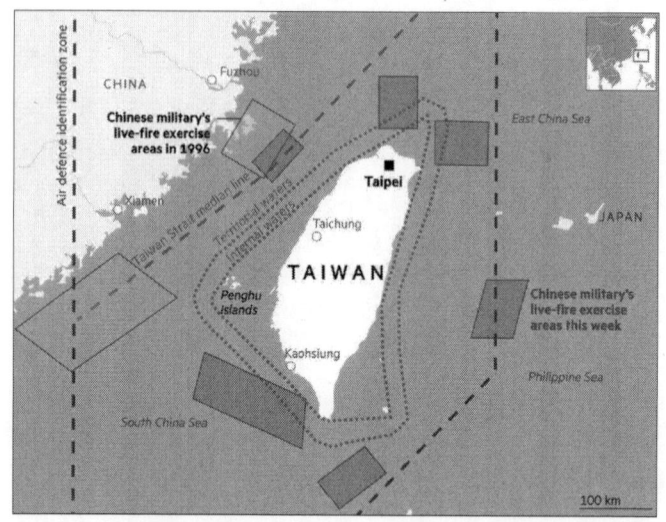

Xiamen, Fukian Province, Southern China, 28 July

General Hu Zhijian, Commander of the PLA's 73rd Army Group, knew this was going to be a busy day. From his desk in his base at Xiamen on China's southern coast in Fukian Province, Taiwanese territory was only four miles away. A small island admittedly, but for some of his colleagues this was unfinished business from the Chinese Civil War.

He had just received orders from General He Weidong of Eastern Command to prepare for a major amphibious landing exercise for later in the year.

These orders didn't come as a surprise: he'd been expecting them ever since the President's snap visit three weeks previously.

General Hu had joined the PLA when he was eighteen, having been conscripted in his home province of Manchuria in the industrial north-east. It had been punishing and dull, particularly for someone whose family origins serving the Qing dynasty still put him under suspicion.

He'd never seen orders for an amphibious exercise on this scale before, but he understood the reasoning. Chiang Kai-shek's Nationalists, having lost the Civil War to the Communists in 1949, had intended to use Taiwan as a base from which to retake the whole of China – a pretence that had continued to the present day. Therefore, both Beijing and Taipei claimed to be the legitimate government of all of China. However, many in Taiwan no longer wished to rejoin the mainland, having seen the tender mercies of Xi's government in Hong Kong. The financial crisis and the shootings in Fujian had polarised Taiwanese opinion even further, with politicians there now openly calling for a formal declaration of independence. For Taiwan this was a statement of the obvious, but for China it was a huge provocation.

General Hu understood what was being asked of him. They were to put on a massive show of force, to send a message to Taiwan that they should not move towards an official declaration of independence. An exercise – but a political one.

He knew what was needed: the requisition of civilian cargo ships and car ferries to provide capacity for perhaps half a million men and vehicles. He needed supplies. He'd coordinate with the navy and air force. Then, for the show itself, they'd carefully curate footage for Taiwanese and international consumption: landings, missile launches, cargo ships and ferries unloading vehicles on shore. The message had to be clear.

This would all take time to organise and he'd have to visit the capital. The thought cheered him: he enjoyed going up to Beijing.

It soon became clear to him what he was required to do. He would produce a scenario based on an amphibious landing on Taiwan. This would involve many stages – a preliminary missile and air attack on the island fortress of Penghu in the Straits of Taiwan close to potential invasion lanes – followed by a simulated mass landing on what would supposedly be the south-west coast of Taiwan. Not too difficult he thought, he had outlined similar scenarios before.

In the meantime, under the pretext of missile tests, the navy would encircle the island and close off certain areas of ocean, simulating a blockade to prevent any reinforcement of Taiwan.

Similar plans in the past had always concluded that such an operation against Taiwan was feasible, and the requisite resources were in place. This was the answer that the Central Military Commission required and the one he'd always supplied.

In reality, he knew that an invasion of Taiwan faced many serious problems. The island was well defended and motivated. Anti-ship missiles were based on Taiwan and Penghu. Taiwan itself was largely surrounded by cliffs, reducing his landing options to a few beaches in the south-west – something Taiwan knew perfectly well. It would also require far more troops than he could muster for an exercise. To gain the minimum three-to-one advantage that an invader needed would require mobilising perhaps over one million men who would need to be transported across the straits once air and naval superiority had been achieved.

Air superiority, despite the bravado of the air force, was not assured. They had some fine planes: the J-20 Chengdu 'Mighty Dragon' was more than a match for the Taiwanese

F-16s, but Taiwan was protected by a Patriot missile defence net that would neutralise their advantage. Beyond the J-20s, the PLA air force represented easy pickings for the Taiwanese.

General Hu knew of all these difficulties, but the unrealistic nature of China's plans never concerned him unduly. He could not write a report suggesting an amphibious invasion of Taiwan was impossible, and in any event, what would be the point? They were not going to invade Taiwan, now or in the near future. By the time they were ever ready to do so, he'd be happily retired.

Hu knew his subject. He'd studied the amphibious landings on D-Day in Normandy, Inchon in the Korean War, Anzio, Leyte and Okinawa. Surprise was the key to success. Without it, as was seen at Okinawa, fighting could be brutal. He knew there was no possibility of a surprise landing on Taiwan – at least not one accompanied by air and naval superiority.

China would need to come out on top in a protracted period of naval and air warfare before any landings could happen, but this would give the Taiwanese the chance to reinforce their beaches and call up their reserves. Landing against a dug-in and motivated enemy would lead to a bloodbath.

He also knew that his troops were capable, but untested. Endless classes on Marxist-Leninism did not make up for their lack of leadership and technical skills.

On D-Day the Allies landed 156,000 troops from one of the largest fleets ever assembled, gaining a three-to-one advantage over the defending Germans. Hu would need to land over a million all at once with perhaps only 300 landing craft.

The plans therefore involved requisitioning large sections of the Chinese merchant and auxiliary fishing fleets to act as small landing ships. The organisation would be complex and the chances of landing troops in good order from fishing boats onto a contested beach were, he thought, low.

He knew the navy and air force doubted the possibility of clearing the way to Taiwan. The Taiwanese navy would cause havoc if they got in amongst an invasion fleet, and there were only so many places to land on Taiwan. The far side of the island was hemmed in by the Philippines and Japan, while the China-facing coast was heavily defended and populated. They would also need a port.

No. This was a fool's mission and everyone knew it. But for political reasons it was best to keep up appearances.

If he had been asked for a serious report on the possibilities of an invasion, he would have concluded the chances of success were fifty-fifty at best, and at a huge cost in terms of men and material. But none of that would be a concern as long as the exercises remained just that: exercises. They were designed to force Taiwan to continue with the status quo and keep the Americans from interfering.

With that in mind, Hu spent the next few days with his staff preparing an outline of the proposed exercises, and then boarded the three-hour flight to Beijing to attend a planning meeting.

18. The Union

Sunderland, 28 July

It had not been a restful night for Richard, what was left of it. Images of Malcolm MacIntyre snarling in his grating Glaswegian accent kept coming back to haunt him. The longer he lay awake, MacIntyre's accent began to warp into the Ulster accent he remembered from the Troubles. He fought it back, but the image remained. By the time he awoke, Richard was exhausted and full of dread. The new Parliament had the potential to be utterly miserable.

Later that day he caught the train back to London to be ready for the inevitable turmoil ahead.

They were barely a few hours into the new Parliament and Summers' intention of settling the issue of Scottish independence once and for all had achieved the exact opposite.

Richard along with all the other parliamentary candidates, had signed up to Summers' manifesto commitment to negotiate with the SNP and vote for any negotiated solution. Would she now bind them into voting for a deal that weakened the Union still further? But what was the alternative? With opinion polls again showing a majority for independence in Scotland, a referendum was surely off the table.

But doing nothing was also a bad option. As his friend Duncan had explained, the Nationalists were skilfully using their existing powers to ensure no alternative view got an airing. Unlike the Conservatives north of the border, they were organised and well-funded. Any delay would just allow more time for corrosive Nationalism to take hold and become normalised. Something needed to be done before it was too late. But what?

Richard found his office in Portcullis House much as he'd left it, partly tidied in case he lost and needed to pack it all up. He fired up his computer and looked at his emails. Amongst the congratulatory messages was one from the 1922 Committee Chairman Sir Richard McLean.

> *Dear Colleagues, The Prime Minister has accepted my invitation to address all members of the parliamentary Party on Wednesday to update you on her plans for Scottish Government reform.*

This was followed immediately by an email from Sir Bill Howard MP, a former Cabinet minister of many years standing, and the chairman of an influential backbench group to which Richard was loosely affiliated.

> *Given the Prime Minister's intention to speak to the 1922 Committee we thought it wise to hold a discussion on the question of Scotland. If you are free, please attend in my Office on the 2nd floor above the Committee Corridor on Tuesday at 2 p.m.*

Good, at least someone else is concerned, thought Richard. Perhaps the stark nature of the election result meant the penny was finally about to drop? Well, he would attend.

On Tuesday Richard made his way across the glass-covered atrium of Portcullis House, full of the buzz of MPs fresh back from the elections chatting with journalists over coffee. Sir Bill's office was one of those reserved for senior ex-Cabinet ministers in the old Palace of Westminster, high up on the second floor overlooking the Thames. Arriving a little early, Richard was shown in. The room was oak-panelled and retained much of the original Pugin-designed furniture that most took for granted there.

Sir Bill was already chatting to another ex-Cabinet minister, while Duncan Turnbull sat on the sill of a bay window overlooking the Thames. Richard sat down on one of the green leather chairs. Eventually twenty-four MPs and several peers arrived, including one minister.

Sir Bill introduced the meeting. 'Thank you all for coming at short notice and congratulations to you all for your re-election, and commiserations to Duncan here. Very bad luck.

'I thought it'd be worthwhile sharing thoughts on the Prime Minister's meeting tomorrow. We know what was in the manifesto. I for one was not happy with the way it was sprung on us, but felt we had no choice but to agree. But I guess the question is – what have we agreed to? What will she say tomorrow and what do we want her to say? We can try and make our voices heard before then, but whether they're listening in Number 10 is another matter. Who'd like to go first? Duncan perhaps?'

'Thank you all for your kind words,' said Duncan. 'Although I'm no longer an MP, I thought I'd share some thoughts. The situation's dire in Scotland. All you hear up there is the SNP's shrill tones, their endless grievances. You have to be of a certain age to remember anything different. We did run a dreadful campaign, but MacIntyre's clever, unscrupulous and driven.

'They have resources we can only dream of, and their media

operation is first class: they can hammer out their lines, true or false, and get them into people's homes. I think we'd lose a referendum, but buying more time by conceding even more power will make matters worse.

'I think we have no option but to play for time, see how long he can maintain this atmosphere. It won't be easy, but surely at some point his bubble has to burst?

'And don't forget, if we fail in Scotland, there'll be an immediate boost for the Nationalists in Northern Ireland, and the Loyalists may well take matters into their own hands if they think they're being deserted. And we all know where that can lead.'

'Apart from that, all is well,' he concluded, with a dry laugh.

Most seemed in agreement. An increasingly forlorn Sir Bill summed it all up. 'Well, we can make our views known to others. There's no need to compound the effects of a poor campaign by conceding yet more power. I'll ask her to re-confirm that she's ruling out another independence referendum.'

Richard then asked if the MPs in the room would support his re-election onto the Foreign Affairs Committee so he could contribute to the Government's new policy on the Indo-Pacific region, something he knew about from his time in Singapore. He joked that Tommy Rosenfield may well use his position in the Foreign Office to try to block him, but their support would be invaluable. With that, the meeting broke up.

• • • •

The following day Richard turned up early knowing that up to 200 MPs might be present. The meeting was to take place in Committee Room 9, the largest on the Committee corridor, its two huge mullioned windows overlooking the Thames and seats arranged in aisles so that it resembled a miniature Commons debating chamber. Richard decided to sit near the back.

The room soon began to fill up. Some MPs took up positions on the window ledges at the back, while others of a more sycophantic frame of mind tried to gain a ringside seat from which to express their adulation of the current Prime Minister, just as they had of the last. There was a buzz of expectation.

On time, as was her habit, the Prime Minister entered. The sycophants started the traditional banging of the desks, trying to outdo each other in their show of loyalty. All eyes were on Summers. She began.

'Colleagues. When I called this election, I had hoped to settle the question of Scottish Nationalism for good. There can be no issue more important to us all as Conservatives and Unionists than the unity of our country, the United Kingdom.

'I wish I had better news for you all. Yes, we won this election, but don't underestimate the trouble we're in. We've failed to win the argument for the Union, and so we must continue to make the case while also displaying some flexibility. This will mean hard choices.

'I am grateful to you all for putting your faith in me. I will therefore be talking to the leader of the Scottish National Party with a view to a new and lasting constitutional settlement. We will look at everything.

'To that end we will call a constitutional convention on Scotland with a view to publishing a revised White Paper on the way forward in the next few months.'

There was an audible murmur of disapproval before the Chairman wound the meeting up. There followed another bout of congratulatory desk banging by the usual suspects, and Summers left.

Afterwards, Richard said to Sir Bill in the corridor, 'That was all very depressing. A full sell-out – is that the plan?'

'It would seem that way. More money no doubt, and now we have this idea of some form of independent military and foreign policy. In short, it's a slippery slope to full independence. But what do we do?'

Richard snapped back: 'Oppose it, get her to change her mind. What else is there to do?'

19. Beijing Calls

August 1, Building, Beijing, 31 July

At the Ministry of National Defence's compound – the August 1st Building – General Hu Zhijian was ushered into a meeting with his counterparts from the air force and navy. On the wall was a large map of Taiwan, and a photographer was present to record the proceedings, which would no doubt then be leaked to a spooked Taiwanese media as part of China's psychological warfare.

General Hu was expecting to be briefed on training for a simulated invasion of Taiwan, but from the moment he entered the compound he'd been struck by the earnestness of the officials.

After sitting through a number of long, formulaic speeches on the necessity of Chinese unification, his counterpart in the air force explained that long-range missiles would be launched against Taiwanese airbases and patriot missile batteries, putting them out of action long enough for long-range Xiang H-6 bombers protected by J-20 fighters to flood the area with anti-ship missiles and attack the island fortress on Penghu. Fighter jets armed with long-range missiles would then suppress remains of the Taiwanese air force. China had a three-to-one advantage in terms of fighters, and due to Taiwan's proximity, even the aged MiG-19s could be of use and make up for the lack of the superior quality fifth generation J-20 'Mighty Dragon' aircraft.

Hu listened sceptically, knowing the plan made little sense in reality. The massed numbers of MiG-19s were a throwback to the Korean War and no match for Taiwanese planes. Yes, they might put some runways out of action for a while, but runways could be repaired quickly, and how many missiles did they have? Along with the rest of the room he clapped and made sure he was seen to be clapping.

He then listened to the naval preparations. The Taiwanese navy was formidable, but lacked submarines. The plan would be to clear an invasion route for Hu's ships, and station submarines around the perimeter to prevent Taiwanese ships interfering with the landings. This had some merits but limited the invasion to one area – the south-west – where the water was deep enough. Even then, the Chinese would be vulnerable to detection in some of the shallow parts, and exposed to anti-shipping missiles based on Penghu, inconveniently located in the very centre of their area of operation.

Lastly, it was Hu's turn to make his presentation to the room. Standing up in front of the large assembly of military and political staff, he explained the numbers he would deploy for the exercise and the shipping requirements once the navy and air force had cleared the way.

He would commandeer civilian ports on the south coast and mobilise Chinese fishing boats to practise mass landings. The merchant ships would stay offshore, while the smaller boats would ferry groups of soldiers onto the Taiwanese beaches. The ferries would follow up to offload more equipment once a Taiwanese port had been captured, presumably Dongshi on the coast closest to Penghu – a vital early objective. This would be coordinated with a large-scale missile attack, while land defences would be dealt with by the 105mm guns mounted on amphibious tanks.

He knew the small numbers he had available for the exercise were woefully inadequate, but he needed to impress the Politburo. A short video then showed the simulated attack ending in complete success, with a staff officer claiming they had war-gamed the scenarios using Artificial Intelligence, and came up against only ineffectual Taiwanese defensive strategies.

Nobody mentioned the possibility of other states intervening in the conflict: the American navy remained an elephant in the room, while the British Royal Navy didn't even rate a passing mention.

Hu was happy with his presentation: it had been well received, unsurprisingly he thought as many in the room had recently seen him make a similar presentation to President Xi. There'd been no difficult questions. He retired to the government accommodation for senior military personnel where his thoughts drifted back to Taiwan. Like most Chinese officials, he believed that the reunification of China was a strategic necessity: it had been a feature of his training as he rose through the military ranks. It was only natural that a newly powerful China should seek to put an end to the artificial division caused by the Civil War. Hong Kong and Macau had returned to the fold – Taiwan would be next.

It was not the end of Taiwanese independence that concerned him. Unlike others, he had no family on Taiwan and although he wasn't particularly bothered by the constant attacks on the Party that Taiwanese politicians indulged in, they didn't endear him to them either. But he was worried how seriously the Party leadership was taking the invasion plan. While in the past there had been an element of ritual about these exercises, the atmosphere seemed to have changed. Was this to be more than just an exercise?

If so, he had concerns, in particular the use of submarines to screen his invading troops. Hu knew that Chinese submarines had a weakness: they were easily trackable and the US would no doubt inform the Taiwanese of their whereabouts. This had come to light several years earlier when Chinese submarines shadowing a British Carrier Group had been contacted and harassed by submarines from both the US and British navies.

Of even greater concern was the inability of the Chinese navy to track British, American and Australian nuclear-powered submarines. When his invasion ships moved out into the deeper waters around the south-east coast of Taiwan, what would happen?

The South China Sea had long been the focus of China's naval expansion, but it was a confined space. There was only one entry point: the Malacca Straits via Singapore to the west, and the Taiwan and Luzon Straits to the east. Other entrances were too shallow and too far away: through the Sunda or Lombok Straits in Indonesia or the Philippines. Even a small number of submarines could patrol these confined spaces and deny China access to the Indian Ocean and its oil supplies. And what was the alternative? Well, they could sail south around Australia, but that would only increase the risks.

If the Australians, British or Americans imposed an oil blockade, there would be little China could do short of direct confrontation and nuclear war.

Hu mulled this all over in his lodgings, becoming more and more distraught. Would he be responsible for a disaster? There were too many variables: what about bad weather? What if they failed to overcome Taiwanese shore installations, or to capture the island fortress of Penghu and its anti-ship missiles? The risks had always been too high for an invasion to be seriously considered, but had something changed?

He needed to do something to stop things getting out of control, but he'd seen the room, the clapping. He'd even clapped himself! But any sign of defeatism and he and his family would be in deep trouble. There was only one person who might listen to his concerns. Fortunately, he was due to meet with him the next day at the Ministry of State Security to discuss the security aspects of the plan. But was it worth trying?

20. South Armagh

South Armagh, Northern Ireland, 31 July

The quiet country lanes, drystone walls and rolling green hills of South Armagh could, to an English eye, easily be mistaken for the Lake District. But this was once known as 'Bandit Country', where for over twenty years IRA snipers took their toll on British Army patrols, before safely disappearing down the back lanes and over the border to the Republic.

Driving from his home in Dundalk in the Republic, Aidan McGuire crossed the border and headed for the town of Crossmaglen, passing the police station, still encased in an ugly shell of corrugated iron, protecting it from the bombings of yesteryear.

Aidan was in his late forties and had grown up in Belfast towards the end of the Troubles. He was from a Roman Catholic, middle-class, non-political family.

Although a bright child, Aidan had not been the university type and had surprised his family when he announced he'd decided to join the British Army. He was soon at Pirbright going through his basic training.

His family, mindful of the complications that having a son in the army would cause them, told anyone who asked that he'd gone to university in Scotland. Nobody suspected he was now Second Lieutenant McGuire, 2nd Battalion, The Rifles Regiment. The longer he was away, the less people asked. When he came home for holidays, he told his parents stories of Bosnia and Iraq, and any enquiring friends about his work for various building firms. He got on well with his soldiers and over time his accent mellowed.

Ironically, it was only after the IRA had agreed a permanent ceasefire in 1998 that the now Captain McGuire joined Army Intelligence in Northern Ireland.

It took several years for Aidan to enrol in the Real IRA, a group that remained active in cross-border smuggling and occasional violence. His big break had been meeting old friends in a Nationalist pub in Dundalk still sympathetic to the cause. He moved closer and closer to the inner circle of the Real IRA until finally he was trusted to run small errands for them.

And so it was that he was now involved in one of the biggest errands in the last few decades of the South Armagh IRA, off to inspect a consignment of weapons.

The days of German submarines or steamers surreptitiously landing arms in Ireland were long gone. There was no need. Terrorists could import them directly into the Belfast docks: all you needed was a paper trail from a legitimate company with a track record in legitimate trading.

But it had become even easier. There were no longer any border controls between the Republic and Northern Ireland, no long queues waiting to cross the border, no soldiers likely to search your vehicle for weapons or explosives. It was an open border: the Troubles were over.

Rotterdam was the main point of entry for containers arriving in the EU from destinations around the world. Among the 25,000 arriving that day was one marked 'Harmony Trade Shipping Company of Guangzhou Province, China.' Its manifest detailed electric motors, but nobody checked the manifest. Less than 1 per cent of containers were inspected, and this wasn't one of them.

From Rotterdam, the sealed container was driven to Cherbourg, where it boarded the *Armorique* ferry bound for Ireland.

Only a few days earlier Aidan was tipped off by the OC of the South Armagh IRA brigade to expect 'something special'. Aidan knew better than to press for more information, but he could guess.

He knew what to do. The container would be unloaded at a building materials company near Newry run by an old IRA man. He would be out for the day as the delivery was made. Aidan would then shift the delivery in smaller loads over a few days to secret bunkers constructed years ago throughout South Armagh.

Aidan's car drew up in the deserted timber yard on the outskirts of Newry. Sitting on a pallet of timber, he waited in the surprisingly warm mid-morning sun. Eventually a truck entered the yard. The engine cut and the driver emerged from the cab.

'Hi, where do you want it?'

'Over there by the wall would be grand,' said Aidan, gesturing across the forecourt.

It was unloaded in a few minutes. Aidan waited until the truck was out of sight and went over to the container; he had the keys to the padlock, and once he'd twisted the lock rod at the back, he yanked it open and peered in.

Inside in the dark he could see wooden cases stacked up to the ceiling of the container. It would take a fair few journeys to transport, he thought to himself, but there was no hurry. For now, all he need to do was report that it had arrived intact and undetected. Aidan locked up the container, took off his gloves and returned to his car.

••••

Later that day Aidan drove the forty miles to Lisburn on the outskirts of Belfast on the pretext of going shopping, and texted his contact. At the appointed spot he parked up in a side street, got out and waited. When a white transit van pulled up beside him, he got in and it drove off.

'So, what is it?'

'It's the whole shebang: rifles, explosives, mortars, RPGs…'

The van did a circuit of Lisburn while the Special Branch operatives worked out the container's journey. It wouldn't be long before they tracked it back to Rotterdam and beyond.

Little did Aidan know that that after years of low-level criminality, the arrival of a huge consignment of weapons in South Armagh would cause major ripples to fan out around Whitehall.

The news caused alarm at MI5. Notes for the Prime Minister were prepared and read, but little concrete action was taken. The container, known IRA arms dumps and IRA operatives coming to disperse the weapons were carefully tracked.

Aidan spent the next few weeks behaving as if nothing had happened. He revisited the container and divided the cache into smaller shipments destined for concealed sites around South Armagh and Belfast.

The timber yard had been well chosen. Nobody thought anything of loads being picked up from the container at the back of the yard amongst a steady stream of legitimate deliveries and customers.

••••

Aidan returned to his life of semi-retirement in Dundalk and MI5 continued to monitor the new arms caches.

A few weeks later he met up again with the OC of the IRA brigade in the bar. 'That was good work you did. We've been busy for the last few months with our new friends; it's been a lot of work but I think it's all in place now.

'I have another job for you. We need to make contact with our new friends. I think you need to tell your family you'll be away for a few days.'

21. Singer & McColl

Washington DC, 31 July

Washington DC is a one-industry town, and that industry is politics, a whole ecosystem feeding off it like a carcass on the African plains. Unlike other great cities such as Paris and London, which double as finance and government centres, Washington lives for politics alone.

Amongst the huge undergrowth of lobbyists, strategists, think-tanks and consultants stand the offices of Jack McColl and his business partner Simon Singer – the eponymous Singer & McColl, lawyers and political consultants.

Jack had been in politics for many years, including spells working for the Democrat Governor of Pennsylvania and then for a senator on the Hill. Over the years he'd grown to loathe the cynicism and futility of many of the campaigns he'd been involved in. As he often said to his friends, 'Once you've seen the sausages being made you don't want to eat sausages,' and so it was for laws.

A master of the process and workings of the US political system, Jack had decided to move into the world of business consultancy, eventually setting up his own firm with his college friend Simon Singer. Although it paid the bills, the firm hadn't been the runaway success the two of them had hoped for: it was still a small firm with only five employees.

'What do you make of the Indo-Pac request that came in?' Jack asked, walking into Simon's office.

'Not quite sure it's our thing, but no harm inviting them in. They seem to have money, which is the main thing. We are pretending to run a business, after all.'

'Sure, I'll invite them in and give them a pitch,' said Jack.

And so a few days later Jack was shepherding in two middle-aged executives from a telecoms consultancy to discuss US and UK views regarding the Indo-Pacific area.

'We'd like your firm's help on the political situation in the Indo-Pacific, and Taiwan in particular,' said one of them. 'Our firm represents some major investors in the western Pacific area who are very interested in US, UK and Australian intentions in the area in case of, let's say, tension in the region that might impact their investments.'

Jack knew what this was about and had seen it before: political intelligence and risk management. The current US administration had been sending out mixed signals on Taiwan since the retreat from Afghanistan. The defence budget had been trimmed and commitments in the western Pacific quietly scaled back. The new President was decidedly uninterested in what she saw as a hobby horse for her opponents. Given all this, it was understandable that the Taiwanese wanted to know what would happen if the worst came to the worst: a full-scale Chinese invasion.

'I understand,' said Jack. 'We've worked with insurance companies on political risk in the past, and we're well known for our analysis and contacts on the Hill.'

'That's why we're here. What are the chances of Taiwan being offered protection? I know you're not the CIA, but we can present your analysis to our clients.'

'What we can do,' said Jack, 'is commission opinion-polling of key decision makers and conduct focused interviews with some of the leading opinion makers in all three countries. That'll give your clients a clearer picture.'

Jack was surprised when his visitors didn't demur. The meeting closed, he showed them out to the foyer at ground level and hurried back up to see Simon.

'What do you make of our mystery guests?' Simon shot at him.

'Strange, I have no idea who they are. Perhaps they represent our friends in Foggy Bottom, getting someone else to do their work for them?'

'That was my thought too. Well, if it is, they'll pay, which is the key thing. We can play along with their game. They know we're trustworthy.'

Jack replied, stroking his chin as if in deep thought. 'I've done some digging: they have a website, some case studies on their political strategy and due diligence work, a phone line, switchboard. I think we can say we've performed due diligence on the company.'

Simon smiled. 'Good, let's see what transpires.'

Jack said, 'I'll ask for some money on account if they agree the pitch. I don't mind going to Australia and the UK if needed.'

• • • •

Two days later an email arrived confirming acceptance of their proposal. The money safely in their account, Jack and Simon went out for drinks in a bar they knew in Georgetown.

'So, Jack, you'll be off to London now with our new mystery client?'

'Actually, I've started work on that already. I've found a company there to do some polling, and we have the names of three MPs, one of them involved in UK foreign policy who the client suggested. They seem to be in quite a hurry. We'll also meet a UK think-tank and two US journalists based there.'

'Good, so long as the cheques keep rolling in; we could do with some more mystery clients!'

The next day Jack set to work organising meetings for his trip to London. First among them was the politician his client had suggested he meet – Richard Reynolds MP.

22. Mei Ling

**Ministry of State Security, Haidan District, Beijing,
1 August**

Mei Ling was in her early thirties, unusually tall, attractive and, like most of her generation, with a taste for Western brands, on the surface just a typical member of the educated, wealthy Chinese middle class that had ridden the wave of economic growth over the last few decades. But her apparent wealth had an unlikely origin.

Mei had just walked into the Ministry of State Security, the government department overlooking Kunming Lake, part of the gardens and ruins of the old Imperial Summer Palace.

Mei walked across the busy foyer and headed towards the lifts. People momentarily stopped to look. She exuded an air of affluence that set her apart from the other state employees in the building.

Mei was one of China's elite foreign agents, and she was in a hurry because she had just been informed that Chen Wenquing, the minister in charge of the MSS, wished to speak to her.

Mei had been in a few meetings with Chen, but this felt very different somehow. So it was with some anxiety that she made her way up to his office.

Mei was from near Harbin in the industrial north-east of China. She was at least partly Manchu, something that explained her height. During the cultural revolution of the 1960s her family had hidden their ancestry and adopted a majority Han ethnic name. They'd been tough times, and her father had by necessity been brought up as a loyal Party man in Harbin.

She remembered him well, always scrupulously loyal to the Party. Sadly, he'd died when Mei was still at school, but his connections had eventually helped her to join the Ministry of State Security.

The Party had sent her to Sydney University to study computing. She could have stayed in Australia and severed her links with the Party, but her indecision was overtaken by events when she accepted a well-paid job for a Chinese state-owned construction company in Singapore.

There, her ostensible role was in IT, but in reality, she helped manage a network of Chinese informants throughout Singapore, Malaysia and Indonesia, using a string of construction projects as cover. She discovered she had a flair for recruiting agents to work for China, and she acquired a reputation for opening doors. So much so that she'd been entrusted with carrying out tasks in the UK and the USA.

The inevitable recall to China came: a promotion, a job in MSS headquarters centralising the data held by various directorates on hundreds of thousands of individuals in target countries: names, dates of birth, bank details, phone numbers and addresses hacked from social media accounts. The project was now seen as something of the jewel in the MSS's foreign operations crown. Mei was well paid, had a nice modern apartment in Beijing and liked to holiday in Hong Kong and in Europe, from where she'd just arrived.

• • • •

Chen Wenquing was sitting behind his desk as she walked

in. He was in his mid-fifties, short and slightly overweight, wearing an old-fashioned suit and even older glasses that contrasted jarringly with Mei's modernity.

'Please sit; we have something to discuss. Comrade Ling, how would you like to return to Singapore?'

This was a surprise. Mei had been expecting the sort of dull data project she'd become quite good at. A little flutter of excitement went through her body.

'I am of course at the Party's disposal, Comrade Minister. I know Singapore and our team there. I would greatly enjoy the opportunity to serve there again.'

Chen smiled. 'I'm well aware of that. We have an important assignment that requires your level of knowledge and loyalty to the Party.'

Mei was finding it hard to restrain her excitement; she liked Singapore and the chance to escape the constraints of her current job was something she'd been longing for. Chen then leant forward and his demeanour changed. He said, in a conspiratorial manner, 'Did I ever tell you that I once knew your father?'

Mei was intrigued. She did not. She could remember many of her father's friends, but she was sure he'd never mentioned Chen.

'Are you also from Harbin?' she asked.

Chen wasn't offended by her informal manner; in fact he was rather enjoying letting her in on his secret. But for now he was keen to move on. He smiled again in a conspiratorial manner. 'I'll have to tell you more about your father when we next meet. He was a good and loyal servant of the Party and of China, and cared deeply for its safety. I know that I can trust you as I once trusted him.'

Mei could not hide her surprise. Was Chen responsible for the success of her career so far?

'Minister, my father—'

'Not now. We have more urgent matters to attend to. One of our directors will brief you on your mission to Singapore. It is at short notice and of great importance, but for someone of your ability… We'll speak again when you're back.'

Her time was up; Chen rose and showed her to the door. Outside, his deputy Tan Geng was waiting. Mei suspected he'd been listening all the while and he scuttled in to see his superior as soon as she left.

Her meeting with the director and two other ministry officials, specialists on Singapore, dragged on for the rest of the day. Eventually Mei was given a new passport and access to funds.

She was now an employee of a Chinese state-owned telecoms company visiting a subsidiary in Singapore. She had copies of company plans, meetings she was to attend and details of various items being shipped into Singapore. All superficially convincing, all genuine company documents, but all fake.

23. A New Parliament

Portcullis House, Parliament, Westminster, 2 August

'So, what are you going to do now Richard?' said Alistair, the now former Secretary of State to the now former Foreign Office Minister. They'd met for a coffee in Portcullis House, a rather public place but only a short journey to their ministerial offices.

'I don't know really, there are a few things I want to follow, see how they develop.'

'Yes, wise plan. Quite brutal, the way one's job is terminated around here. I had expected it I guess, but nonetheless it's a shock. I was called in to Number 10 and the PM told me I was being sacked. Of course, I'd worked that out already: it was early in the day and it had been suggested the car drop me off at the Cabinet Office to avoid the public walk up Downing Street. Coming out I was told I'd be taken to the Commons; all the stuff from my office had already arrived – the civil servants knew before I did!'

Richard was mildly shocked by this; he knew politics was brutal but hadn't considered the mechanics before. No goodbyes or leaving drinks, just out!

Richard knew the chances of him re-entering government in the foreseeable future were somewhere between slim and zero. He'd helped run a rival leadership candidate's campaign and resigned, and the new management were hardly likely to give him a medal. Besides, he was hardly enthused by the government's direction under Summers, and he'd find his views very hard to disguise.

He would have to get used to his current role as a backbench MP, but it did have its benefits. He could write articles, develop thinking on areas that interested him, carve out a niche and a reputation as an 'expert'. The Far East, the future of the UK constitution – there was a wide range of subjects he could write about. It wasn't the end of the world not having to go through the red boxes every day, his diary and time managed by the department, fighting an unceasing battle against a Civil Service enthused with values he little understood or cared for. He would not miss that.

But he wasn't prepared to give up politics and slide into the uneventful life of a government loyalist. He had a plan, the start of which was to get himself elected to the influential Foreign Affairs Committee.

He had a fight on his hands, and he knew it. He suspected Foreign Secretary Tommy Rosenfield would ask the Whips to try and block him. While the Government was forbidden from influencing elections to the Committees, they could easily lean on loyal MPs to vote for their favoured candidate. A quiet word here, a promise there. 'Did you know that Mr Reynolds was unsound on…' He knew the drill, having been on the other end of those conversations in the past.

He would need to meet fire with fire. He already had the support of his immediate circle of allies, but for good measure he fired off messages reminding them he was standing. The real key was to access the new intake of MPs before they were told what to do by the Whips.

This election was an internal Party contest, and so he had to reach the whole Party and convince them to vote for him. Richard decided to treat this as a real election and printed a short flyer –

> Vote for Richard Reynolds for the Foreign Affairs Committee on 15th September
> - Former minister – I know how to hold the FCO to account.
> - I have lived in the Far East and wish to contribute to the Committee's work on scrutinising China's role in South East Asia and the Government's Indo-Pacific policy.
> - Stronger defence in NATO and more Government engagement in the Indo-Pacific, including the UK's Five Powers Agreement with Malaysia, Singapore, Australia and New Zealand.
> - Will continue to fight to change the culture in the FCO to focus more on UK interests and less on FCO interests.

With his leaflets back from the printers, Richard set off on a *chevauchée* around the parliamentary estate in search of Conservative MPs' offices.

Having been in Parliament for many years, Richard was still surprised to discover new corridors. Amongst the 330 Conservative MPs, he knew at most fifty to speak to, and a wider group as acquaintances. That left a huge number of MPs he hardly knew or even recognised.

Tramping the corridors of Parliament took him the best part of a day, the garrets up in the rafters of the House of Commons, more spacious corridors in the Norman Shaw Building, spacious suites for former ministers and tiny basement offices for the most junior MPs, all allocated by the Accommodation Whip, who always became incredibly popular the moment they were appointed.

Circling the building he became aware that Parliament was in a state of organised chaos. Defeated MPs were still packing up their offices and the new incumbents were congregating in the committee rooms waiting for their IT logins to be set up.

It was from one of these new MPs that Richard discovered who he was up against – another former minister, a friend and political ally of Tommy Rosenfield, Julian White MP. White too had been talking to MPs, but enquiries had also been made by the Whips on his behalf. He'd be the one to beat.

Well, this would be an interesting contest, Richard thought to himself. The truth was it was only a junior position, albeit one that came with the potential to travel and highlight interesting issues, but the thought that Rosenfield had decided to try and stop him made Richard even more determined. If his leaflets and conversations hadn't reached everyone, he'd also write some online articles, including on a Conservative blog. They'd be loyal and would attack Labour, but also independent and highlighting issues he knew were of particular concern to MPs: the increasing instability emanating from China and, to a lesser extent, Russia – all subtly explaining why he was the best candidate. He could post the articles on various MPs' WhatsApp groups and get his friends to comment on them.

The day came, and Richard was tense. He was therefore relieved that shortly after the ballot closed, the Chairman of the 1922 Committee rang to tell him he had been successful.

• • • •

The first meeting duly came around. The new Committee Chair was to be Sir Gareth Smith, an MP on the Right of the Labour Party and someone Richard respected.

It is a quirk of the system that whereas committee positions are allotted to Parties and the members elected from within those Parties, the Chairs are also from a designated Party but then elected by the House of Commons as a whole. So Sir Gareth had been elected on the back of Conservative votes, including Richard's.

Before the first meeting, Richard introduced himself to his fellow members and canvassed some ideas he'd like to pursue, including the question of increasing Chinese influence both in the West and in South East Asia. Newspaper investigations had recently exposed Chinese money in UK and foreign universities. Richard suggested this was something that could be usefully publicised.

Secondly, and allied to this, he felt the Government's increased focus on the Indo-Pacific region should be looked at in more detail. Was it in the UK's interest to oppose Chinese influence in this area, or should they leave it to the Americans?

'Maybe we should visit the Indo-Pacific and take a look!' Richard suggested only half-jokingly to one of the Labour MPs.

24. Curious Visitors

3rd Floor, 1 Parliament Street, Parliament, Westminster, 6 August

Richard stood in his new House of Commons office amongst packing cases. His demotion from ministerial office had been sharp and brutal and he hadn't quite recovered. Shortly after his resignation he'd received a message asking him to pack up his Minister's Parliamentary office on a gloomy corridor near the Commons Chamber. He was being relocated to a new block overlooking Whitehall. There'd been little time to organise things before being barred from the Palace of Westminster for the duration of the election campaign.

His removal from the Foreign Office had been even more brutal; he'd never been back into the building and his possessions, such as they were, had appeared in a box the following day.

So, there he stood, wondering how to organise his new room and admiring the third-floor view over Parliament Street to the Portland stone bulk of HM's Treasury opposite, and down Whitehall past the Cenotaph and into Parliament Square to the left; a good vantage point to observe the daily protests.

Without a ministerial job, Richard was busy with other responsibilities, much to the chagrin of the two staff who'd been running his parliamentary office while he was across the road in the Foreign Office. Constituency school visits and meetings with local businesses had taken over from foreign trips.

He'd previously entrusted constituency emails and invitations to his secretary Adele to sift through, but he now had the time to go through them himself. One immediately aroused his curiosity: an invitation from a Washington DC law firm, Singer & McColl.

The reasons the firm wanted to speak to him were vague, but seemed related to US/UK relations generally and the Indo-Pacific region in particular. Richard was wary of this sort of thing: might it be a newspaper sting from a fake company offering money? He'd never been on the receiving end himself, but there was always a first time, he thought. He looked up their website and googled the name on the invitation – Jack McColl, previously a staffer on Capitol Hill. It seemed to check out. Well, it might be interesting, he thought, scrawling 'ACCEPT' and placing the invitation on the pile for Adele.

He thought little of it until the day came around, an uneventful Tuesday with little parliamentary business. When the two Americans arrived, Adele picked them up from reception and showed them into his still spartan office.

'Gentlemen, I trust you had a good trip over. How can I help?'

They proceeded to ask several reasonably straightforward questions about Richard's views on defence, in passing asking for his views as to how the Scottish issue could be resolved.

Richard answered blandly – the usual platitudes about NATO being the cornerstone of UK defence, the Scotland situation being of deep concern due to Trident etc., interspersed with a few anecdotes about his resignation and the reason for the packing cases.

After a while McColl, the lead American, seemed to run

out of things to say, and Richard thought he'd turn the tables. 'Gentlemen, if you don't mind me asking, who exactly am I speaking to? I mean, I know of your firm, I've looked at your website, I see you once worked for the Democrats, but it might help if I knew what your clients were actually after?'

Jack McColl waited a second, then replied. 'Fair question. Let's just say we represent the "unofficial" thinking of the current US administration. Between these four walls, some in Washington are interested in finding out who are the big names in UK foreign policy without officially asking, if you understand me.'

Richard said he had nothing to tell them that he wouldn't be happy to talk about in public. He then changed tack. 'May I now ask you some questions? I was in Afghanistan shortly after 9/11. Nothing too dramatic, but the end of the US engagement there in 2021 still came as a shock. President Harris says she's committed to NATO, but that's balanced by a clear desire not to get entangled in global problems again. How does that leave allies such as the UK? Not to mention other states that rely on US guarantees: Taiwan, the Gulf states etc. Should they look beyond their partnership with the US?'

Jack replied: 'That's a good question. The administration will tell you that they're engaged in the world, but privately that view is not shared across Washington, and certainly not by the President. The Department of Defense, as you might expect, puts great store on NATO. The State Department traditionally has been far less keen. There is a certain current of isolationism within the US psyche – we saw it before World War Two and we're seeing it again now. That's potentially something you, as a trusted ally, can help us with.'

Richard considered this. Now perhaps they were getting to the real purpose of the meeting. So, elements of the United States machine really wanted help in winning their domestic arguments?

'For instance, the United Kingdom has interests in the Far East. Some in Washington appreciate that the stronger the UK presence is in that part of the world, the more reliable US guarantees appear to our partners. We're very interested to know how the UK's defence policy might develop; it may well inform our own.

'Malaysia and Singapore are a case in point. If the UK is implicitly guaranteed to cooperate with Singapore, then US disengagement would be so much more difficult.'

With that, Richard's mind wandered to Singapore.

'Well, as I explained I have an interest in the area myself and I'm glad people in Washington share my concerns.'

With that, Richard decided to bring the meeting to an end.

25. HMS *Prince of Wales* Sets Sail

HMNB Portsmouth, 6 August

'So, you're planning to sail HMS *Prince of Wales* to Singapore?' joked Captain Barker to Commodore John Fisher in the briefing room of one of the Royal Navy's Queen Elizabeth-class aircraft carriers.

'Yes, that's why I requested you, someone who knows about the Chinese. You're aware the Japanese navy will be joining us; we'll do a deal with them – no talk of 1941 and we won't mention… well, some details about how the war ended.'

They all knew the significance of the joke. There had not been an HMS *Prince of Wales* since 10 December 1941, when the pride of the Royal Navy had been sunk by long-range Japanese bombers with the loss of 327 lives.

The latest incarnation of the *Prince of Wales* featured a replica of the doomed ship's bell; one seaman's grandfather had even served on it.

It was Commodore Fisher's first major command – to take charge of the annual Royal Navy Carrier Strike Group exercise in the Far East. It was hoped the force would be engage with allies en route – in the Mediterranean and Indian Ocean

– before joint training with Singapore, Malaysia, Australia and New Zealand as part of the Five Powers Defence Arrangement, otherwise known as the Durian Pact.[4]

Fisher had also been briefed about the political background to his mission, about China's expansionism into the South China Sea and 'Freedom of Navigation' of the shipping lanes that carried a significant percentage of UK and world trade.

The exercise was designed to display the UK's commitment to its partners and its role as an effective deterrent if necessary.

Fisher, having joined the Royal Navy thirty years earlier, had served on the carrier HMS *Ark Royal* during the Second Iraq War, as well as a spell as a defence attaché at the British Embassy in Washington.

However, this was the command he was most proud of. At 65,000 tonnes with an air wing of F-35 jets, the *Prince of Wales* was an impressive ship. But his remit also included air-defence ships, submarines, tankers and auxiliaries. This was no ordinary task. He was commanding the mainstay of the UK's naval power.

Fisher was old enough to remember the Falklands War; some of his earliest memories were of watching Harrier jets taking off from *Ark Royal* and *Hermes*. This and the love of sailing he'd acquired from his father had taken him into the Navy, a decision he'd never regretted. And now he was in command of a Carrier Strike Group of twelve ships. This was a great honour and one he was determined to make the most of.

---

[4] The 1971 Five Powers Defence Arrangements between Australia, Malaysia, New Zealand, Singapore, and the United Kingdom commits the parties to cooperate in the event of any form of armed attack or such threat against Malaysia or Singapore.

One of the fleet's duties was to demonstrate the international right of navigation. This would involve sailing close to what were regarded as illegal artificial islands built by China in the South China Sea. He was told to expect harassment, but that it was important politically not to concede control of the water to China and to insist on the right of navigation. 'A robust defence of freedom of navigation along with our allies,' was the line from the top.

Returning to Portsmouth from briefings in London, Fisher had many plans to see to: continued liaison with allied navies; last-minute equipment to be loaded. Fortunately, the Carrier Strike Group had exercised together for a few years now, and each ship knew its role.

Fisher said to Barker with a knowing smile, 'I think we should go and have a look at the arrival of our new cargo.' Barker knew exactly what he was talking about as he had been briefed extensively about the new equipment and its forthcoming test.

'Aye, aye, sir, coming aboard to HMS *Diamond* shortly. She's alongside: we can walk along.'

HMS *Diamond* was an air defence destroyer, equipped with a top-of-the-range Sampson radar and a large complement of Aster surface-to-air missiles. Two of its launch tubes had been converted for the use of a new missile – the CVS401 Perseus, brand new to the Royal Navy. Powered by a Rolls Royce jet engine and capable of delivering a 200kg warhead at Mach 5 over a 300km range, it was the Royal Navy's secretive first experiment in hypersonic missiles.

'That's a gleaming piece of kit, Captain Barker. We'll be lucky to see it on its first test.'

'We also have some other surprises for our Russian friends

under the water,' said Fisher. 'All in all, I think this is perhaps the most powerful Royal Navy force to go east of Suez since the war.'

The next day four harbour tugs attached themselves to the carrier; slowly it slipped its moorings, with the crew lined up on deck watching a crowd of family and well-wishers on the Portsmouth waterfront as the huge ship slowly passed the historic fort at the harbour's mouth and moved out into the Solent, where its escorts were already waiting in the sun. It was to be a long journey to the Far East: Gibraltar, Italy, Cyprus, before transiting the Suez Canal and on to an engagement in Oman.

26. Scottish Separatism

Westminster, 8 August

Malcolm MacIntyre, the leader of the Scottish National Party, had been passionate about Scottish independence from an early age. He'd joined the Party at Glasgow University, but had primarily been interested in student politics of a more general nature, organising the university's 'Stop the War' campaign and getting elected to the Student Union council. He'd picked up an acute dislike of what he saw as 'rich English'. His was not a world of expansive horizons, but of black and white certainties.

He'd become active in the SNP while working in a Glaswegian law firm, eventually working in Holyrood for a Nationalist MSP. He'd campaigned during the 2014 referendum and like many of his friends had been bitterly disappointed by the result. He'd nearly given up on politics, but was offered a place on the Scottish parliamentary list and won an unexpected victory in 2017.

His skills at crafting winning lines and campaigns had allowed him to quickly progress through the Party ranks to deputy leader. It came as a complete surprise to him when he eventually became leader in the tumultuous years following Nicola Sturgeon's resignation in disgrace in 2023, spearheading the party's remarkable resurgence.

He kept many of his student views with him throughout his career. While revelling in the imagery of Scottish regiments and an independent Scottish army, he remained staunchly on the left – anti-war and opposed to NATO, an issue that still smouldered beneath the surface of the Party.

But his abiding political belief was a dislike of what he saw as the 'British State'. At university many of his friends had Irish Republican backgrounds, and he'd visited Northern Ireland on many occasions. While too young to remember her himself, he often conjured up the phantom of Margaret Thatcher as a bogeyman symbolising the UK Government. He was motivated, unscrupulous and had one aim – independence for Scotland, with himself as President.

By contrast, Caroline Summers was not afflicted by similar burning beliefs or ambition. Having appeared from nowhere without any obvious effort or talent, she saw Scotland simply as an intellectual problem to be solved. She took SNP pronouncements literally: a desire for further tax-raising powers could be discussed; tailored immigration rules could be adopted; a UK framework within which to discuss particular UK issues could be formed and the SNP could be accommodated within it.

With this in mind, Summers had agreed to hold talks with Malcolm MacIntyre in Scotland following the election. She was determined to continue with her plan, but she'd fallen straight into a series of carefully choreographed traps laid by the wily SNP leader.

Firstly, he'd managed to frame the talks as an invitation from the Scottish leader, creating a carefully curated image of himself as the legitimate voice of Scotland.

From then on it got worse. The Prime Minister's team had been kept waiting on the First Minister's doorstep and an SNP press release claimed she had come offering nothing and would walk away empty-handed before the discussions had even begun.

MacIntyre presented her with a list of unrealistic demands he knew Summers would never be able to accept – tax, immigration powers, even a Scottish defence framework that would effectively have given the SNP a veto on British use of military facilities in Scotland, particularly the nuclear submarines based at Faslane. Caroline Summers was horrified, but had as good as promised MacIntyre a response.

She decided to call his bluff, give him what he wanted and, she hoped, pop his balloon. She had warned her Party she was prepared to make tough choices and the resulting White Paper was met by Richard and many other Conservative MPs with horror.

Later that week, Scottish Secretary Robert Lacy put on a brave face at the Despatch Box. Taking hostile interventions from his own side, he failed to spell out exactly how the new proposals would work. A separate Scottish immigration policy without a border between Scotland and the rest of the UK? What would a Scottish defence agreement entail? There was nothing he could say because there were no answers.

The proposals were immediately met with a furious response from MacIntyre, who denounced the 'weak package of measures' as an 'insult to Scotland'.

Two days of debate would be followed by a vote. Richard saw it as a disaster in the making. Sir Bill Howard kicked off a meeting in his office of what they'd decided to call the 'Union Group' of MPs. 'This is even worse that we thought, he said. 'I'm just amazed the Secretary of State has gone along with it; apparently it sailed through Cabinet this morning with little discussion and no resignations.'

A former Cabinet minister added: 'Well, Lacy has a Welsh seat: the SNP gambled that he's not particularly principled on the Union and so they took him to the cleaners. And as for the Prime Minister, I don't think she has a clue what's going on.'

'Should we ask to see them?' added another MP.

Richard waited for a gap in the comments before saying, 'I told my Whip I'd vote against the White Paper. I suggest others do the same; perhaps they'll pull it if there's enough opposition?'

Sir Bill replied, 'They didn't even ask me. I guess they know my reply! I'm afraid we don't have any other option. We can't tweak it – it's so far off the mark it needs to go.'

A backbench MP in the room asked, 'What will Labour do? If they support this then what's the point in voting against it?'

'We'll have to wait for the Government motion. Perhaps they'll word it in an uncontroversial manner?' pondered Sir Bill.

In the end MPs were simply asked to support the White Paper. Given an opportunity to defeat the Government, this made it highly unlikely Labour would vote for it.

The day came and, in a packed Commons, the Prime Minister set out her case, reading from a prepared script.

'I was elected as a Conservative and Unionist. I will not be the Prime Minister who puts the Union in peril. Now is the time to show flexibility...'

Each line was met with a half-hearted 'hear, hear' from the usual crowd of ambitious loyalists, but a few feet down on the Government front bench the sullen expression on the face of the Chief Whip told another story. He knew he was defeated. And he was right.

The division bell rang and MPs trooped off to the Aye and No lobbies. Richard followed Sir Bill and others towards the latter, avoiding the Government Whips hovering by the entrance.

He spotted the Education Secretary Alan Stewart who, although he represented an English constituency, was Scottish and held strong views on the Union. He was surrounded by a throng of MPs all trying to speak at once 'He's just resigned or is about to,' thought Richard. 'This is just the beginning.'

Fifteen minutes later the Speaker read out the result. The Government had lost. A jeer went up from the Labour bench.

Richard looked over to the Scottish Nationalists. Surprisingly, they showed a mixture of responses. MacIntyre was finding it hard to contain his glee, but others looked concerned. The Government had lost by 180 votes to 450: a massive defeat for the Prime Minister.

The Leader of the Opposition then stood up and hesitantly requested a vote of confidence in the Prime Minister. A mistake, thought Richard. Labour would have no chance in the General Election that would inevitably follow if she lost.

The Government Whips, fresh from one defeat, ran around reassuring themselves and others that they were going to win this time.

Richard wondered what might now happen. Alan Stewart, as the most senior figure opposed to the devolution White Paper, must now be a serious contender for the leadership, well placed to pick up the pieces if Summers were to falter.

He was the one to beat.

But then an awful thought hit him. He hadn't seen Tommy Rosenfield in the voting lobbies. Had he also spotted an opportunity to run for the leadership and voted against and resigned? Asking around it transpired he was somewhere in the Far East and had missed the devolution vote, of course. 'Cunning,' thought Richard. Either way there were now two candidates.

27. The South China Sea

Xiamen Harbour, Southern China, 8 August

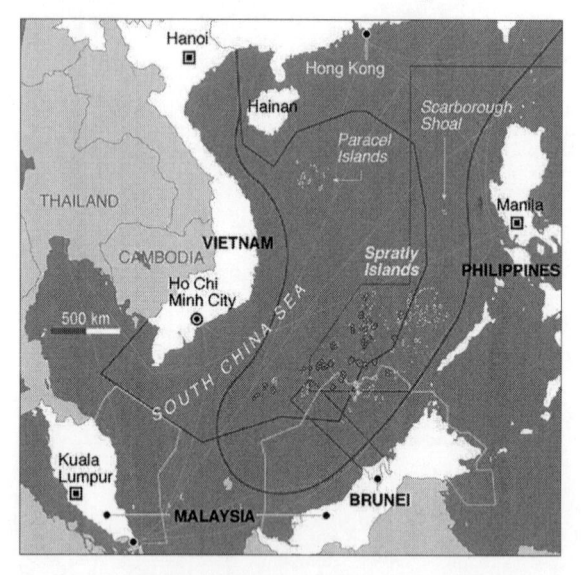

General Hu looked as if he were happy with the way things were developing. He enjoyed getting out to see his troops and today, as he looked out to sea from a headland overlooking Xiamen, there was a marvellous sight to behold.

The harbour was a flurry of activity. The last of the roll-on-roll-off ferries had arrived, now converted for military use with their cargoes of tanks and armoured vehicles.

Offshore, larger amphibious assault craft waited in the light swell at anchor, while landing craft and helicopters buzzed backwards and forwards carrying troops and their equipment out to them. The exercise was going well so far. It was an impressive sight.

It had started two days previously with a barrage of surface-to-surface missiles fired into the sea surrounding Taiwan, followed up by overflights from a mix of Shenyang J-11 fighters, including the long-range Xiang H-6 nicknamed the 'Badger', visibly sporting an array of YJ-12 anti-ship cruise missiles.

The primary purpose was of course political: to put maximum pressure on Taiwan and deter any interference from the West; they also made for good propaganda – rockets being fired and anti-ship missiles flying over the strait sent an obvious message.

General Hu had received detailed instructions. This was a large-scale exercise to test amphibious capabilities. It was to include a simulated landing on a contested shore, aerial bombardment, missile tests and a major naval exercise to clear and protect invasion lines. Nobody actually came out and said it, but there was no doubt this was a practice for a future invasion of Taiwan.

• • • •

One thousand miles to the south of Xiamen, in the middle of one of the world's busiest shipping lanes, lies Fiery Cross Atoll. Once just a speck of sand barely breaking the surface of the South China Sea, it was now a major Chinese PLA base.

It consisted of roughly 700 acres of reclaimed land midway between the Philippines, Vietnam, Malaysia and Brunei, occupied by China but claimed by the Philippines, Taiwan and Vietnam. However, none of it had actually existed at all prior to 2014, when the Chinese navy moved in with a fleet of dredgers, pushing out the local fishermen and building a new island fortress.

It boasted a two-mile runway, a harbour, shelters, barracks for troops and early warning radar, on land that shouldn't exist, surrounded by waters that nobody recognised as Chinese. It served many purposes: to control, intimidate and project Chinese power throughout the region.

General Hu had visited Fiery Cross a few times, but this evening's flight would be different. A special plane had been sent to collect him and he was to be briefed on board by a staff officer from Beijing.

In the late afternoon, General Hu's car took him to a military airfield outside Xiamen. He waited outside in the humidity, watching the strip as his driver listened to the radio. Hu was consumed by his thoughts – why take him to Fiery Cross? The exercise was taking place in the Taiwan Straits and the surrounding coastline. He'd been ordered to hand over to his second in command for the next three days, something he was most unwilling to do. He also resented the appearance of an officer from Beijing. This had the hallmarks of something political, and that concerned him greatly.

Soon he could see the outline of a small executive passenger jet, painted grey, making its descent and eventually taxiing to a halt a short distance from the car. A young officer from the central military staff appeared at the top of the steps and beckoned Hu to join him on the plane. It was spacious, plush seats grouped around polished tables. The plane took off, banked and headed over the South China Sea. Below, the small armada of ships and landing craft shrank to specks before the plane rose above the clouds and headed south.

The staff officer then turned to Hu. 'General, are you aware of Operation Red Ocean?'

'No.'

'It is of the greatest importance to China,' said the officer, producing a folder from his briefcase.

'Soon, General, all your training will be put to the test. The reunification of China. You will be playing a vital historic role, a role you've been training for all these years. You know of our plans for Taiwan, in fact I believe you helped design them. They are very thorough, but they lack a significant element which needs rectifying immediately. This will be your task.'

Hu looked uneasily at the staff officer, concerned that his face would betray the utter astonishment and dread that was creeping its way around his body. A real invasion? Surely not. And what would his role be? The unease had spread to his stomach and he began to feel he might be sick. He was trapped.

'Please continue, Comrade', he forced himself to spit out. 'I would not wish to overlook any element that could aid in the success of our plans.'

The officer studied his face closely; Hu thought for a second he'd detected his concern, but he wasn't sure.

'General, the reunification of China will be met by fierce opposition from the West. We saw how they interfered in Ukraine. We believe there will be a similar attempt to interfere in our plans for Taiwan.'

'They will fail,' said Hu, recovering his composure. He'd studied the Russian invasion of Ukraine; China was a far larger state with a far more disciplined and professional army. Besides, Taiwan was an island; it was almost impossible for hostile nations to resupply it.

'China is not Russia,' continued General Hu, 'and Taiwan does not share a land border with NATO. We need not concern ourselves. The United States will bluster and the

United Kingdom can do little. Our missiles will prevent their naval forces from approaching.'

'I don't doubt it, General,' said the staff officer. 'That is not what concerns Beijing. We do not fear the United States or its allies, but we are vulnerable in other ways. I presume you studied Japan's wars of aggression at Military College?'

'Of course.'

'You will remember that the Japanese advanced south in pursuit of oil, oil that the Americans had denied them with their sanctions. Well, we are also dependent on oil –from the Middle East and Angola, oil that's shipped across the seas to our south. We cannot allow the United States to cut off our supply. That means we must secure the seaways.'

Hu was lost in thought. Japan had been left with a choice of complying with the US and ending the war in China, or waging a wider war. It chose the latter.

'Is that why we're going to Fiery Cross?'

The staff officer turned away to look out the window. They were high up and the clouds had cleared. Specks of land began to appear in the distance: the contested atolls of the Spratly Islands.

'No, they're not concerned about the strength of our defences here. The Straits of Malacca is our problem, and Singapore is the choke point. If the United States get hold of the straits before we do, they'll cut off our oil, and without it we're doomed.'

The officer's eyes pierced into Hu's. 'Our orders are to prepare for the occupation of the straits and deny Singapore to the Americans and the British. It will be our gateway to the Indian Ocean – our shield.'

The General stared in amazement. He was already

concerned about the invasion of Taiwan. Now he was being told they were going to widen their operation into a confrontation with the United States. This was madness, but there was no way he could come out and say that.

'I am honoured to be a part of such an historic mission for the Motherland, Comrade. There is much work to be done.'

Hu looked out of the window. More ships were visible and the plane was starting to descend. Once they landed and the door was opened, a blast of humid tropical air wafted into the cabin. They were met at the bottom of the steps by a senior PLA naval officer, who they followed to what looked like a headquarters building a few hundred yards away.

They were ushered down long corridors to a planning room, where Hu was introduced to a Vice Admiral Li of the Southern Command, who pointed to a large map mounted on a table in the centre of the room.

'We are here on Fiery Cross,' said Li. 'This will be one of the major launch areas of the operation; there are others. One is up here,' he pointed to the coast of Cambodia, 'where we have a deep-water port. Our forces in Myanmar will approach the straits from the west. We are also strengthening our forces in Djibouti.'

Hu was not aware of a naval force in Cambodia, but he knew China had been expanding its presence.

'Now Admiral, shall we move on to the operation itself?' said the staff officer.

'Yes. We will have nearly 100,000 troops for this part of the operation, on various ships, both military and commercial; indeed some are pre-deployed in the area and ready to appear when needed. We have planned three phases.

'Phase One: we move the troops to their formation points,

under the cover of an exercise. We also need to move our ships from Africa and Myanmar without causing too much concern. We already have plans for that. Serious piracy incidents in the Bay of Bengal involving Chinese vessels are allowing us to transfer ships to the area undetected.

'Phase Two: embarkation. This needs careful coordination with the air force; their long-range aircraft will need to protect the ships on their way in.

'Phase Three: our forces will take Singapore's Changi Airport, coinciding with the landing of the main force on Singapore and Malaysia. This will also require significant submarine and air activity.

'Now, General, your troops have been picked for one of the main invasion corridors. The training you have undertaken is vital for the success of this part of the plan; if we cannot secure the seaways, the Taiwan part of the operation will not succeed.

'I am sure you have many questions. Please feel free to ask.'

Hu was doing his best not to look shocked. He knew from experience that any sign of weakness would lead to his dismissal or worse. He kept his composure and replied, 'Yes, two questions if I may. Firstly, how many of my troops will be here and on the ships? Will there be a designated landing zone? Where are the other zones? And secondly, what assumptions do we have as to the enemy? Is Singapore well defended? What of the Western forces? Do we have any intelligence?'

'Good questions. About 20,000 troops will depart from here in waves, with reserves following up. This facility will be very busy and well defended. Your landing zone will be in Singapore itself. If surprise is maintained, it will be the north coast, the area of the naval base. If our special forces fail to secure the landing zone, we have a secondary option in Malaysia, opposite Singapore.

'We do not anticipate any Western interference. Our long-range bombers with their anti-ship missiles, lots of them, should deter their ships and they won't have time to move air assets into the area. Singapore's armed forces won't fight for long, especially once we've taken them by surprise. They can't survive without access to the sea.'

General Hu had one last burning question: 'What are the expected timings for these plans?'

The staff officer replied, 'The President is adamant that this must be completed in time for the eightieth anniversary of the fall of Nanjing and the end of the Civil War.[5] Troops will be moved into position in two weeks' time and the invasion will start a week later. This timetable cannot be altered, but I presume this won't pose a problem for you: your troops are well trained and acclimatised to amphibious operations. Anything else?'

'Nothing other than to say that it is a great honour to be part of this historic mission,' Hu replied. He was fighting back a strong mix of fear and anger at the plans, but to say anything would be fatal. His troops would be in the open, preparing an amphibious landing on a well-defended coast. He also knew a little about the combined US, Australian and British naval forces – could Beijing really guarantee they could keep their submarines away? They'd sailed through the

---

[5] In April 1949 the Nationalists capital fell and on 7 September 1949 the Nationalist Government of China retreated to Taiwan, leaving the mainland to Communist Party rule.

Taiwan Straits before – why wouldn't they be in Singapore?

The meeting came to an end and General Hu was left on his own for a moment, before a staff officer came over.

'You have a special visitor from Beijing, who is coming to see the plans for himself and to check you have everything you need for the task ahead. The Minister for State Security Chen Wenquing. We'll brief him on the necessary security matters, including plans for a civil administration in Singapore.'

Interesting, thought Hu, maybe his message had got through. If anyone could try and stop this madness it was Chen, but how?

Chen's plane landed the following morning and Hu was told that a meeting was planned for the two of them at 10 a.m. General Hu entered the briefing room and greeted Chen formally, disguising the fact that they'd known each other for many years.

Chen ran through security requirements, especially the need to keep the mission secret. It would remain an 'exercise' until the very last moment. He then went on to detail how his department would ensure security in Singapore and Malaysia after the invasion. He had details of local officials who would cooperate with the Chinese army. There was also a plan to move large numbers of Chinese security officials into the area to maintain order.

Singapore was a trading city and would be cut off without access to the South China Sea. China would use Hong Kong as a model: the two territories would maintain their current administrations subject to a new security law. Chinese security officials would arrive shortly after the first troops had entered the city and secured key points.

After a while Chen asked his staff officer to leave as he had some direct security questions for Hu.

'General, never did I imagine meeting you on an island in the South China Sea on the cusp of such a great disaster for our country. I received your message. How did we get to this?'

'Thank you for coming' replied Hu. 'In hindsight I somewhat blame myself. We'd been studying Operation Red Ocean for some time and I'd been asking about entry and exit points into the South China Sea.'

He lowered his voice. 'I even wrote a note – "How could we guarantee access to the Indian Ocean at a time of conflict with Taiwan" for Eastern Command. I'd hoped this would have been enough to dissuade Beijing from such an adventure. But I seem to have made things worse. The whole idea is madness. Stretched supply lines over the open ocean. Landings in a densely built-up city. Nobody's ever done anything like this before.

'The Americans and British invaded Sicily, but they had thousands of landing craft and hundreds of thousands of men. The only thing going for us is surprise.

'But if we were discovered en route we'd be at their mercy. I don't rate our chances, but Beijing seems adamant.'

Chen replied thoughtfully, 'I think our President takes a simple view. The invasion of Taiwan must go ahead, therefore every mad plan required to make that invasion a success must also go ahead.

'But have you considered what might happen if we succeed? Without even considering Taiwan we'd have a restive city to guard. The destruction of Singapore might spark an even worse recession at home. We could end up with a revolution.

'And if we fail? Well, we'll be cut off and humiliated; the Party will be to blame and it'll be the end. Revolution.

'No, for the good of the Party and for China – this must be stopped.'

Chen looked troubled – as if he'd only just appreciated the full implications. 'That's why I came here. A failed invasion would be a disaster. We're in a precarious position at home. The economy and the people are hurting. If we add a chaotic defeat into the bargain, then I can't tell what might happen. There are reports from all over the country of food riots and disturbances. The President believes a victory in Taiwan would strengthen the Party's position, but the chances of success are far too low. But how do we stop this?'

General Hu replied, 'I'm accustomed to following orders, not working out ways to disrupt them. We're all ready. There's no switch I can pull to stop it.'

Chen looked pensively at Hu. 'I may have an idea, but it means taking a huge risk. Still, with your support I'll start working on it.'

28. Number 10 Downing Street

The Prime Minister's Office, Number 10 Downing Street, 14 August

Sir Bill Howard was a veteran MP, an elder statesman. He'd known Caroline Summers for much of her career, and knew her as a trusted friend.

This had led him to back her when she'd stood for the leadership of the Conservative Party, and she'd repaid his loyalty by agreeing to meet him in private whenever he had concerns. With this in mind, he'd attempted to speak to her before the vote on the devolution package, but had had been blocked by her office. But he'd finally managed to catch her in the voting lobby where she agreed to meet him and one or two of his colleagues to talk her through their concerns. The two colleagues were Sir William Mostyn and Richard.

The three of them met up in Sir Bill's office, a large corner office in one of the spherical towers that cornered Portcullis House. Bill had a panoramic view over to Westminster Abbey. Mostyn was already there when Richard arrived.

'Well, what should we tell her?' asked Bill as Richard walked in. Richard sat down and replied:

'We must let her know the strength of feeling in the Party. The policy needs to be reversed. The bill should be put back out to consultation, and we should make the case for an alternative. We can beat Malcolm MacIntyre. He can't walk on water: his electorate are tiring of him and his incessant droning on about referendums while the public services are failing.'

Mostyn interjected: 'If she's in the mood for listening. I had a look through some of her earlier speeches – she used to be a strong Unionist. The irony is, her desire to maintain the Union is driving her to all the wrong conclusions.

'We know what she's like: she can be rather wooden, inflexible. So how do we change her outlook when the Cabinet Secretary's pouring defeatist nonsense in her ear every day? She's a mandarin's dream of a Prime Minister, accepting every word of advice as gospel truth.

'Still, we have to try. Appeal to Party unity, survival even. She's a loyalist at heart; it's one of her virtues.'

Ever since the election Richard had been toying with the puzzle of Malcolm MacIntyre and the apparent invincibility of the Nationalist vote. He thought he'd share some of his findings.

'Bill, William, as you know I've been very concerned about the Scotland issue for some years. I've spent the last few weeks looking at the polling and I've come to a rather different conclusion from the mainstream media. I'd like to raise some concerns about it with the Prime Minister, if I may.'

'Go on,' said Sir Bill.

'Well, the top-line figures are very bad – 60 per cent plus for independence. But it's worth looking into the background detail. Firstly, the questions asked, the sampling and the expectations of those who might vote. Some of the polling firms take very different approaches, but the ones quoted always seem to be from this new firm, Salisbury Partners, which consistently show a stronger vote for independence.

'So, take the question "Do you want to separate from the UK" compared with "Do you think Scotland should be allowed to be independent" – same question, but a very different result.

'Reading between the lines, only a small minority want independence above all else; others seem more fickle.

'In fact, I think we have cause for optimism. But this hasn't seeped through to the media. The headwind from the election result has disturbed people who are normally fairly well-balanced. I'd like to share these findings with the Prime Minister as part of planning an alternate strategy.'

Sir Bill looked over. 'By all means. We have twenty minutes, shall we slowly walk over?'

And with that they filed out of his office, down into the glass atrium of Portcullis House and across the road to show their credentials at the Downing Street barrier.

Walking the remainder of the street to the famous black door and running the familiar gauntlet of the cameras opposite, Richard wondered whether their appearance would lead to any speculation.

Inside Number 10 they were ushered up the main staircase past the portraits of former Prime Ministers, into the Terracotta Drawing Room.

Summers got up to greet them and beckoned them over to a sofa and chair opposite her on the other side of the fireplace.

'Thank you very much Prime Minister for agreeing to meet with us,' said Sir Bill. 'The last few weeks or so can't have been easy.'

Summers didn't respond, leaving an awkward silence that lingered for a few long seconds until an attendant appeared with tea. Once the minor commotion caused by the pouring of the tea had subsided, Sir Bill tried to pick up his train of thought.

'Prime Minister, we are loyal supporters. I backed you for the leadership; we're also fully aware of the problems facing us and the weight placed upon you. We are very keen to be of help.'

Summers looked straight at Sir Bill and said, 'Thank you for your understanding. These are indeed difficult times for those among us who believe passionately in the United Kingdom.'

'That is why we have some suggestions for you,' said Sir Bill. 'We're not convinced this current legislation is the right approach to ending the Nationalist threat. Handing over more and more powers is a slippery slope that has led us to this moment. We need a new strategy. This legislation has been defeated and must be replaced by a broad, optimistic package.

'Richard has been working on the polling numbers. They're not as bad as you might think. You can rescue this situation. We should take the fight to the Nationalists and make a positive case. Back MacIntyre into a corner, where all he can do is demand endless referendums in the face of positive UK Government action.

'We should treat it like an election – aim to win over certain groups with specific messages and policies.'

As Sir Bill reached a crescendo he studied the Prime Minister's face. There was not even a flicker of acknowledgement.

'Thank you, Sir Bill, that is very interesting.'

Sir William Mostyn decided to fill the resulting awkward silence. 'Prime Minister, my concerns with this Bill are manifold. It would not only do irrecoverable damage to the Union, but also damage our Party. How can one Kingdom have two immigration and defence policies? It's playing straight into the Nationalists' hands.'

Again, they were met with silence. Richard decided it was his turn to fill the gap. 'Prime Minister, as someone who comes from a Anglo-Scottish family and has served alongside Scots in the army, I'd be deeply sad if we allowed MacIntyre to play games with our Union. But my main point is that this is all so unnecessary. The polling isn't at all as bad as you may believe. You, Prime Minister, could rescue the situation with a bold campaign for the Union. Go up to Scotland and be relevant. Support for the SNP isn't as strong as it seems. We must challenge them.'

Richard attempted to hand a copy of the polling report to the Prime Minister, but when she ignored his outstretched, he placed it on the coffee table between them.

Sir Bill then interjected. 'Prime Minister, if I may, perhaps you could explain to us why you believe this legislation is necessary?'

'This is not my preferred choice,' Summers finally said. 'But there are certain realities that I have to take into account. The political environment in Scotland is volatile. The demand for a referendum is persistent and I cannot ignore it. I am not at liberty to say too much, but I have intelligence as to what the more extreme ends of the Nationalist spectrum are planning if a referendum is denied. I don't want to be faced with violence on the streets.

'I have no choice: the legislation must be passed. I don't like it, but one way or another we have to move on.'

The three MPs glanced nervously at each other. There was little more they could say. Sir Bill changed the subject and the four of them chatted for a few more minutes before the

Cabinet Secretary came in to announce that another meeting was imminent.

'I'm so sorry gentlemen, I have to leave you, but I trust that was useful.' With that, Summers saw them out. As they reached the door, Richard looked back to see the Cabinet Secretary remove his polling report from the table.

Out on Whitehall Sir Bill said, 'Well, that was one of the most depressing meetings in my whole career in politics. Anyone for a drink?'

They went into the Red Lion, a Victorian pub with a long wooden bar and heavy Victorian panelling overlooking Whitehall, frequented by journalists, politicians and civil servants. They headed for a secluded nook where Mostyn seemed keen to talk.

'She's asking us to concede the future of the United Kingdom to a rabble-rousing monomaniac, without providing any coherent explanation. And the saddest thing is that many of the Party are going along with it without any real thought for the consequences.'

Richard added: 'What struck me was her total disinterest. She didn't engage with us at all. She wasn't remotely interested in any alternatives. And what did you make of that talk of violence? I suppose her officials have fed her that. I had hoped we could change her position, but seeing that wooden performance I don't see how we can work with her.'

Sir Bill replied, 'That's always been a danger with her. Her reliance on others and her inflexibility. I've been racking my mind to think if there's anyone else she trusts who might get through to her, but I can't think of anyone. The officials have her where they want her. The Cabinet Secretary's ultimately to blame and is possibly our biggest enemy in all of this.'

Mostyn said: 'It looks to me like we have no choice. If the Prime Minister refuses to change, then we'll have to change the Prime Minister.'

Sir Bill nodded. 'Yes, I've come to the same conclusion. We have little time to lose.'

29. Singapore

Singapore, 17 August

Mei arrived at Singapore's Changi Airport at 11.20 p.m. on a Thursday evening.

It was late at night and the passengers that came off the flight were mostly returning Singaporeans. Her new passport didn't raise any suspicions.

Mei wheeled her hand-luggage-sized black case through the main doors and was hit by a blast of warm air. It was still cold in Beijing at this time of year and the familiar warmth enveloped her. After a short journey to the centre of the city, Mei asked her taxi driver to stop a block away from her destination – an apartment owned by a company that acted as a front for Chinese interests in the city. Her cover was as an executive working for a genuine company – CathayCom – a subsidiary of Environ.

She made her way inside and up the staircase to the apartment. A modern apartment on the twentieth floor of a fairly nondescript block like many others in the area, but one with a good view over the city.

Tired from the flight Mei soon went to sleep and was woken by the sun streaming in. She checked her messages: there was one from the Chinese Embassy, instructions for a meeting in a café well out of the city centre to avoid being spotted by Singaporean intelligence.

Trying not to draw attention to her height, Mei walked into the Tanglin shopping centre near the Chinese Embassy and browsed in a few shops, checking to see if anyone had followed her. She then headed for the agreed meeting spot in a café up on the second floor.

The official, a man in his mid-fifties, was actually the Chinese Defence Attaché and a former PLA navy officer.

'Good to see you at last,' he said. 'Your reputation goes before you.'

'That's very kind of you, it's good to be back. Now, perhaps you could enlighten me as to why I'm here!'

'Of course. I trust that my old friend Chen Wenquing has provided some background.'

'Yes, a visit by British and Australian MPs to inspect their military exercises in the South China Sea. That's all I know.'

The official told her they knew the dates of the military exercise and, more importantly, where the MPs would be staying – the Raffles Hotel.

The plan was for Mei to engage with the MPs and find out as much as she could about the mission: its purpose and the strategy behind it. Her Australian connections had marked her out as the ideal candidate.

This was why she'd been checked into Raffles and given the cover of working for an Australian firm. They'd even booked her a room on the same floor as the MPs.

'Here are your booking details,' he said. 'I also have some details on the targets; photos, biographies etc.' He handed over a memory chip.

Mei smiled. She'd been to the hotel before and it would make a welcome contrast to Beijing. 'That's very useful, I'll report back when I've made contact.'

30. Chairman of the 1922 Committee

**Sir Richard McLean's House of Common's Office,
17 August**

Three days after the fateful visit to Number 10, Sir Bill called another meeting of the group of MPs he chaired. The mood was sombre as they joined him in his office. He kicked off with an unusual notice.

'You're all aware of our usual rules, and nobody to my knowledge has leaked the contents of any of our meetings, but for reasons that will become apparent, I'd like to remind you that the matters discussed at this meeting must not leave the room.'

He detailed their meeting with Summers before concluding slowly and deliberately, 'I'm afraid we're going to have to work to remove her as Prime Minister.'

There was not one murmur of dissent from the twenty MPs present.

'That brings me to what I think we need to do. I've prepared a short plan and I'll distribute printouts, but I must ask for them back at the end. Firstly, we need to ascertain the mechanisms for a leadership challenge. I need to visit Sir Richard McLean, the Chairman of the 1922 Committee, and sound him out.

'As I understand it, we need 15 per cent of MPs to put in letters to Sir Richard requesting a leadership ballot. That's fifty-two; we already have twenty in this room. We do need to consider a whole range of other issues, however. When the vote's held we'll need to either win or get close enough so that Summers can be persuaded to resign.

'Key to persuading our colleagues to vote against her is providing a workable alternative to the current devolution legislation. We have the outlines, but we're not quite there yet.

'We also need our own mechanism to persuade our colleagues to send their letters in and then to vote against her. In effect we need a parallel Whips' Office. That will be no easy task. You know our colleagues.'

Sir Bill continued, over a subdued laugh from his colleagues. 'We also need to win the argument in Scotland. We need to set up a campaign drawing on press relations and social media. I suggest we contact Duncan Turnbull, see if he wants to help. We also need a political strategist. I suggest Chris Stuart: he used to work for me and is now at the *Telegraph* – he can be trusted and understands the dynamics. The social media side is easier and I have some plans for that. We also need some money, of course. Any questions?'

Richard raised his hand. 'Some of you have seen the polling report I compiled. I believe part of our strategy should be to turn the figures around. Now some of you know my views on polls, I've bored for Britain on the subject. I think it's one of the most corrupt and powerful area of politics, yet the Nationalists have run away with it. We need to commission some new polls to rebalance that perception and, if possible, discredit some of the polling coming out of the SNP.'

After an hour or so the meeting began to wind up. A plan was formulating and the MPs were feeling a little more confident.

• • • •

The next day Sir Bill, Richard and Mostyn were shown into Sir Richard McLean's office in the Palace of Westminster.

'Gentlemen, for what do I owe the pleasure of your company?'

'Advice, Sir Richard, on a subject close to your heart' said Sir Bill.

'Well, do come in. I'll make some tea: my secretary's away today.'

'Sir Richard, speaking confidentially and indeed purely hypothetically, I wish to pick your brains on the rules that you oversee as Chairman.'

'Pick away. I'll help you if I can.'

'Firstly, in order for there to be a vote of confidence, is there any particular format or wording required for the letters sent in to you?'

'Well, they should express clearly that you have no confidence in the leader of our Party and that you're requesting a ballot. I will hold such letters until such time as we reach the requisite fifty-two, and at that point notify the Prime Minister. A ballot will then be held within a few days.'

'May I ask how many letters you hold at present?'

'Ha! As you know, I can't even tell the Prime Minister that!'

Mostyn now chipped in. 'And if there were a confidence vote, what should the margin be?'

'It's a straight vote of all the Party's MPs, including ministers. A conclusive vote of no confidence would trigger a contest.'

Sir Bill asked: 'What practical level of support does a Prime Minister require? Surely a vote of, say, 51 per cent in her favour would shoot her authority to pieces.'

McLean replied: 'I don't make the rules, but they are what

they are. In those circumstances, of course there would be some politics to contend with, and like you I'd like to see a leader with the support of the overwhelming majority of the Party. But that's all I can say.'

Sir Bill looked up from his notebook. 'Thank you, Sir Richard; that's been very helpful.'

Leaving the room Richard turned to Sir Bill and Mostyn. 'Very interesting. He'd see what happens if we get close to but just fail to reach 50 per cent, or that's how I read it. A second vote if she refuses to change course. So that makes it much more achievable.'

They went their separate ways.

31. Foreign Affairs Committee to Singapore

The 'Battlebox', Fort Canning, Singapore, 11 September

Fort Canning is now a public park on a hill close to the Singapore River in the centre of the modern city. Surrounded by museums, and the restaurants and bars of the boat quay, it's a popular spot for escaping from the heat.

The tranquillity of its lawns and flower beds belies a turbulent history. It served as General Percival's HQ during the fall of Singapore and it was here that the decision was taken on 15 February 1942 to surrender the island.

Richard and his fellow MPs on the Foreign Affairs Committee descended the stairs into what was now a museum, leaving the modern park and entering a replica of 1940s Britain.

Their guide ran through the history: the British in Malaya, the Japanese, the sinking of the *Prince of Wales* and *Repulse* and the eventual surrender. They were led through the complex: the cipher room with its coding machines, a telephone exchange.

'The next room is "Commander, Anti-Aircraft Defence", where the decision was taken to surrender Singapore,' said the guide.

The room was not unlike the Cabinet War Rooms in London, life-sized wax works of eleven uniformed generals standing around a table in the process of conducting their fateful meeting.

For a moment Richard was taken aback; he hadn't visited the museum in decades and the figures took him by surprise.

The guide continued the history, describing how some historians had questioned not only how it had gone so badly wrong for the British, but why the defences to the north had been neglected. Had Percival really ordered a halt to the building of defences there because the digging up of golf courses would have dismayed the civilians?

Turning to the waxworks, frozen in time for posterity, the guide wondered whether they'd made the correct decision: might a counter-attack have succeeded?

The MPs had arrived earlier in the day. The Singaporean Government was taking this year's Five Powers military exercises very seriously and had spared no expense in putting them up at Raffles Hotel.

They were a mixed bunch, some were genuinely fascinated by the tour, others giving the impression they were only there for the drinks and dinners. This trip had been a particularly popular one.

Of the eleven Foreign Affairs Committee members, five had agreed to go. Luckily the one SNP MP had made his excuses.

The MPs had been briefed on the background to the Five Powers 'Durian Pact' and on international laws concerning freedom of navigation that the exercise was designed to uphold. They were also briefed on personal security. Travelling MPs had in the past been targeted by 'hostile' states, the male MPs finding it particularly amusing to be told to be wary of 'honey traps' set by attractive and attentive women!

Since the first UK Carrier Strike Group had joined the exercises in the Far East in 2021, interest had grown in what had become known as the 'Indo-Pacific,' but this was the first visit by MPs to an actual exercise.

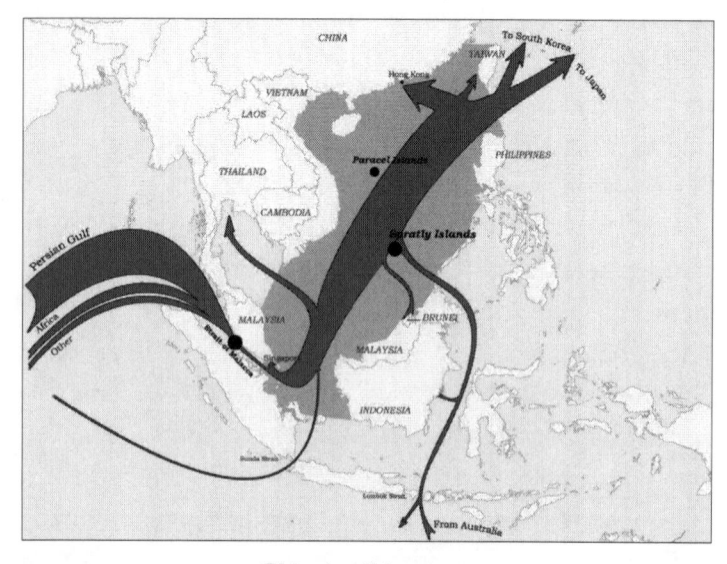

China's oil imports

The day after their arrival they were up early to be taken to a Singaporean military base in the north-east of the island for a briefing.

It started calmly, enough with a senior officer in the Singaporean Defence Forces explaining Singapore's position astride the shipping lanes that supplied a large proportion of China's oil, as. well as Singapores' recent investment in defence technology, its fighter planes and the massed reserves it could call upon.

The strategic position was also set out. Singapore had no direct military alliances except the Durian Pact. Moving closer to the USA would raise the hackles of ASEAN partners and the unspoken threat, China. Therefore, the Durian pact was of huge importance to Singapore and Malaysia.

They were taken through the importance of the Integrated

Air Defence System (IADS) for Malaysia and Singapore, based at Royal Malaysian Air Force (RMAF) Butterworth to the north, which they'd soon be visiting.

While many of the MPs weren't taking this particularly seriously, Richard found it fascinating. A whole security network in which the UK played a potentially vital role, yet few in the UK had heard of it. The MPs were then to be taken on a short plane journey from the city up to RMAF Butterworth before returning to see HMS *Prince of Wales* and her escorts arrive at the RN facility on the island's north coast.

At Butterworth they were met by an array of international military personnel – Australians, New Zealanders etc., who manned the air defence systems for the peninsula. As part of the forthcoming exercise, the Malaysians had constructed an exercise scenario – Exercise Durian IV, in which an unnamed aggressor with designs on the peninsula planned to invade from the north. Very similar to the Second World War, Richard thought to himself, with the Chinese playing the role of the Japanese. He wondered how they'd fare this time.

The group then set off for Georgetown for lunch, a short tunnel away on the island of Penang. This was an interesting visit for Richard; he could remember the stories his grandfather had told of pre-war Malaya, trips to Penang, Selangor and the Sultan's palaces. It had all sounded very exotic. His grandfather was always keen to talk about the period before the Japanese arrived, but would change the subject when it came to the war itself. It was understandable, thought Richard; like many others, his grandfather's story had ended in defeat, captivity and near starvation. The pre-war Malaya of shooting parties and expeditions into the jungle had given way to a jungle of leeches, the ever-present Japanese and the constant danger of death.

Lunch was followed by a briefing on air defences, designed to cope with any conceivable threat long enough for reinforcements to arrive. But could an invasion down the peninsula be stopped, wondered Richard, and with what? And where would the invasion come from? Thailand? Myanmar?

Back in Singapore that evening a drinks party was held in the Foreign Ministry for the various representatives observing the exercises. Richard started chatting to an Australian MP, Bob McDonald. A straightforward Queenslander with a broad accent and a penchant for laughing at his own jokes, he was clearly enjoying the trip. Richard asked him about Australia's view of the Durian Pact. McDonald joked, 'It's like the Singapore Strategy of the 1930s. We rely on the UK to defend us and then, when something happens, it turns out you're otherwise engaged and the rest of the strategy is just smoke and mirrors. Everyone knew this island fortress wasn't really impregnable, but we all so wanted to believe it.

'We felt the fall of Singapore much more keenly than you in Britain. It left us on our own. We'd sent our best troops to help the British in the desert against Rommel, and Britain failed to protect us.'

Richard replied, 'To be fair, the fall of Singapore was a shock to us as well. We'd been complacent about the Japanese, but unlike us they were battle-hardened from their wars in China, and had trained in the jungle.

'My grandfather was in Singapore at the time; he was captured like many of your countrymen, so I guess we can share the blame. Yet here we are: it's still important to us.'

Bob shot back, 'So now it's heating up in the South China

Sea, you send us HMS *Prince of Wales* again, just like old times... I'm joking of course.'

It was at this point that McDonald revealed something that Richard hadn't really appreciated.

'You know for years this agreement was given little thought. We turned up, we discussed things, but it wasn't expected to actually do anything. But it's now one of the key pacts in South East Asia. You see, Singapore and Malaysia have no other Western alliances, and they're not automatically defended by the United States. Taiwan, yes, but not Malaysia or Singapore.

'The unofficial plan we're working on is if the worst happens – China invades Taiwan – then we'd do our bit here in the straits. It makes sense for us to be here – close the straits, to Chinese shipping, oil, arms – what have you. The Royal Navy's part of that; the US wants a carrier group in the Indo-Pacific area, but now the UK's committed here, you're on rotation to free up their capacity.'

Richard digested this. If he'd heard it right, in the event of an US–China confrontation, the UK, with its allies in Australia and New Zealand, would move to protect Malaysia and police the Straits of Malacca. That would no doubt place the UK bang in the centre of a potential war.

32. Raffles Hotel

Raffles Hotel, Singapore, 13 September

That evening at Raffles Richard and the rest of the party had been invited to dinner with some of the Five Powers military staff in a grand private dining room. Over dinner Richard was chatting to Captain Bill Lauder, an Australian naval officer who'd been with them at Butterworth. After a glass of wine, he decided to ask him something that had been preying on his mind.

'Tell me Captain, I presume the Durian Pact is now all about China and that's why we're all here, but what could we actually do if China did decide to overrun the neighbourhood?'

'Well, the short answer is,' said Lauder, 'if it were a protracted war with a fully committed China – not that much. We could buy time, we could close the straits, but if the Chinese Army came down the peninsula... We know what happened in World War Two. But we're not in that business. We're here to deter Chinese aggression, raise the bar of risk so they don't attempt anything.

'It of course largely depends on whether the USA comes to our aid... The Chinese could potentially risk a war with the UK and Australia, but the USA?

'In any event China's not our direct neighbour: they'd need to get here first. They have expanded into the South China Sea, as you'll see in the next few days, but naval and amphibious operations are risky and they have bigger fish to fry. I think if there was a genuine threat to Malaysia there'd be some sort of warning. In the meantime, all we can do is prepare, deter and deal with smaller problems – pirates, terrorists and the like.'

After dinner they retired to the Raffles Hotel Long Bar, an impressive venue with fans stirring the air and a plaque marking where a tiger had supposedly once been shot. To add to the slightly ersatz atmosphere of a frontiersman bar, the floor crackled as they walked over the shells of discarded peanuts. At the bar Richard turned to Bill Lauder.

'We should probably have a Singapore Sling, I guess.'

It was at that moment that they noticed Mei. Tall and wearing a black evening dress, she was hardly attempting to be inconspicuous. She introduced herself to Lauder and, noticing his accent, explained in her equally Australian-accented English that she'd graduated from Sydney University. They chatted for a few minutes before Lauder thought better of it and broke off the conversation, turning back to Richard to pick up his drink. They then rejoined the rest of the party, where one of the British MPs joked to Lauder that he was in danger of falling into a Chinese honey trap!

It was getting late and Richard decided to retire. He took out the magnetic card to open his room, heard the click and walked in.

The lights came on with a clunk. He immediately felt he wasn't alone. He then felt his heart jump. The woman in the black dress stood at the far end of the room, pointing a gun equipped with an elongated silencer towards him.

'Don't be alarmed,' she said. 'This is for my protection. I have no intention of harming you.'

Richard's heart raced. The drinks he'd had earlier were having an effect, and he tried desperately to concentrate.

'For *your* protection! You break into my room and *you*

demand protection?' Fear and shock rolled around his body. Ideas ran though his mind: blackmail, theft, but nothing really made sense. He was a junior MP, unimportant in the scheme of things, of no value.

'Please, whatever it is you want, I'm not your target. I know nothing of interest and I don't have any money.'

'Sit down over there; there's something I want to discuss with you.'

Richard complied, walking slowly over to a chair in the corner of the room. Mei lowered the gun but remained standing.

'I do apologise for introducing myself this way. I was going to do it less... formally downstairs in the bar, but you and your Australian friend managed to avoid me.'

Richard fought back the urge to apologise, then realised how ridiculous that would have been: she was the one threatening him with a gun!

'I am Mei Ling. I work for the Chinese Government in the Ministry of State Security, but that's not why I'm here. You are aware of the situation in China I believe?'

Richard nodded.

'It is not very good; people are angry, and some are beginning to starve. The Party is being blamed for the crisis. If you understand Chinese history, you'll know that times like these present great dangers. We are a large country and maintaining stability is the Party's constant endeavour. We have chosen you to help us.'

Richard remained silent, wondering if this woman was either mad or some sort of fanatic, but as the gun remained in her hand, he said nothing.

'There are some within the Party and the military who see

the solution to our problems in patriotism, in the reunification of China. While the West is concerned about its economy, they think we should seize a historic opportunity to invade Taiwan. Plans are advanced. But this would be a mistake. Military adventurism is not the way forward.

'Tomorrow you will board the *Prince of Wales* in the South China Sea. You will see for yourself. You have been chosen for an extremely delicate task, but I will explain. I represent powerful figures within the Chinese Government who wish for better relations with the West; an attack on Taiwan is a risk for China that we should not be taking. If it succeeds, we risk war with the West; if we fail, we endanger the very stability of China. I want you to help us prevent this tragedy.'

Richard was stunned. This was not what he'd expected. He'd expected to be asked for the few scant crumbs of information he possessed. But this was fantastical.

'You said you'd chosen me. I don't see why. I'm a junior MP. You could go to the Government, to our secret service. I'm in no position to help, even if I wanted to.'

Mei considered. It was a fair question and one he'd need to have answered if he was going to be of any help.

'Mr Reynolds, we know more about you that you realise. Your military record, your time in politics; you're well connected and trusted by your colleagues. If you put your mind to it, you can really help us.' She looked straight at him.

'We also know that you'll want to help us. Let me explain. If we do nothing, millions of Chinese soldiers will converge, not just on Taiwan, but Singapore and Malaysia also. Your grandfather was in Singapore in 1942. The Japanese caused much suffering here when Britain left Singapore to its fate.

'We believe you have a personal reason to prevent that

particular chapter of British history from repeating itself. Your question was a good one, but even you don't know who you can trust in the British Government. Your politicians are greedy, Mr Reynolds. If I spoke to your Prime Minister, it would only be a matter of time before the information leaked back to China. Furthermore, we don't even know who the Prime Minister will be in a few weeks' time.

'You have been selected because you have no contacts with China. You have an interest in the area and you'll want to help. Mr Reynolds, all we want is to prevent a tragedy.'

Richard had many questions. He had no idea whether this woman was a fantasist, a con-artist or a blackmailer, but she held the cards and the gun, so he thought he'd hear her out.

'You forget that the UK has a defence arrangement with Singapore,' he said. 'You don't need me. You also seem very well-informed about our politics. But if you'll forgive me, I have a few questions. How do I know you're telling the truth? And even if I did choose to believe you, how could I, a comparative nobody, prevent this "tragedy" from happening?'

Mei looked at him, deep in thought. 'The Chinese Central Military Commission are planning a military exercise near Taiwan. This is common knowledge. But it won't just be an exercise.

'And what can *you* do? A lot! Your country can block the Straits of Malacca, to which Singapore is key. If Beijing cannot rely on subduing Singapore and the straits, then they will not risk an invasion of Taiwan.

'Now, your government is weak, your Prime Minister is weak, the United States is weak. But you don't know *how* weak, and things are about to get a lot worse. And that is how I am going to help you, and why you are going to help me. You are uniquely placed. I think I've told you enough for now. We will meet again after you've returned from your excursion; by then you'll realise that what I've said is indeed true.'

Mei fished for something on a string around her neck and threw it onto the bed.

'This is a memory stick containing information on Chinese informers in your government. They're not the only ones, but this information should be enough to convince you I'm not lying.

'Lastly, you must never say a word about this to anyone. If you do, there will not just be outrage in your country. Names can easily be added to the list I've handed to you. I think we understand each other.'

And with that she quietly left the room, leaving Richard to his thoughts.

33. South China Sea incident

The British Defence Singapore Support Unit, Sembewang, Singapore, 15 September

> ...*to exercise that kind of vague menace which capital ships of the highest quality whose whereabouts are unknown can impose upon all hostile naval calculations. How should we use them now? Obviously, they must go to sea and vanish among the innumerable islands. There was general agreement on that.*
>
> Winston Churchill on the deployment of HMS *Prince of Wales* and HMS *Repulse* in 1941

Richard was up early and waiting in the foyer of the Raffles Hotel waiting to be transported to the Sembawang naval base in the north of the island. From there they were to fly out into the South China Sea on board one of HMS *Prince of Wales*'s naval air squadron helicopters.

Once at the base they were ushered out of the coach and into a classroom where a Navy pilot explained the day's activities.

'Now if the helicopter should land on water...' he said gleefully, taking great delight in attempting to terrify the would-be passengers. They were then led to two waiting helicopters.

Once airborne, they quickly ascended before heading out to the east of the island over a never-ending procession of commercial ships heading through the straits. Passing the port side of the Horsburgh Lighthouse, they soon spotted the looming silhouette of the *Prince of Wales*, its bull-nosed ski jump and twin towers appearing out of the haze, surrounded by a number of smaller ships.

The helicopters circled the carrier, giving its occupants a good view of the vessel and its escorts, before coming in to land on the flight deck. The MPs were swiftly ushered away from the still-whirling blades towards the forward island, where Captain Barker was standing. As the noise from the helicopters died down, he attempted to welcome the party but his voice was drowned out and he beckoned them inside.

Richard had only ever been inside museum ships when he was a child and he now felt the same childish thrill, taking in the atmosphere and the smell of machinery as they climbed up a companionway towards the flight operations room. He was immediately aware that the crew behind the various consoles were wearing their full-body white 'flash' suits, designed to protect them from fire during a missile attack. That was taking it rather seriously: was that normal for an exercise?

Captain Barker briefed them in the wardroom over plans for the next day and a half. The Carrier Strike Group now consisted of fifteen ships: auxiliaries, air defence frigates, mostly Royal Navy but also including Danes, Australians, New Zealanders, Malaysians, Singaporeans and an US ship with a Japanese observer.

Barker explained they'd first sail northwards, eventually entering Brunei's territorial waters, from where the MPs would take a short civilian flight back to Singapore.

The captain then revealed a map detailing all conflicting claims to the South China Sea. Their course would take them through waters claimed by China.

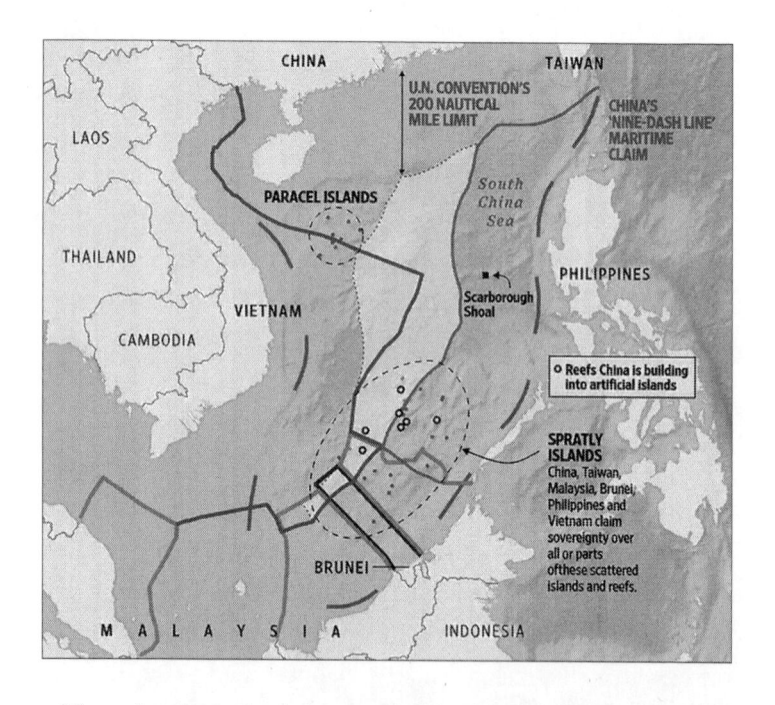

Next, he described the artificial islands the Chinese had been building. One in particular was close to their planned route; satellite imagery showed that it was equipped with an airstrip, radar and barracks. Finally, Barker said, 'Ladies and gentlemen. We are not trying to antagonise the Chinese, but merely to uphold international law, in this case freedom of navigation. This is one of the busiest shipping lanes in the world, vital for trade. Everything from oil and gas, from high-tech equipment to plastic toys, is shipped through the South China Sea. If it became inaccessible, the entire world economy would grind to a halt.

'So, what can we do? Well, under the United Nations Law of the Sea, we are allowed to navigate the high seas. We can also pass through the territorial waters of neighbouring states, exercising our "Right of Innocent Passage", which basically means we can travel where we want but shouldn't linger in territorial waters.

'That brings me to artificial islands. They don't get their entitlement to territorial waters; in fact, we don't recognise them at all. Therefore, when we transit close to a Chinese artificial island, we're not duty bound to sail straight through: we can deviate, linger, treat it as we would the high seas – and we will do just that near this island.'

He pointed to a small island called Fiery Cross Atoll.

'Now, some of you may have heard about this place. It's in international waters and didn't even exist until 2014. The Chinese have built a large military base there. As you can see, it's also close to Malaysia and Brunei's Exclusive Economic Zones. It's a potential threat to our allies in the region.

'We're aiming to demonstrate that we don't recognise the rights of the occupiers to territorial waters here. We'll sail past before continuing our operations and organising your onward flights to Singapore after a visit to the British forces in Brunei.

'So, ladies and gentlemen, that's the plan for the next two days. We're now underway; this is one of the most powerful Royal Navy-led fleets to sail east of Singapore for decades. We are very proud to be sailing with our partners under the Durian Pact.

'Over the next two days we'll be organising several tours to different parts of the fleet. I'd like to point out some key features of the fleet. Firstly, the Type-45 destroyers. These remain the most potent air defence ships afloat.

'We'll also want to impress you with our flight operations. We'll be treating these waters as hostile for the sake of the operation, and will be conducting combat air patrols and anti-submarine patrols.'

With that, Barker wished them well and a junior officer escorted them to their berths.

Richard felt a childish excitement. He'd been in the army of course, but the sights, sounds and smells of a large ship were new to him. His fellow MPs were also in a jovial mood, correcting each other on the correct terms for berths and galleys and joking that the entire Chinese navy would soon be upon them.

The fleet continued northwards for the remainder of the day, soon passing Tioman Island on the port side. At this point Barker announced via the ship's intercom system that they were passing near to the wreck of the former HMS *Prince of Wales*, sunk in 1941 and now lying in about 250 feet of water to the west. One of the smaller ships in the group would be laying a wreath over the wreck.

Richard had heard the story many times. It was a curious coincidence that the new HMS *Prince of Wales* was also in Singapore.

The MPs were then given tours of various parts of the ship, including the interior of an F-35 jet. They were taken to the flight operations room in the forward tower, where they could see the regular taking off and landing of the F-35s, constantly circling above the ship protecting it from enemy planes.

The following day, after breakfast in the officers' ward room, Richard was to visit HMS *Dragon*, part of the escort force. He donned naval overalls and was given a fresh briefing on the helicopters, particularly on how to escape should they ditch in the sea. The briefing officer attempted to lighten the mood with a joke about the lack of sharks in the South China

Sea, and before long they were out on the flight deck and up in the air.

The fleet was a majestic sight, the *Prince of Wales* surrounded by its escorts, the large auxiliary ship, the smaller frigates and the Danish destroyer.

They landed on the rear flight deck of HMS *Dragon*, which featured a large, grey pyramid at its centre, topped by the 'golf ball' housing its radar.

They spent the next hour being impressed by the radar and operations control room; a dimly lit room full of blue-tinted screens. They were told that the ship was capable of tracking thousands of aerial objects simultaneously throughout the South China Sea.

'You can see us here on the screen,' said the officer escorting them. 'Fiery Cross Atoll is here, there's already some air activity around the island, quite a build-up, an exercise perhaps. Here you can see a patrol, most likely a pair of Chendu J-20 'Mighty Dragon' jets, somewhat similar to the F-35, although as we can see them, their stealth capabilities need some improvement.'

Richard chuckled, but he knew these were serious planes, the product of years of economic espionage.

They'd been in the operations room for about twenty minutes when suddenly an alarm sounded: 'Action stations, Action stations'.

The officer told the MPs to stay where they were and rushed out. Returning moments later, he told them to follow him up to the bridge, the alarm still sounding.

The captain of the *Dragon* was calm but alert, sending messages from his headpiece to the control room on the *Prince of Wales*.

He said to the MPs: 'I thought you'd better see this. We'll soon be joined by some Chinese PLA jets, who will no doubt wish to show their displeasure.'

A junior officer then shouted out 'Visual contact! Two jets to the north-east!'

Richard went over to the window and peered out. Sure enough he could see two dots on the horizon which appeared to be getting bigger.

'They're Chinese jets based on Fiery Cross. We'll shortly be sending up another two aircraft to join the jet we already have up there. This isn't unusual for the Russians or Chinese. It's international airspace after all and they'll want to get a good look at us. We'll continue about our business. You can see our course here – we're still fifty miles from the atoll.'

Richard watched as the dots on the horizon took shape, until they were recognisably aircraft.

'They're getting quite close, said the captain. 'They really don't want us here.'

As he spoke the jets could be heard over the destroyer's engines; they are heading directly for the *Dragon*. Moments later one screeched overhead, its red star markings clearly visible. The second followed shortly afterwards with a roar that could be heard on the bridge; the aircraft then banked and headed into the gap between the destroyer and the carrier half a mile away.

'Well, that wasn't exactly a professional fly past,' said the captain. 'It looks like they're going to have another go.'

Sure, enough they could see the two jets turning, this time followed by an F-35. A warning alarm sounded and the junior officer shouted, 'They have a radar lock.'

'Carry on. It's just intimidation.'

They then saw one of the jets attempt to close in on one of the F-35s, which banked away to the right. With that, the two Chinese jets left the Carrier Group, but could still be seen on the screens, circling at a distance.

Richard spotted that one of the other MPs in the party had been videoing the whole affair on his phone. He quietly put it away in his pocket before anyone spotted him.

'Well, there you are, welcome to the sharp end of life in the Navy,' exclaimed the captain.

The Carrier Strike Group continued on its route undeterred, scanning the radar for any repeat attempt by the Chinese, but they seemed content they'd made their point.

• • • •

Back at Raffles the next day, Richard was packing for his departure when he decided to turn on the news. He was surprised to see the banner on CNN:

BREAKING NEWS: British warship harassed in South China Sea

He watched the footage of Chinese jets taking off from what looked like an island base. Oh well he thought, no harm done, they'd expected as much.

The next item made him jolt.

China military exercises in Taiwan Straits

He saw images of missiles being launched and troops being marshalled; amphibious assault ships. The tone of the commentary was disarming: 'Long planned', 'regular', just a 'response to statements on independence by Taiwan's President in the run up to the election,' etc.

Yes, he could remember similar exercises, but might this be ideal cover, gaining a few days' head start before US satellite reconnaissance could work out what was really going on?

Up to now Richard had buried the incident with the Chinese woman, hoping it would go away, but the news story bought it all back. He remembered her words: 'The Chinese Central Military Commission are planning a military exercise near Taiwan. This is common knowledge.' This was now clearly happening, yet he still had no idea what they were planning to do with him.

Amongst the jokey text messages from his colleagues back home asking if he'd seen off the Chinese, there was a startling piece of news:

'Singapore and Malaysia request HMS *Prince of Wales* and its Carrier Group and the air defence destroyer HMAS *Brisbane* to stay on for a period after the end of the Five Powers exercise while tensions persist in Taiwan.'

This was getting serious. He stopped packing and thought he'd contact the Australian MP Bob McDonald to see what he knew They agreed to meet up in the bar.

'Well, we didn't expect to be in the middle of a blooming war now did we?' Richard half joked. But he was beginning to feel that none of this was remotely funny.

Bob seemed calm. 'It looks like we've all received this call for assistance. I wonder what it is they're concerned about. Most people in Australia have never even heard of the Durian Pact, still less believe it could tangle us up in a war. Remember last time we came to help you in Malaysia,' he said with a grin. 'Some of my constituents do!'

'Yes, you don't need to remind me' said Richard, slightly irritated that the joke was being overused. 'What are you going to do?' he asked. 'Go back to Canberra I presume? I haven't heard anything yet but there may well have to be a debate in Westminster about this so shouldn't we get back.'

Bob replied, 'Yes, but while we're here we should talk to the Singaporeans, find out what's spooked them. Surely, it's not the Chinese planes? There must be more to this.'

They didn't have long to wait. The Singaporean diplomat who had been overseeing their visit came into the bar and announced that the Defence Minister wished to brief them the following morning.

They were up early for the short drive to the Singaporean Ministry of Defence. Once out of their cars, they were ushered to a mini theatre, where the Defence Minister introduced a presentation from a general in the Singapore Defence Force.

'Ladies and Gentlemen,' the general began. 'You have no doubt seen the news. Not only the incident regarding the British aircraft carrier but also the provocative acts by China with regard to Taiwan.

'In response to that, Singapore and Malaysia have now officially requested assistance under the Durian Pact and discussions are ongoing as to what cooperation is appropriate.

'I would like, however, to share with you some further details that have not been made public.

'Firstly, we do not believe that Chinese action is limited to the South China Sea/Taiwan theatre.

'As you know, China has been building up its military resources on several of the contested islands. What we have discovered more recently however is highly disturbing. There are now Chinese troops in Myanmar and Cambodia, where the Chinese have constructed a new airport and marine port, ostensibly for civilian use, but clearly with a dual purpose. We believe that China could, if it chose, rapidly expand its military presence in these two locations, and with the addition of the artificial islands in the South China Sea, pose a direct and immediate threat to the Malay Peninsula.

'Now, we cannot be sure this is China's intention – we regrettably have little direct human intelligence as to their motives – but it is a concern and one that is best prepared for.'

The Minister of Defence then interjected. 'We are therefore planning for all scenarios. I am sure you can appreciate the delicate nature of this information and request it remains with yourselves or your respective Ministers of Defence only. Now, I fear you have planes to catch.'

And with that, the talk came to an end and they all left for the airport.

34. A London Paper

London Heathrow Airport, 16 September

On the way through the concourse back at Heathrow, Richard stopped at a newsagent to buy the Sunday papers, keen to see how the *Sunday Times* and *Telegraph* had covered the incident. And there it was on the front page, as he expected.

'Royal Navy Carrier attacked by Chinese jets' from *The Times*; the *Telegraph* ran with the dramatic but incorrect 'China fires on Royal Navy jet as UK threatens reprisals'.

The *Telegraph* journalist had obviously done his job well, being briefed on various COBRA meetings and the tumult surrounding the planned UK response. Tommy Rosenfield had come out of it looking good:

'Foreign Secretary Tommy Rosenfield immediately demanded to see the Chinese Ambassador and informed them that the Carrier Strike Group would from now on use force in self-defence. It was this communication that persuaded the Chinese military to stop their harassment...'

Interesting, thought Richard, that Tommy Rosenfield had been quick to take the credit.

The *Sunday Times* led with a double attack on the Ministry of Defence and on Nicholas Braithwaite, former Defence Minister and now Chairman of the Defence Committee. Apparently, he'd lobbied for a 'dialling down' of tensions and withdrawing the carrier from the immediate area. The paper quoted conversations with anonymous colleagues claiming this was seen as 'appeasement' within the Foreign Office. A deliberate attack, thought Richard, and a sign that the phantom leadership campaign was underway. Rosenfield had clearly spotted an opportunity to get the better of two potential adversaries, but unusually there was no obvious indication as to who had briefed the paper. There was also a mention of a new group called the 'Conservative China Group', cobbled together to raise awareness of the increasing threat from China. It was chaired by Toby Watson MP, an ally of Tommy Rosenfield. 'So is that it?', thought Richard. 'A cover to organise MPs for a leadership contest? Clever.'

Later in the day Richard called Sir Bill Howard to find out more about the China Group. Sir Bill said, 'Yes, the first I'd heard about it was earlier in the week – friends of Tommy Rosenfield mostly, but there are a few other names, and they send out a newsletter on China – quite hawkish. Seems to have some money, run by that PR chap – Rossi, was it? – who's also close to Rosenfield, as far as I can tell.'

Richard added, more himself than to Sir Bill, 'I wonder who's funding it, and why, for that matter? I mean, it can't be cheap… There's no lack of people concerned about China, but precious few who see Rosenfield as the solution!'

Sir Bill laughed. 'What is also curious is what Lacy thinks about it, isn't he the one Rosenfield is shilling for? I mean, don't we have our concerns about him and his pals' hunger for Chinese gold? Presumably we were wrong.'

'It would seem so. Rosenfield and Lacy will be off the Beijing Christmas card list, which is no bad thing in my book.'

35. The Leadership Contest

Houses of Parliament, Westminster, 18 September

'It is therefore with regret that I inform you that I have no confidence in the Prime Minister and request that you organise a vote of no confidence in her at the earliest convenience.'

With that, Sir Bill signed the letter more carefully than usual, put down his pen, folded it and placed it in a light, creamy-yellow-coloured House of Commons envelope. Sealing the envelope, he then wrote:

Rt Hon Sir Richard McLean MP
Chairman of the 1922 Committee, House of Commons

Sir Bill then set off at a leisurely pace towards Sir Richard's office. He and the envelope he was carrying attracted little attention. He may as well have been walking to the local shops. Having delivered it, he returned to his office; said nothing to his secretary, made himself a cup of tea and busied himself with other correspondence, a weight lifted from his shoulders.

This was not something he'd done on a whim; it was the culmination of many weeks' deliberations since the Government's heavy defeat on the Scotland Devolution Bill.

It was also nothing personal; unlike some of his colleagues, driven by a desire for office, perceived slights or petty jealousies, he'd long passed the point in his career when any of that mattered. No, this was solely about the legislation.

Since the defeat of her devolution package the Prime Minister had been nearly invisible, making very few public appearances. But that hadn't really mattered. Parliament had been in recess for the past few weeks and the lack of any other major political events had allowed her to remain out of the public eye. But that couldn't last forever. With the end of the recess MPs were now back at Westminster.

Yet for all the silence, it was clear to all that a 'phoney war' had begun. The Prime Minister may not have had plans to vacate Downing Street, but others certainly had plans to move in. Foremost among them was Tommy Rosenfield.

Through articles, blogs and interviews, Rosenfield and his allies had been carefully raising his profile. His new invention as a leading 'China Hawk' was a clever way to capture the hour.

Yet, while Tommy Rosenfield saw himself as (and indeed was, for now) the main contender, many more experienced MPs still saw him as little more than a cypher for Robert Lacy, who it was assumed would attempt his own new leadership bid. There were other contenders yet to reveal themselves, still hiding their ambitions for now. Chief among these was Chairman of the Defence Committee and former Defence Minister Nicholas Braithwaite.

While Sir Bill and his group had been leading the opposition to the devolution package, they had decided not to link the issue to the fate of the Prime Minister. This had all changed, of course, after their depressing meeting with Summers, but their plans had not yet altered.

Sir Bill now felt the time had come to share his views and move on with the inevitable, before the Prime Minister had the chance to bring forwards her legislation for another vote. Summoning another meeting of his group he set out the issues as he saw them.

'I'm afraid Summers is her old inflexible self, and it's unrealistic to expect any movement from her. She's as terrified of what the Nationalists might do if we vote down her legislation as we are if it passes. It's irrational, but as always it probably comes from her senior civil servants. They're terrified and easy to terrify. The latest thing doing the rounds is this threat of violence, imagined or otherwise.'

Alistair Murray interrupted. 'It's the same old playbook they used in Northern Ireland: the police recycle threats to an incredulous PM and the terrorists don't even need to actually say or do anything themselves.'

'Yes, quite so,' said Sir Bill, before continuing, putting on a self-consciously serious voice. 'Now, I've discussed this with a few of you personally and I think we all agree that there is nothing for it but to change the leader of our Party. We all know the rules.'

Alistair interrupted again. 'I've heard a rumour that some of Summers' ministers have put in letters to Sir Richard, knowing they'll be told when fifty-two has been reached, allowing them to then withdraw their letters and warn her of the imminence of the vote.

Sir Bill replied: 'Yes, that may well be so, all sorts of games will be played. But I'd ignore that for now. What we need is a figurehead. There was a time – John will remember,' he said, pointing to Lord Strachan, 'when all you needed was a stalking horse and a few backers. That's not necessary, but I think we still need a horse that can stalk. I suggest Sir William Mostyn.'

Mostyn was a bit taken aback by this suggestion coming

out of the blue. 'Oh, I'm happy to help in any way the room feels appropriate, but what exactly do you have in mind?'

Sir Bill explained: 'We need a public challenge to the PM, and that needs a credible challenger. I don't know if you have any ambition for the leadership, but you're well known, and you coming out in favour of a contest would kick it all off. I suggest we summon as many MPs as possible to discuss the leadership issue, take the temperature and then announce to the assembled media that we're sending in letters to Sir Richard.'

Chris Stuart then added, 'I'd suggest the following: we plan a meeting and tip the media off about it. We want to get as many potential leadership candidates there as possible. We build up some tension. We do an 'op note' and get the broadcast media to assemble outside the door onto College Green and then Sir William can produce a copy of the letter he's about to send and make some comments. The media can count. If there are, say, twenty to thirty MPs there, then it's game on.'

Sir Bill: 'Right, that sounds like a plan. Do we all agree?'

Commons Committee Room 14 began to fill up as soon as Sir William Mostyn had sent his WhatsApp message – 'To discuss the current state of Conservative Policy – to most of the Conservative back-benchers.

Sir Bill and Richard arrived there together from Bill's office, where they'd been planning the choreography of the meeting. Mostyn was to open and explain why he'd lost confidence in the Prime Minister, and this would be supported by the other MPs.

Chris Stuart sent out a message to the press to assemble outside the door from the Lords onto College Green. But word had spread and the corridor outside began to fill with journalists, chatting and feeding off each other's morsels of information. Once the crowd of MPs inside the room had stopped growing, Sir Bill called the room to order and invited Sir William Mostyn to speak.

Mostyn began with recent history, the constitutional issues, the fall of Prime Minister Edwards and Summers' missteps. Summing up, he stressed, 'The reason I'm sending this letter is simple. I have no confidence in the Prime Minister and her handling of the Scottish question. If you feel the same as I, then we should have the integrity to say so and demand a confidence vote.'

With that, Mostyn left the room and Chris Stuart helped to clear a path through the assembled media and down the main staircase of the House of Commons out onto College Green, followed all the way by lobby journalists baying 'Sir William! Sir William!' but receiving little in return.

Opening the small door, Mostyn walked out and was stunned. The railings opposite held back the biggest media scrum he'd ever seen. But he'd been born for a moment such as this.

'I would like to thank you all for coming to hear why my colleagues and I have no confidence in the Prime Minister and her approach to the issue of Scottish devolution.' He was in his element, the world's media a captive audience hanging on his every word. Questions soon began to be shouted from the expectant audience.

For the second time in as many months, a British Prime Minister was on borrowed time.

36. Garden Party

Chelsea, London, 19 September

John McVey was a successful entrepreneur, well known in Conservative Party circles. He'd made a fortune from a successful venture-capital firm investing in early-stage bio-tech companies, which he'd then invested in property, including a large house in a secluded square in Chelsea.

Richard had known John for many years; most recently they'd both contributed a paper on the rise of China to The Centre for British Policy, of which McVey was a board member. Richard counted John as a true friend and one of the few people in politics he trusted.

McVey's annual garden parties at his home in Chelsea had become one of the 'must attend' events, in the week just after MPs returned from the summer recess. Given the looming prospect of a leadership contest and the political drama unfolding in Scotland, Richard had been looking forward to it more than in previous years. Besides the interesting politics, it was a lovely afternoon and there'd be Pimm's and canapés!

McVey's house was an elegant Georgian building; a large marquee had been set up in the spacious rear garden. Richard could hear music drifting into the square.

John and his wife Helen were hovering around greeting guests in the impressive entrance hall, beckoning them to move through to the marquee and the garden, the source of the music a string quartet playing chamber music.

Richard had arrived fairly early but he recognised a fair number of people: newspaper columnists, think-tank figures and veterans from various campaigns, along with fellow Conservative MPs and peers. He went over to talk to a well-known constitutional lawyer, Sir Justin Thompson KC, a regular commentator in various newspapers and always a useful sounding board.

'What do you make of the latest devolution problems, Justin?'

Justin smiled. 'Well, Tony Blair has a lot to answer for, but we are where we are. The way out isn't clear. Legally the Government doesn't need to do anything; nothing says there has to be another referendum, and only Westminster can call one. Our Nationalist friends can whine as much as they want, but they cannot hold a vote themselves. But can we hold the line politically?'

This was, course, the ten-million-dollar question.

'I suggest we ride it out,' said Richard. 'No Party can maintain that level of monopoly for long.'

Thompson took a mouthful of Pimm's. 'You say that, Richard, but one-party states can last a very long time and tend not to end in a peaceful change of Government... and I think that's what we're seeing develop. I agree we cannot hold a referendum and they legally cannot force one, but I'm not convinced time is necessarily on our side. We have no voice in Scotland and the more time passes the more the two sides drift apart. I can see no simple solution.'

'Well, forcing the BBC to reduce the Nationalists' coverage and include a bit of UK news would help,' replied Richard. 'As would more interventions from us in Scotland say boo to the nationalist goose. If we started from scratch, we could create a far better form of devolution, by changing or reducing their powers. But they'd explode. We have to stop things getting worse.'

Thompson laughed; he'd been around this buoy before. 'A counsel of despair, Richard. You are in a jolly mood! Anyway, on a lighter note, what are you doing with what is left of the summer?'

Richard was glad of the change of topic. 'Well, I have just come back from that Foreign Affairs trip to Malaysia, rather livelier than I expected! No real plans for the rest of it. Hopefully Cumbria for a few days, I go there fairly often. And you?'

'Yes, I read all about your exploits,' said Thompson. 'It looked rather exciting, but also rather dangerous. I have a rather laborious case dragging on at the moment, but I'll try and get away later.'

Richard intimated he was going to get another drink and wandered around the garden. Animated by the Pimm's, the atmosphere was more febrile than usual. There was chatter about the Government defeat. What did it mean? Who were the runners and riders in the potential contest? What did it all mean for Scotland and the Nationalists? There was blood in the water – specifically Summers' blood – the MPs were beginning to sense that she could not survive and were beginning to plan.

But as of yet there was no vacancy and no credible candidates. McVey's MP friends were mainly, but not exclusively, on the Right of the party; many had supported Brexit in 2016 but that was no longer the label it had once been. Now the same MPs were divided on the Union, tax and the direction of the Party generally, but also now – with the incident with China – foreign policy. Should the UK put its weight behind the 'league of democracies' standing up to China or follow the EU's lead and intimate this was a purely a United States affair?

Richard then spotted Tommy Rosenfield chatting to a group of MPs, including Matt McCarthy, one of Richard's friends. He observed from a discreet distance. Rosenfield was laying on the charm, laughing in response to one of the MPs' comments. He then made his excuses and circulated on to his next victims. Having recharged his drink Richard wandered over to McCarthy and friends.

'Good evening, all! Great party as always – John has really mastered it!'

McCarthy chipped in: 'Yes, I've never seen such canapés – well since last year anyway – I'm waiting for the chocolates: they were amazing last year!'

One of Richards pals Andrea, an MP for a Welsh seat, responded as Richard had hoped she would. 'You never know who came over to show an interest in us Richard. Tommy Rosenfield. All sweetness, and he made a convincing pretence of actually wanting to listen to what we have to say! Now that's a first, is it not?

'Remarkable!' said Richard. 'I wonder what came over him? A man of such exalted intellect and skills, suddenly interested in the opinions of mere back-benchers? A shocking lapse!'

Andrea laughed. 'Stop it, Richard! I'm sure he was just being pleasant – well, we shouldn't rule that possibility out anyway.'

Richard smiled. He knew Tommy Rosenfield wasn't popular among his friends, but he was an operator. He could see him now at the other end of the marquee flattering a more senior MP. He was on a mission all right. He was closely followed by his former PPS – an MP who was appointed to help him liaise with Parliament and his own Party – and a public relations executive was never far away from him.

Richard pointed him out. 'Look at him now. Next victim. So, we have a leadership candidate do we? He and twenty others, if it's anything like last time.'

Andrea chipped in: 'Who else do we think will run? Nicholas Braithwaite, I presume? How about Robert Lacy, will he try again? There's no one overwhelming choice as far as I can see. Someone who can stand up to this Scottish nonsense is the immediate priority, I guess?'

This was going to be a busy few months, Richard thought to himself. Only the ever-ambitious Tommy Rosenfield seemed to be in the running so far, but others would feel the need to join the shadow campaign. A Cabinet Minister, but which one? Someone would have to break ranks on the Scotland policy, but the ministers were aware that the assassin is rarely the one who goes on to wear the crown. Richard saw McVey on his own and slipped away to say hello.

'Fantastic party again, John. Have you seen Rosenfield? What do you think he's up to?'

'Yes, not particularly subtle. I hadn't actually invited him, but Rossi, who seems close to him, talked me into it. I still count him as a friend.'

Richard changed the topic. 'John, what do you know of spies? Chinese spies to be precise?'

'Not much; we were hacked several times when I worked in consulting. They were trying to get access to the databases we built for the Government. Why do you ask? This sounds interesting…'

'Well, strictly between us, I have a bit of a dilemma.'

'Sounds fascinating. Pray tell.'

Richard then explained about the woman in Singapore,

the encounter and the odd fact that nothing was really asked of him. 'What do you make of that?'

John looked cheered. The party had so far thrown up a few amusing anecdotes, but this one had blown them out of the water.

'Well, that is very odd. I don't mean this the wrong way, but you're not the sort of senior MP that could be of any use to them.'

'No, nor would I want to be of use to them. But it did happen, and the Chinese had put some effort into planning it.'

John was excited about the intrigue, but calmly listed the possibilities. 'Well, it could be a plan to compromise you and turn you into an accomplice.

'Or, as she said, dissidents within China wanting to sabotage a government plan. Or perhaps it's an elaborate ruse by the Chinese state to get you to do something for them.'

John paused, searching for an even more ingenious explanation. 'Or maybe… it's not China at all but a criminal sting! And was she pretty? I need a full description!'

Richard smiled. 'Always the important points! Very tall for a Chinese woman, Western-educated and smartly dressed. An Australian accent, I think.'

'But why contact you and then do nothing? I'd be rather careful if I were you. Have you been to MI6 or the police?'

'No,' replied Richard carefully. 'I did have some dealings with the secret services when I was a minister, but I hardly want this landing on Foreign Secretary Rosenfield's desk: it'd be all over the front pages tomorrow! And what would I say? If I stroll into Vauxhall Bridge House and tell them what I've just told you, they'd either laugh or lock me up as a fantasist.

So, I'm not of a mind to do anything, but that does leave me with a problem.'

John replied: 'I can see. You say she gave you some information about Chinese agents?'

'Yes, I have it on a memory stick. I haven't looked at it yet; I presume it's infected with all manner of Chinese viruses. I don't want to be blamed for allowing them to hack the parliamentary IT system!'

John thought about it. This had cheered him up: a genuine bit of intrigue. 'I could get some of our IT people to look at it. See if there's anything on it. I'll swear them to secrecy.'

'Sure', said Richard, happy to get rid of the thing. He took the memory stick out of his wallet and handed it to John, feeling its weight leave him.

'Don't worry, it'll go in the safe the moment I'm back indoors! I'd also suggest you follow me over to speak to an American friend of mine, Tom Gracey. Nominally he's a political counsellor at their embassy, but he's actually their spy, or so I'm told. Let's see what he thinks you should do – without providing any details, of course.'

Richard agreed and followed McVey into the crowd.

Moments later John spied the American and beckoned him over. 'Tom, may I introduce you to my old friend Richard Reynolds MP?'

After a bit of small talk and jokes about spying and how it was all in fact rather dull, Richard decided to try Tom out. 'Between you and me, I have a spy anecdote. Last week I was in Singapore and…' He ran through the incident. 'What do you make of that? Should I report it?'

Tom explained he'd best log it with the British, if only for his own protection, in case something happened later.

'Thanks. Actually, I did meet some of your people a few weeks ago when they came over, I thought I might talk to them.'

Tom suddenly looked troubled. 'Oh, who did you talk to?'

Richard fished in his wallet and brought out McColl and Singer's business cards. Tom's face darkened. 'No, I don't recognise them. If you don't mind, may I check up on this and get back to you?'

'By all means.'

'I'll also let you have our MI5 contact,' said Tom. 'It's probably nothing, but it might mean something to them.'

John and Richard made their goodbyes and walked on.

'What did you make of that, John? He's probably right about contacting MI5.'

'Yes, but that's very odd about the other Americans; they don't seem very joined up.'

Having spoken to Gracey, Richard felt some of the weight lift from him and felt he now had no option but to contact the British security services. However, he had an instinctive wariness about explaining anything in detail. People could easily jump to the wrong conclusions and putting his trust, as a Conservative MP, in the hands of an instinctively hostile Civil Service seemed to him a major error.

But the next day he locked himself in his office and reluctantly dialled up the number on the card that Gracey had given him.

37. A Crunch Vote

House of Commons, 20 September

For Richard the summer recess came to a shuddering halt with the news that the Prime Minister would put her devolution legislation to a new vote the first week Parliament returned after the break. Any thoughts that Summers and her team might have used the summer to quietly shelve the idea and tackle Scottish Nationalism head on disappeared. She had opted for a different confrontation, not with the Scottish separatists, but with her own Party.

Sir William Mostyn was rapidly becoming the public face of opposition to the devolution legislation. Over the summer he'd filled numerous news slots, giving short, succinct sound bites:

'Sovereignty or Separation? Yes, to the UK.'

He'd even debated directly with Malcolm MacIntyre on *Newsnight*, and had momentarily forced the Nationalist leader to stumble on the economics of separation and whether he'd accept an end to independence in exchange for the Prime Minister's deal. MacIntyre's answers were slippery, and the audience knew it.

But Summers still had cause for hope.

The leadership contest had failed to gain momentum. While the rules specified that fifty-two letters had to be sent in to trigger a vote, according to Mostyn's spreadsheet they had at least fifty-three, but nothing had happened. Clearly some MPs had failed to fulfil their promises.

Suspicions abounded. Who was double-bluffing? Was

Sir Richard McLean telling the truth? Was he trying to protect the Prime Minister? Nobody knew. And without an imminent leadership contest, Summers could keep trying to ram her legislation through time and time again, until enough MPs gave in through exhaustion. The Whips explained that two days of debate would be given to the legislation, followed by a second-reading vote.

The debate was due on the first Thursday after the recess, and Richard registered his desire to speak in the Chamber. It was late at night before he was called. Speeches were curtailed to three minutes due to the sheer number of those wishing to make their views heard.

Richard ran through his arguments: this was not the way to protect the Union, there was an alternative... but in the feverish atmosphere he was interrupted numerous times and despite the best efforts of the Speaker to keep the Chamber calm, little was heard.

And then a surprise. Foreign Secretary Tommy Rosenfield got up to speak from the backbenches. The Chamber fell silent as MPs cottoned on to what was about to happen: it could only mean one thing. He was going to resign. Rosenfield, after a dramatic pause, began to explain that he'd been toying with his conscience for the last few months but had come to the conclusion that he could not vote for a piece of legislation that might spell the end of the United Kingdom.

'I will therefore be tendering my resignation to the Prime Minister and will resume my role on the back benches.'

Caroline Summers, sitting a few rows in front of him, listened to him impassively, looking straight forward, but at the mention of her name, and Rosenfield's assertion that no Conservative Prime Minister could vote for this bill, she turned and glared at him. The Chamber erupted in jeers from all sides, and the shouts of 'Order!' from the Speaker fell on deaf ears.

The debate went on for several more hours late into the evening as Government ministers and Whips furiously tried to persuade Conservative MPs to back the bill. Promises of new roads, bypasses, hospitals, knighthoods, peerages and even space ports were bandied about in a vain attempt to stem the seeping away of the Prime Minister's support.

It was not until one o'clock in the morning that the Secretary of State for Scotland Robert Lacy was able to pick up the debate and 'wind up' the Government's case for their legislation. But it was clear that things had not gone well and the opposition scented blood.

When the division bells rang, the chamber was alive with hurried conversations and Whips running around trying to persuade their wayward flocks from voting the wrong way: 'What did this mean?' 'Is he running for leader?' 'Can the Prime Minister survive?' They were all very good questions, to which none of the MPs had good answers.

The result of the vote came fifteen minutes later and again it was a defeat for the Prime Minister. Tommy Rosenfield left the Chamber straight into a pack of cameras in the Central Lobby. He spoke slowly and deliberately.

'This is why I have lost confidence in the Prime Minister's approach to the Scottish Nationalist problem. This is why I will be writing to Sir Richard McLean to request a leadership ballot. I can confirm that I will be a candidate.'

The next morning the BBC reported that McLean was calling a press conference at noon on behalf of the 1922 Committee. The reason was obvious: the requisite fifty-two letters had now been delivered. Rosenfield and his supporters had cleverly withheld their letters to give him a boost. There were now three serious candidates – the former Defence Secretary Nicholas Braithwaite, Sir William Mostyn and Tommy Rosenfield. The momentum was with Rosenfield, who, it was cattily remarked, had suddenly become very popular with his colleagues.

The next day Rosenfield was the surprise guest alongside Malcom MacIntyre on BBC *Question Time*, broadcast live from Edinburgh. It was billed as the great showdown between the leaders of the two camps, hyperbole Rosenfield did nothing to stop. The audience, as Richard had often observed was the case with BBC audiences, started off hostile towards Rosenfield as a 'Conservative', but gradually shifted as the exchanges went on.

Then something surprising happened. MacIntyre stumbled on the economic case for Scottish independence and seemed to accept that Scotland would require UK support for its currency and economy. The audience sensed weakness and Rosenfield hammered his point home, scoring a second hit on pensions and then a third on the armed forces, stressing his own role fighting alongside Scots in the British Army in Afghanistan. By the end of the programme MacIntyre looked defeated and Tommy Rosenfield seemed unstoppable.

The papers the next day duly reported a triumph for Rosenfield. A snap poll of Conservative Party members published by the *Telegraph* had him as the clear favourite after Nicholas Braithwaite.

38. Greenslade Limited

Chelsea, 20 September

John McVey retrieved an old laptop computer from a cupboard in his office and plugged it in. It came to life. He checked that the Wi-Fi was disabled and plugged in the memory stick that Richard had given him.

The drive appeared on the screen. It contained numerous documents, many of which were in Chinese. Scrolling through, McVey picked up an occasional UK company and various other names which meant little to him. But slowly and surely some familiar names began to emerge.

An investment company called Greenslade Limited, known to have several former senior British civil servants on its board and payroll, appeared in one document. Much of its work appeared to involve investments in British technology companies, acting as a holding company for various Chinese investors.

Next up was Sedwood Investments LLP, apparently an insurance company with a former MP on its board. Salisbury Partners, a lobbying company linked to a Conservative peer came up several times. This one interested him as they were active in Conservative political circles, employing former Party advisers. John had no idea who their clients were but they would occasionally appear in the media, commissioning polls or commenting on contentious policy and polling issues.

Polling was something that John knew quite a bit about as a veteran of many campaigns going back to the Brexit Referendum in 2016. Most commentators ignore the motives of the people who commission opinion polls, but John was well aware that polls don't only tell you how people might vote, they actually influence their voting choices.

If you commission a poll with the aim of showing how popular your particular cause is, you can build momentum and then attract those who want to be on the winning side of the argument; conversely, a poll that shows your opponent's policy or Party haemorrhaging support could well increase that effect. Control the polling and you control the parameters of a political debate, which is why so much money is spent on it.

Salisbury Partners had been heavily involved in the cause of Scottish Nationalism, publishing opinion-poll-based commentary on the rise in support for independence.

With this in mind, McVey opened a Salisbury Partners file containing invoices from Greenslade Limited related to the conducting of polls that had caused a bit of a stir recently, showing one of the biggest majorities for independence since 2014.

McVey, with his knowledge of the dark arts of polling, was intrigued. He knew that a well-crafted question – a leading question such as 'Should Scotland be independent?' with a correctly weighted sample – could deliver the results the polling agency's clients were after. But why would Greenslade Limited, a company stacked with former British civil servants, have a fascination with Scottish polling? It made no sense.

But that was not all of it. McVey also discovered a file containing lists of payments to a Scottish property company, a major donor to the Scottish National Party. He was amazed. Was that where they got their money from? From an investment company that appeared to be part of a network of Chinese companies? If so, this would be dynamite.

But what should he do with this information? There were some well-known names on these lists, none of whom would take kindly to being exposed as part of a Chinese web of influence.

He could turn it over to the police, but would they understand the significance of what they were looking at? Would they dare to investigate these companies? How could he explain how he'd discovered the files? He could hardly saunter into a police station and say he'd found a file of national importance that a Chinese spy had given to a pal of his in Singapore!

Perhaps he should try a different route – a journalist could dig out the information and give the SNP an airing? That would remove McVey and Richard from the story and put the SNP on the back foot. That seemed a better option: once out in the open the security services could find it all out for themselves. But which newspaper should he go to? How could he approach them? How would they then explain how they'd come across this information?

Then an idea came to him. He could ask his old friend Tommy Rosenfield. He had the contacts to deal with it properly. With his new-found love for the Union and hard line on China, he was the perfect choice – he could make hay with this information.

McVey decided to contact Rosenfield's office and arrange a meeting, hinting he had interesting information on Chinese infiltrators that might help his campaign. Rosenfield told McVey he was intrigued.

'You never know who might be working for the Chinese. They have serious money and our officials are a greedy lot!

'Promise me one thing, though,' said McVey.

'Sure.'

'Please keep this information away from Robert Lacy. Don't tell anyone I said this, but I don't quite trust him on China. This is best kept between us and the security services.'

'I give you my word. No Lacy.'

39. MI5

Thames House, 12 Milbank, Westminster, 21 September

Richard sat at his desk listening to his MI5 contact's phone ringing. He didn't want to speak to them – or anyone else for that matter – about the woman in Singapore, but he now felt he had no choice. The five buzzes it took before he heard a woman's voice answer seemed like an eternity.

Callum Burn's secretary took his details; he was then left on hold. He sat at his desk nervously playing with his pen. Eventually a man's voice came on the line. 'I think it's probably best if you come down here. Are you in Westminster? I'm free at 2.30 if that would suit.'

It didn't, but Richard was keen to get this matter over with as soon as possible, so he set off for the short walk to Thames House, an unmarked building a few hundred yards upstream from Parliament.

He was escorted upstairs into a meeting room. It was small, had no external window and contained unremarkable office furniture. Tom's contact arrived shortly afterwards.

'Thank you for coming, I'm Callum.'

He was a short, slight man with a weak voice and smug disposition. The fact that he was wearing his security pass on the obligatory rainbow lanyard over a plain white shirt immediately made Richard wary. He had come across civil servants like this before and had always felt he was being judged for some non-existent crime. He made a mental note to say as little as possible.

Richard tried to make his encounter with the Chinese

woman sound as dull as possible, occasionally stopped to see if Callum would say anything in response, but there was little in the way of reaction. He concluded with his meeting with Tom at McVey's garden party.

'I thought I should let you know in case it means more to you than me.'

Richard had had enough and wanted to leave. He looked up at Burn, whose face showed a mix of disgust and condescension.

'We've seen this before, MPs abroad targeted by young women after information or trying to compromise the individuals concerned. You were right to report it to us. Please let us know if you have any further contact with her.'

Richard resented the implication but let it go, desperate to leave without any further discussion. 'What will you do with this information, if anything?' he asked.

'We'll let our sister organisation in Singapore know, and possibly update our advice to MPs travelling abroad. This looks like a failed contact from a foreign actor, but as it was in Singapore there's little we can do about it.'

Richard was glad to escape the building. The meeting had served its purpose.

40. Unexpected Visitors

3rd Floor, 1 Parliament Street, 22 September

The next day Richard arrived in his parliamentary office a little later than usual. His secretary Adele mentioned that Jack McColl was back in London and wanted to meet him, preferably today.

Richard was minded not to accept his request, but casting his mind back to the previous meeting, the strange timing of his reappearance intrigued him. Why would McColl, who claimed to be working on behalf of the US Government, want to see him again?

In the end curiosity got the better of him and later that afternoon he was exchanging pleasantries with McColl and a colleague in his office, happy to relate with added colour the incident on the *Prince of Wales* earlier in the summer. With that, McColl suddenly changed tack.

'We've been following your exploits in the Far East. In fact it was that which prompted us to ask for another meeting. We're aware you're of some interest to Chinese intelligence – the Ministry of State Security – and we wanted to give you some advice on how to deal with them.'

McColl told him they'd become aware that a Chinese spy had contacted Richard, with the intention of ensnaring him into a network of political figures they could ask favours from under threat of blackmail.

'The operative's well known to us, tall for a Chinese woman, goes by the name of Mei and has an Australian accent, having gone to university there. But she is a Ministry of State Security asset and operates under various aliases.'

Richard sat in silence, not wishing to engage. McColl finished with a question.

'We were wondering if you could help us by explaining what it was she wanted from you, what her story was?'

Richard was shocked. How on earth would the Americans, if indeed that's who they were, know about the spy in Singapore? There was no way he was prepared to explain to them what had happened. After all, he had no real idea who these two characters were.

Without confirming or denying anything, Richard tried to treat it as a joke and thanked McColl for his advice 'about tall Chinese women' before changing the topic in rather a clunky manner to US politics and the China/US relationship.

The meeting dragged on, but Richard sensed that McColl was dying to bring the conversation back to Singapore. Eventually Richard looked at his watch, exclaimed that he had another meeting and he was so glad they'd found time to see him, and asked Adele to see them out.

Afterwards, when Richard asked her what she'd made of them, Adele replied that they seemed pleasant enough, but McColl had asked her in the lift about Singapore and if she knew whether Richard had any further plans to visit. 'Of course, I said nothing, but that was very odd, don't you think?'

'Yes, they are two very strange characters, and well done for not telling them anything. I don't think I'll be talking to them again!' She left him to his thoughts. Perhaps they were right: Mei's story was merely a ruse to compromise him and gain his cooperation. But then she did seem genuine, and her story about needing help also seemed credible. He had no way of telling the truth, but if McColl and his partner were indeed right, then the Chinese plan to compromise him had failed, and that was probably the end of it.

• • • •

The next day John McVey called. 'Tom wants to see you urgently, but didn't say what about exactly. I think you should meet him: he seemed genuinely agitated. I've known him for years; he can be trusted.'

Later that day Richard set off for the new US Embassy south of the river. The outline of an outsized US eagle cut into a stone wall loomed behind the reception desk, surrounded by the names of previous US Ambassadors. Richard was searched, given a security lanyard and asked to sit until Tom appeared.

'Thanks for coming,' said the American. 'I thought it best to talk in person.'

A lift took them up to a meeting room on the fourth floor, empty save for a table, chairs and some instantly forgettable modern artwork. The view to the south over some modern blocks was equally uninspiring. Richard was wondering why on earth he'd been called here for a meeting. He felt as if he was about to be told off for some grave misdemeanour, but kept telling himself he'd done nothing wrong.

'Richard, I've run some checks on the American lobbyists you met,' said Tom. 'I'm afraid they're bit of a mystery. They're certainly not on our books; in fact we know very little about them. The firm does exist and has a few clients, but nothing substantial.'

Richard went through his meeting with McColl, sparing no details except for the memory stick. When he'd finished Tom rolled back in his chair and breathed in heavily.

'Well, we have ourselves a mystery. A double mystery perhaps. Who is Mei and who does she work for? And who are these fellow countrymen of mine, taking such a close interest in you, dare I say it, a junior politician? It doesn't really stack up.'

'Well, they're all real enough, and their interest in me seems pretty serious. What should I do if Mei contacts me again?'

Tom replied, 'For now I'll limit myself to Jack McColl and his friend. We'll keep them under surveillance and do some digging. They may have their fingers in other pies. I'll also ask the Singaporeans what they know about this Chinese woman.'

'And me?' asked Richard.

'McColl won't bother you again. As for the Chinese woman, if she gets in touch, you should contact your security services. But I doubt she will. They seem to have bigger things on their mind at the moment.'

The whole business seemed to be getting out of hand and Richard was beginning to wonder whether it would land him in serious trouble. He'd now provided the Americans with more information than his own Government, but, as he kept telling himself, he'd done nothing wrong.

Back in his flat near Gloucester Road, he poured himself a glass of wine before settling in an armchair and sinking into despair. Not only was his Party and Government in complete disarray, but he was now caught in a bizarre plot involving a Chinese spy that could explode at any moment and engulf his career.

Meanwhile, with the UK in political meltdown, Singapore had slipped out of the news. Was Mei telling him the truth? If so, what was McColl up to? Richard had always prided himself on knowing exactly what was going on; it had been the secret to the little success he'd achieved so far in his political career. But now he was at the centre of something he did not understand.

41. The Ministry of State Security

Ministry of State Security, Haidan District, Beijing, 26 September

Mei had received a troubling message. It wasn't the content that concerned her – a request to return to Beijing for further instructions – but the fact that it hadn't been sent from her usual contact in the MSS. This was unusual and worried her. Was there a problem? Was she in trouble?

She tried to ring her contact but the phone was dead. She tried another contact in Chen Wenquing's office, but she sounded so panicky that Mei quickly ended the conversation.

What had happened? She was now convinced her contacts were in trouble, but it was unclear why. She searched Chinese social media and eventually discovered a curt announcement stating that Chen Wenquing had been arrested for corruption.

This was a shock. Corruption was often used as a pretext for other, more, political 'crimes'. If he was indeed under arrest, what would happen to her when she arrived back in Beijing? Prison? Interrogation? A labour camp even? She remembered the stories her grandparents told her of their suffering during the Cultural Revolution. A single denunciation and that was it.

No, she couldn't risk that. She couldn't go back to Beijing and risk being caught up in a witch hunt. But where else could she go?

Meanwhile in Beijing Chen Wenquing didn't have the luxury of a choice of destination. His day had begun with the arrival of a detachment of police and an official from the President's office marching into his office and arresting him. They'd taken him to a military base on the outskirts of Beijing.

He hadn't been told why he'd been arrested, but he was fairly certain his mission to Singapore had been compromised. But by whom, and how badly? He refused believe it was Mei: he'd known her father in Harbin.

As he sat in his cell, his mind settled on his deputy, Tan Geng. Any whiff of disloyalty from Chen and he'd be on to him without a thought or qualm.

He must somehow have found out about the mission, but Chen had only told his family and close friends. Perhaps it was the British politician? Was he a Chinese agent? It was not unknown for other agencies to run agents he was unaware of but the President would have to know. Reynolds was a junior politician and so, surely he would have been told, he was after all supposed to have control of all Chinese agents.

They were in serious trouble, him and Mei. Hopefully she'd stay out of China; her father would never have forgiven him if he got her into trouble. Where was she? Had she been arrested? Had she told them of their plans?

There was little he could do now. Geng would be in control of the Ministry and in Chen's absence his agents would be picked off one by one. The entire network would be exposed.

• • • •

Tan Geng was rather pleased with himself. In one day, he'd unearthed a serious plot against China, been appointed to run the Ministry of State Security and been praised by President Xi himself in a personal audience. Not bad for someone without any of the advantages and family contacts of other senior Party officials.

He'd never liked Chen Wenquing, a career diplomat who'd become far too friendly with the westerners. In Geng's mind that made him suspicious.

Because of this, Xi had secretly instructed him years ago to keep a close eye on Chen, ensuring that the MSS could be relied upon in a crisis. The sort of crisis they were experiencing now.

But Chen was a loyal Party man, and however hard he tried, Geng failed to uncover any legitimate cause for suspicion. His relations with Western intelligence agencies had always been strictly professional. He'd occasionally objected to some of the harsher measures suggested by the Politburo, but had never openly defied the Party. Until the last few weeks there had been no reason to doubt that Chen was anything other than a loyal Party servant.

That had all changed with news of a major breach of security in London. Someone had attempted to leak a list of Chinese agents to the British. Geng had then managed to persuade Xi to allow him to investigate the MSS, including Chen, for the source of the leak.

Many hours scouring the databases had produced a list of people who had access to the leaked information. His next task had been to work out how the British had got their hands on it.

This was easier said than done, but hours of trawling through itineraries, emails and documents had produced a possible source. A young spy called Mei Ling. It was a breakthrough, but he needed to know who had authorised it.

With this information he was then granted approval to contact the American lobbyists they'd used in the past to collect low-level intelligence on political figures without arousing too much suspicion. It was a high-risk approach: the British might realise what had happened and prevent a similar case happening again. But it had worked, and to his secret delight the Americans had produced just enough evidence to enable him to order Chen Wenquing's arrest.

Yet for all his success, one key fact was missing. A spy in the heart of the Ministry of State Security and a loyal minister betraying a whole Chinese network – why? What was their motivation? For now, Chen was refusing to talk.

But Geng was now in control, with the authority to close down this threat to national security. They had to get Chen to talk.

42. John McVey

Chelsea, 27 September

Richard had agreed to meet John at his house in Chelsea at 11 a.m. When no one answered the doorbell, he tried to phone, but again there was no reply. He sat on the steps and waited. After twenty minutes he was beginning to think McVey had forgotten, but there was no reply from his office either. He then called John's wife, who ran a small fashion company in the West End.

'That's very odd,' said Helen. 'He said he was going to be in all day. Wait there, I'll try and find him.'

Richard waited for another half an hour and called her back. 'Sorry,' said Helen. 'I can't get in touch with him either. Stay there, I'll come over.'

'Sure, I hope he's okay.'

Helen McVey arrived shortly afterwards in a taxi, looking agitated. Richard followed her up the steps as she unlocked the front door into the main hall. She called John's name.

Nothing.

Richard decided to head for his study which overlooked the garden at the back of the house. He knocked on the door and called out.

There was no reply.

Opening the door, he looked around the room. Nothing seemed out of place.

Walking over to the window he spotted a leather armchair at the far end of the room. To his horror he saw John slumped there. A sudden panic overwhelmed him. He ran up to him and shook him, but it was clear that something was very wrong. His eyes were fixed. He took John's right hand and felt for a pulse, but realised from the coldness of his skin that there was no point in continuing.

Richard was overcome with all manner of emotions – shock, horror and panic. He'd never seen someone dead like this before; in Afghanistan yes, but not a place and person he knew so well. The mundane awfulness of it surprised him.

He went back into the hall and looked over to see Helen. Seeing Richard's expression she asked, 'What is it?'

'I'm afraid he's dead. This is too dreadful.'

Helen began to sob. 'No, that's not possible. Where is he? Let me see him.'

Richard dialled 999, asking for an ambulance and the police. Twenty minutes later the doorbell rang and Richard beckoned the emergency services through to the study.

The officer in charge introduced herself as Detective Inspector Holly Fenton, a woman in her late thirties who, despite her obvious experience, seemed ill at ease under these particular circumstances. She began firing questions at him.

Yes, he'd known Mr McVey for some years.

No, he had no idea about his health.

'Did he have any enemies?' she asked.

'Not that I know of. Why? Do you think there's something suspicious here?'

Fenton replied: 'We don't know anything at the moment, but we need to keep an open mind. One more thing Mr Reynolds, did you remove anything from the office?'

'No. Why do you ask?'

'A computer appears to have been stolen, and someone's tried to break into his desk. They've made a bit of a mess of it. Have you any idea what they might have been looking for?'

A thought was beginning to plant itself in Richard's mind.

'I don't. But I'd be happy to come down to the station and make a statement. This is an awful business.'

Richard was still in shock, but the mention of the computer had added a heavy dollop of guilt to his already confused state. Had John been killed because of the memory stick he'd given him? Surely not...

Millions of theories ran through Richard's mind. Perhaps the Chinese were willing to kill to get the memory stick back? But who would have known that John had it? Someone at the garden party? The two American lobbyists? Callum Burn at MI5? Could he trust anyone?

Richard agreed to visit the police station the following day to provide a statement. He slept poorly that night. Had his actions led to John's death? Was the murderer likely to come after him next? He found himself checking the locks on his door in the middle of the night.

At Belgravia Police Station the following day, Richard was shown through to an interview room. DI Fenton repeated many of the questions from the day before while a colleague took notes

'Do you know of any threats to Mr McVey?'

'No. He had political enemies, but nothing to warrant murder.'

'Was he depressed?'

'No, quite the opposite. What was the cause of death?'

'Well, we only have an initial post-mortem. He'd been dead for a few hours. It seems to have been a combination of a weak heart and possibly a toxin of some kind. We'll know for certain in a few days, but we're not making any of this public. It may have been an accident, suicide or murder – we just don't know. We're looking at local CCTV; there's quite a lot of it in the area, so we're hopeful something will show up.

'We're not having much luck with a motive. Business partners? Must have been someone with considerable resources. There are some signs of a struggle, but it seems he must have known the murderer and let them in.'

Richard headed back to his office. He had no idea what to think. Should he tell the police about the memory stick? But one thought was louder than any other: 'Does the killer know where the memory stick came from?' The thought raced around his mind. 'If they didn't know Richard had got it from Mei, then surely the murderer must have been someone John contacted after their conversation. But who? Perhaps the contents of the memory stick was of far greater importance than either of them had suspected?'

None of this speculation was helping him much. He needed to do something. Richard therefore fished out his phone and asked Tom Gracey to come round for a chat.

43. On The Run

London Heathrow Airport, 27 September

Mei had left Singapore by the first plane she could book that morning, travelling on her Australian passport, under a name the Ministry of State Security would search for as soon as they realised she wasn't returning to Beijing.

She cleared passport control at Heathrow and headed for the centre of London. She knew her chances of avoiding capture and whatever fate was planned for her were better if she was in the UK.

Sitting in the train carriage waiting to depart, she went through what she knew. She'd been sent to Singapore to make contact with British and Australian politicians and to hand over to them genuine – or what she believed to be genuine – information on Chinese operatives working secretly within their governments, presumably as bait to induce them to work with her.

She'd also been instructed to inform the politicians of a plot to invade Singapore, presumably false information that the MSS wished the MPs to believe. She'd done her job. She'd done nothing wrong. So what was going on in Beijing?

Perhaps a particular faction had come unstuck. Perhaps the invasion of Singapore cover story wasn't just a cover after all? This seemed unlikely.

But just possibly could it have been something else? She knew Chen Wenquing had grave misgivings about the Chinese leadership, and was deeply concerned that the Party's future. Could he have decided to do something himself? But what? She had no idea, but by not returning to Beijing she knew she'd immediately become a suspect in whatever was unfolding.

At that point she received a WhatsApp from an unknown number. Her heart stopped for a moment. Perhaps it was Chinese security? She didn't want to open it. Plucking up courage, she scrolled down to the message.

From a friend of Chen Wenquing: Operation Red Ocean

She clicked on the attachment: plans, timings and maps of the South China Sea popped up. Whoever had sent it assumed she'd know what to do with this information. But was it genuine? Who was this person?

She replied:

Who are you? What do you want me to do with this?

A text came back:

I am a friend of Chen Wenquing, we both knew your father years ago in Harbin. He's been arrested on suspicion of authorising an illegal mission to Singapore to contact British and Australian politicians. You should not return to China.

The information given to you by Wenquing is genuine. There is an imminent plan to invade Taiwan and Singapore. It will fail. It would be a disaster for China if this went ahead. I know, because I've been responsible for these plans.

She was astounded. Any friend of her father would have to be in their late fifties or sixties, so who could this be? More importantly, why should she trust them?

> *If you really knew my father, you'll know his nickname.*
> *Little bear.*
> *What was his favourite saying?*
> *Better a diamond with a flaw than a pebble.*
> *Describe his face.*
> *A scar on his left cheek from a mining accident when he was young.*

Mei's mind flooded with memories from Manchuria, the late 1990s. Her father, a local Party official, would often bring friends around to their house for a drink, where they felt safe talking about the events of decades earlier: Pu Yi the 'Last Emperor' of the Japanese puppet state of Manchuria. For her own safety she wasn't really supposed to listen, but the tales they told were captivating. She could remember one man in particular, a local who'd been conscripted into the army. A name came to her. A nickname.

Does Lai Fu mean anything to you? she asked.

Yes, that was my name.

At Paddington Mei walked out through the ticket gate and into the nearest café.

She saw no reason not to believe this man: there was going to be an invasion and it would be a disaster for China. She'd read enough in the media to be cynical about the Chinese belief in the weakness of the West. They were complacent, but they were not defenceless.

Well, she was no longer working for the Party and her

survival was now in the balance. There was no doubt they were already looking for her. She knew she had to be careful, but she had little money and nowhere to go.

She had one option. She picked up her phone and searched for the link to a Dropbox she'd created months earlier. This was her insurance policy. A list of Chinese contacts and informants more extensive than any she'd shared previously. She sent the link directly to Richard Reynolds.

Richard was in the Commons restaurant when the message arrived, a message from an unknown number that he'd normally have deleted. But he sat up with a jolt. It was from the woman in Singapore: he recognised her profile photo. He didn't open the link, but Mei explained exactly what it was.

What on earth should he do now? Ignore it or take it to Callum and be grilled to within an inch of his life and accused, quite rightly, of withholding information?

Then the second message arrived. She was in London and needed help. What cheek, Richard thought to himself She accosts him in Singapore, waves a gun at him, causes him any amount of stress and is possibly responsible for the death of a close friend, and now turns up in London asking for help!

Whatever the cost he should go to M15 and hand the whole problem over to them. If she were genuine then they could protect her; if not, well she'd face the consequences. But was it that simple? He could end up being blamed for everything. And was it possible he was about to report himself straight into the hands of the Chinese Communist Party? No, he was comprehensively trapped. He would have to keep quiet.

He left the office early that day, making an excuse that he was ill, which was not far from the truth. At home that evening Richard switched on an old computer. He wasn't going to be caught downloading a Chinese spy system, but he had to know what was in this Dropbox that had prompted the woman to cross half the world and try to make contact. He typed in the address and the password she'd provided. A list of files appeared, spreadsheets, copies of documents. Most were in Chinese but when he opened one document in English, a list of names sprung up.

'Good lord!' he exclaimed to himself.

'That can't be true!'

'Well, that would explain everything.'

He then looked through the names more methodically: a list of some of the worst people he knew in British politics. A former Prime Minister, a senior civil servant, a handful of MPs and various academics, businessmen and people from think-tanks, the media and NGOs. But one name in particular shocked him.

What on earth should he do? He couldn't bury this information, yet judging from some of the names on the list, there was no way he could just walk into MI5 and hand it over. He needed to think this through.

He replied to Mei: '*Have read your message. Very interesting. What are you doing with this information?*'

'*Keep it safe.*' Came the reply.

Richard hesitated, then replied, *Why are you contacting me?*

Because I think I can trust you and because you were in Singapore. You were our best chance.

That did make some sense. It was just bad luck they'd decided on him. So, should he meet her? Should he try to help her? Without his help would the Chinese get to her first? More than likely, especially if she stayed in London.

· · · ·

On Thursday afternoon Richard's train pulled into Sunderland station. He always visited his constituency on a Thursday and saw no reason to change his routine. He walked towards his constituency house, a million miles away from his troubles in Westminster. He was always able to think more clearly away from London. He had this awful feeling of being dragged into something against his will, a whirlpool which he was paddling against but being sucked into regardless.

It had become obvious that China had a network of informers within the UK political establishment. Some of the names didn't surprise Richard that much: bitter, overlooked MPs who were happy to sell what little they knew. Richard was deeply concerned by two names in particular: a senior civil servant and a disturbingly senior Conservative politician.

But what was the purpose of this network? It had long been thought that China used its wide diaspora to gain technological advantages over Western companies, but presumably they were now also after political influence?

More disturbingly, they also seemed willing to kill. Richard was now more certain than ever that John McVey had been killed because he had access to the information. But who was the killer? Who knew John had access to the memory stick?

What did Mei want in return? To defect? But that didn't make any sense; she could have chosen any number of destinations, the United States for one. There were so many questions and only she knew the answer to them.

Late afternoon the following day Richard drove to Durham, having to concentrate as his mind was on other things. Before long the Norman cathedral was in sight and he parked in a street near the station, near the hotel where

Mei had checked in. Richard walked in and told reception he had a booking for dinner. 'Has Ms Lee arrived?'

'Yes, she's in the restaurant, I'll show you through.'

Richard had requested a corner table so they wouldn't be overheard. He saw Mei at a table by the window. He wondered what to say: should he seem pleased to see her or angry at the chaos she'd involved him in?' He decided on a plain 'Good evening, you made it!' It was clearly going to be an awkward conversation.

'Well, the last time I saw you were pointing a gun at me! So perhaps you could tell me what's so urgent that you've come all the way across the world to tell me?'

Mei smiled awkwardly. 'Yes, I'm sorry about the gun. This is going to be a long story. As you're aware I was sent to Singapore by the head of the Ministry of State Security to contact you and tell you of China's plans to invade Taiwan and Singapore.'

'Yes, so you told me, but why?'

'Well, I didn't know at the time, it wasn't my place to ask. But I now know my trip was not authorised by the Chinese Military Commission. It was an attempt by a faction in China who wanted to, as you say, "put a spanner in the works", prevent the invasion.'

Richard had so many questions. 'Who's trying to stop the invasion? When is it due to take place?'

'Minister Chen Wenquing. He's now been arrested. There are others, some in the military. They are very concerned. They're desperate to stop it. You see, the invasion timetable has moved forwards. We only have a few weeks to prevent this catastrophe.'

'We?' said Richard, slightly indignantly.

'Yes, you have a key role, you and the United Kingdom, you can help prevent this.'

'I don't understand. We're not going to war with China. I doubt we even figure in their thoughts. It's the US you need to talk to if you want to prevent a war, not us.'

Mei looked surprised. 'No, you're wrong. The United States will do nothing. They have no military arrangement with Singapore. They will be caught by surprise and be too late. But the UK, it could. You know yourself: the Durian Pact might be enough to prevent a Chinese invasion.'

She continued 'the US doesn't have an aircraft carrier in Singapore. The United Kingdom does, and now you're allied with Australia – remember your submarine deal – you're very much on the Chinese radar.'

Richard asked, 'Why Singapore?'

Mei explained. 'China needs oil, the oil flows past Singapore. Those US ships, those Australian submarines. What if there were sanctions? Singapore is the key to Taiwan. It commands the routes to the Indian Ocean.'

Richard noticed the waiter had been keeping an eye on them. He called him over and quickly ordered before resuming his questions.

'So, what does the Chinese leadership hope to achieve?'

'A major war is being planned. Things are tough in China at the moment; the leadership is desperate. Unite the Chinese under the Party leadership. That's their plan. But it will be a disaster. They've learnt nothing from Ukraine and the Russian army.'

Richard replied, 'You know my family history. My grandfather suffered enormously when the Japanese captured Singapore. I doubt it'd be any different with the Chinese army.

We saw what happened in Ukraine. Singapore is even more densely populated and dependent on food from outside. I commend your bravery for standing up to this. But I still don't understand what you want me to do?'

Mei looked pained but went on: 'Well, you're a politician; you now know who to trust, who not to trust, you know what's being planned. I also have another key piece of information. I have the invasion plans, the timings, the troop numbers. I have it all. Surely that's enough to convince people in the right places.'

Richard broke out of his gloom and smirked at that. 'Yes, who to trust! You realise the list you sent me means there are few in the UK government that *can* be trusted.'

Mei replied, 'Yes, you need to solve your own political situation. That must be done. Then deterrence. The PLA need to know that they cannot swan into Singapore without getting a bloody nose. They are risk-averse. If the calculation changes, it would give more strength to those opposed to this plan.

'You have the information; now you need a new Prime Minister who's willing to take a stand, and you need to ensure their name's not on the list I gave you.'

Dinner was served; Richard found this all very difficult to digest. A Chinese spy singling him out to save Singapore from certain destruction.

Richard returned to Sunderland in a state of mental exhaustion. It was now past midnight and he'd still not decided what to do. Then he suddenly remembered the discussion in the bar at Raffles with Bob McDonald, the Australian MP.

Yes, he might be able to help. He'd know the background but wasn't linked to any of the names on the list. Richard got through to Bob's office and heard that familiar accent: 'Richard, I was wondering if you might call. Where are you?'

Richard was surprised by the response and paused. 'Well, I wanted to speak to you about something. Do you remember that Chinese lady in Raffles? I think we may have stumbled upon some kind of plot.'

'I think we may have indeed. I was thinking of calling you myself, but it's difficult to know who to trust. But I can tell you more about this in person.'

'In person! I thought you were in Australia?'

'I am at the moment, but my government has decided that I need to be in London, courtesy of this mutual acquaintance of ours. In fact, I'm booked on a flight this evening. I'll be staying with our High Commissioner while we sort out this little mystery.'

44. Black Baron Farm

Dunbarton, 28 September

Allison Campbell was an inspector with Police Scotland's drug enforcement unit based in Tulliallan Castle in Fife. She was a hardworking and competent officer, known throughout her unit for her thoroughness and dedication. Little escaped her.

It was possibly due to her reputation that Allison had received an urgent request to take a team to an address near Dumbarton to follow up a report of a suspected marijuana farm.

This was not unusual in itself, but this particular request had come directly from the National Crime Agency in London.

Black Baron Farm was a collection of traditional stone barns clustered around a small cottage at the end of a long private track. It was unkempt, with various rusting pieces of farm machinery left in the grass around the yard.

Campbell had arrived at the property with two PCs to conduct a search. Taking the precaution of blocking the drive, they headed in. It was deserted. Undeterred, she directed her colleagues to enter the house. Breaking the door open they went up the main stairs but, finding nothing of interest, continued their search in the outbuildings.

In one barn they found brand-new white plastic bags, the type you can only pick up with a tractor. They'd discovered the farm's fertiliser store.

'Inspector, look what we have here,' one of the PCs shouted.

'Enough to grow all the drugs in Colombia! There must be several hundred tonnes here!' Allison had been brought up on a farm not too dissimilar to this one, and immediately realised that this was a huge quantity that would never be required on this farm. 'That's enough to keep a marijuana operation going for decades.' She replied looking at it. 'See if you can find any delivery details, where it came from or who ordered it?'

They still hadn't found the growing rooms they'd been expecting. Such an amount would require a truly vast space. It must be there, but there were no tell-tale signs, no rubbish or compost bags. Barely any signs of life at all. Still, this just made the puzzle all the more interesting. She persevered. Perhaps it was underground.

Campbell pulled a pile of tarpaulins away from the corner of an office room at the back of the barn, revealing a trap door. Pulling that up, she saw steps heading down into a vault below.

'Over here!' she shouted.

The nearest PC ran over. 'Look at that,' he replied. 'It's like *Tomb Raider*!'

'Well, get a torch and we'll check it out.'

Going down into the clammy gloom of the vault Allison shone her torch around the large, empty space smelling of oil and must. Packing cases were piled to the ceiling around the walls.

'We have something here,' said Allison. 'Not marijuana but... Oh God!'

In the darkness of the subterranean room were case upon case of weapons: RPGs and rifles.

Allison climbed back up the steps. 'Right... We need to

seal this off and contact the firearms unit and the Met anti-terrorist command unit immediately. We also need to hope the owners aren't planning to come back in a hurry.'

Later that day the specialists moved in, and the quiet yard became a hive of activity as officers set to work removing case after case of rifles and explosives.

The final tally was impressive: four snipers' rifles, an array of pistols but also twenty Chinese-made automatic rifles and twenty M16 assault rifles, plus tens of thousands of rounds of ammunition, plastic explosives, and timers and detonators that could be used to make fertiliser bombs.

This discovery was a truly disturbing departure for Scotland, something not lost on the police working at the farm, who were told of the importance of conducting the enquiry in strict secrecy.

While the work went on recovering the weapons, links to the participants were gradually put together: names and payments etc. They had to move fast; time was limited before the perpetrators realised they'd been compromised.

On Wednesday afternoon, too late to be brought up in Prime Minister's Questions at midday, the Anti-Terror Commander launched into a press conference from behind a desk in a briefing room in New Scotland Yard.

He talked the assembled journalists through the discovery in as methodical and straightforward a way as possible, before getting to that day's developments. The weapons haul itself was shocking enough but then he said:

'And we suspect a group that call themselves the "Scottish Republican Army", with links to criminals in Glasgow and Belfast.'

Within moments the news had erupted everywhere, with

the BBC reporting:

> **BREAKING NEWS:** Raids across Scotland have led to multiple arrests of militants of the Scottish Republican Army.

Recriminations came thick and fast. Unionist politicians attempted to link the weapons to Malcolm MacIntyre, but without much direct evidence. For his part MacIntyre came out fighting, accusing politicians in Westminster of fanning the flames of violence by not acceding to Scottish demands for independence. The darker recesses of social media were full of conspiracy theories and thinly veiled threats. Scottish politics, always a heady brew, was taking a turn for the worse.

Exacerbating the situation were tensions within the Conservative Party over the Government's Devolution Bill. Opinion polls were again showing that the package had the support of the majority of Scotland's population, but the delay in Parliament was increasing support for full independence. It was difficult to predict how the arms discovery would change opinion.

Christmas had come early for Malcolm MacIntyre, who was doing the rounds of the news channels, carefully condemning violence but also pointing out that there was 'much anger' in Scotland, and there were some who might resort to other means if the constitutional democratic approach failed. He made yet another threat to hold an illegal referendum on Scottish independence if Summers refused to agree to his demands for further devolution. Within the Conservative Party, MPs were beginning to wobble.

Yet for all that, a select group within the security services in Northern Ireland knew that things were much worse than they seemed. The weapons recovered in Scotland were indeed the very same weapons that Aidan McGuire had spirited away from South Armagh. But they were also only a small part of the consignment; the rest had already been moved.

Richard followed the news with increasing alarm. He and his fellow Conservative MPs were now being put under huge pressure by the Government to accept there was no alternative to the devolution package. The weapons haul filled Richard with dread. How long would it be before opponents of the legislation would be accused of stoking the tension? He knew enough about his own Party to predict how they might react under pressure.

Those in marginal seats would be the first to panic: violence and instability in Scotland could cost them their seats, best to do a deal and move on, they'd think. The careerists, accustomed to following the majority view and sensing that the Party was moving away from confrontation with the SNP, would be next.

The media was guaranteed not to fully understand the issues, yet move in lock step with the Government machine; a few articles would appear questioning the wisdom of holding out against further Scottish devolution. Next, senior Scottish policemen would brief select groups of influential MPs, emphasising the threat of violence if no deal was reached. The 'Ground Zero' blog would argue that Conservatives voting against Summers' package risked civil war and the end of the UK. Finally, there'd be a full stampede as the centre-right hurtled off in the wrong direction. What could be done?

MPs were already plotting, the 'Reform' group of Left-leaning Conservative MPs were holding meetings on how to support devolution and 'prevent a 'new Northern Ireland'. To Richard and his fellow Unionists, the stampede looked set on running off a cliff.

And then to make matters worse, the police called him in for questioning. John McVey had indeed been murdered. The pathology reports had confirmed he died of a toxin, a rare and advanced nerve agent related to the Russian Novichok, a chemical that could only be manufactured by a state with an advanced chemical weapons programme.

45. Meltdown in Parliament

House of Commons, Westminster, 28 September

'You'll cause a civil war by voting against this bill!' yelled a junior minister in Richard's face as he walked to his office. It had been a fraught few weeks and some of his fellow MPs were not coping well with the situation.

He found a note on his desk telling him to expect a visit from his Whip in half an hour. 'What's the point?' he thought to himself. 'She knows I'll vote against it.'

After a few phone calls to constituents there was a knock on the door and his secretary showed Julia Cartwright MP in.

'Richard, I know you feel strongly on this but can't you see the damage this is causing? Damage to the Party and to Scotland. Did you see the news about the arms find? This could get very nasty.'

'I know all that Julia, but this legislation is not the right way to deal with it. It's a matter of principle. We can't vote the United Kingdom out of existence as if it were a statutory instrument on the regulation of toasters.'

'No, of course not. But we're not planning anything like that. We have no choice. Can't you sense the anger brewing? Why can't you just vote for it?'

'Look Julia, we've known each other for years. There's no point trying to persuade me with the same old arguments. Yes, I accept this might be the end of this Prime Minister, but frankly there are more important things—'

'But Richard—'

'Please, I don't see any point to this conversation. Could you now leave before I say something I might regret?'

'But—'

'Leave!'

And with that she left. Richard immediately regretted losing his temper, but at least she'd departed before he'd really got going. He really didn't have time for this.

His resolve fortified by the encounter, Richard decided to act. He telephoned the Labour Whips; he knew the Labour Party was more interested in defeating the Government and destroying the Conservatives than the future of this particular piece of legislation, but on this issue they could seal a marriage of convenience. Besides, if the United Kingdom was about to be broken up, did it really matter whether Labour or the Conservatives ran the remaining parts?

Labour wanted to reduce the number of their own rebels who'd vote with the Government, and Richard needed to be able to reassure his side that it was worth rebelling. Nobody wanted to stick their head over the parapet, risk their career and friends for a lost cause. If only he could convince them the cause was not lost.

The Labour Whip picked up his call – as he always did at times like this. 'Hi Gavin, how's it looking from your side?' said Richard. 'Our Whips would have us believe a phalanx of Labour MPs are ready to save Summers' Bill – I assume you've heard that one?'

Gavin chortled before replying. 'Yes, it's rubbish, straight from Number 10. My educated guess is there's no more than two. I think we're okay on our side.'

'That's good to hear. For our part, we're solid.'

Gavin continued: 'You can count on us; we have them

locked down. My only concern is that if your lot suddenly broke ranks and supported Summers then it might discourage some of my pals from voting against; some have been under pressure locally. But what you say sounds reassuring. If you don't mind, we need to get that news out.'

'I can do that,' suggested Richard. 'In fact, I'll Tweet it once we're off the phone: "I'm told that the Labour rebellion in favour of Summers' bill has evaporated" – or something like that.'

'Good, we have some time. The vote will be late, I imagine. Time for some last-minute phone calls should we need them!'

Richard and his fellow 'Union Group' of Conservative rebels had planned a meeting before the debates were due to commence at about 2.30 p.m., invited all the MPs who'd voted against the Scotland Bill last time. Many had changed their mind since.

In the past week pressure had come to bear on some of the newer or more ambitious MPs: fears for the future of the Government, concerns about the threat of violence in Scotland since the arms discovery. MPs were tired and many were beginning to throw in the towel. Sensing a shift in opinion, the centre-right press also began to turn, picturing the rebels as 'die-hards', obstinate, even thick.

But before Richard's group could come together, an invitation went around in the morning inviting every Conservative MP to a meeting with the Prime Minister. Clever, thought Richard, they can use that to pressure the remaining rebels. And that was exactly their plan.

Shortly before twelve o'clock, Conservative MPs could be seen trooping up into the gigantic Committee Room 9, a miniature House of Commons. When Richard and Alistair arrived, the room was already packed and the noise could be heard along the corridor. The intimidation began immediately. A group of MPs, well known for their sycophancy, pointed at Richard and Alistair as they came in and a murmur of disapproval rippled around the room.

The Whips had really gone overboard this time. The noise and pointing continued until the Prime Minister appeared.

'Colleagues, this is the most important vote for decades and one that will have a direct impact on the future of our country and Party,' she said. 'I appeal to you all to put aside our disagreements and think of the future.'

Dreadful, thought Richard, but she momentarily had the room at her disposal and continued to picture herself as the saviour of the United Kingdom, winding up her peroration with a sickly sweet appeal to unity before allowing a few questions.

'Has the SNP agreed to drop calls for independence?'
'Yes.'
'Can we be sure this will keep the UK in one piece?'
'Yes.'

Richard decided to break the cosy consensus. When the Chief Whip chose to ignore his raised hand, he decided to ask his question anyway.

'Prime Minister, this package allows for Scotland to borrow, guaranteed by the Bank of England; it allows for separate immigration policies, even separate elements of foreign policy and defence. Even the monarchy. How can you claim that the UK will remain united or even a Kingdom if this surrender bill is passed?'

The room erupted. The pointing gave way to shouting and a chant: 'Just vote for the damn Bill… Vote for the Bill…'

with many in the room pointing at Alistair and Richard. The Prime Minister had no answer; she turned, signalled that the meeting was over and left.

The shouting began to subside and Richard and Alistair tried to fight their way to the exit. Out in the corridor Alistair turned to him and remarked, 'I didn't disagree with a word you said, but was that worth it?'

'No, but that was such an ugly meeting I would have regretted not speaking up.'

Richard and Alistair walked down the corridor to their own meeting like ships into harbour. A much pleasanter atmosphere, thought Richard. If the Prime Minister's meeting was a display of artificially manufactured opinion, then their Union meeting was a complete contrast. Although Richard and his friends had been ringing MPs all day, there were still a few waverers, keen to see what others were going to do before jumping either way.

Alistair, Richard and Sir Bill Howard set out their case from the front of the room, before the discussion darted around, MPs asking questions or explaining their own way of seeing things. One quoted Rudyard Kipling and another explained how Churchill made up his mind during the 1940 Norway debate. As time moved on the atmosphere became tense as they waited for the debate to begin. When 2 p.m. arrived, the MPs broke up and headed down to the Chamber.

Alistair sat in his usual spot at the back to watch the opening speeches. Robert Lacy kicked off the case for the Government, explaining it was a bill of necessity to keep the United Kingdom together.

Richard sat directly behind Lacy on the green leather benches. The Chamber always felt very small in real life and

Lacy was only a few feet in front of him. It was quite late before the time came for Richard to speak. MP after MP had railed against the Bill; one even went as far as to accuse the Prime Minister of 'appeasement'. And so it continued all afternoon, as MPs spotted who was talking to whom and who had to leave to take phone calls from begging Whips.

The anxiety continued for hours until eventually a government minister wound up the debate. The vote was now imminent as the clock ticked towards 'the knife'. The division bells sounded, calling MPs to vote – the Aye's to one side and the No's to the other. It was another anxious fifteen minutes' wait…

The Commons went quiet as the tellers assembled. As usual, the winning tellers made their way through the crowd to stand to the Speaker's left, in this case, those voting 'no'. Seeing this, a cheer went up from the opposition even before the result had been formally announced. 286 votes for, 344 against. The devolution package had been defeated again.

Through the din Richard turned to Alistair, 'Well, the margin of defeat has been reduced again; will she carry on?' The Commons was in uproar, the opposition treating the Government defeat as if it were a goal at a football match. Malcolm MacIntyre looked subdued. Those on the Government side who'd just delivered the defeat into Labour's hands remained silent. The Prime Minister rose:

'On a point of order, Mr Speaker, the House has now voted on this piece of important legislation for a second time and it is clear that this House does not support the measures set out and agreed by the Honourable Member for Greenock. What this doesn't tell us, however, is how we are now to resolve the undoubted tensions that have built up within our

United Kingdom. We'll need to analyse this result, speak to the political parties in Scotland and come back with further proposals to put before the House.'

The Prime Minister's voice was weak and was drowned out as the murmuring grew louder.

Then the Leader of the Opposition stood up. 'On a further point of order, Mr Speaker, we have now seen a weak and divided Government defeated twice. With the leave of the House I will now be placing a motion, "That this House has no confidence in Her Majesty's Government".'

After a short discussion on the Government front bench, the Leader of the House went to the dispatch box. 'With permission, Mr Speaker, I should like to make a short statement regarding the business for tomorrow. The House will be asked to consider a motion of no confidence in Her Majesty's Government.'

A shocked groan could be heard in the Chamber. There you have it, Richard thought to himself. A vote of no confidence which could lead to a General Election. Would anyone vote with Labour while a question mark hung over the Conservative leadership?

Leaving the Commons and returning to his office Richard became aware that a loud protest had erupted on Parliament Square. One group had even installed a stage from which various minor celebrities were taking turns in singing 'Land of Hope and Glory', adding to the deafening mix of drums from Northern Irish Unionists combined with bagpipes and *Braveheart* from the Scottish Nationalists. One big deafening mess.

An odd mix, he thought to himself as he looked out across the square: anti-war protesters, Green activists and

Nationalists all campaigning for a bill they probably knew little about.

The next morning's papers made it clear that the fallout from the no confidence vote had continued to play out throughout the evening. One report detailed an attempt by Richard McLean to broker a deal which would allow the Prime Minister to resign after her deal had gone through.

'After?' thought Richard. 'What's the point of that?' He was mystified as to how some of his colleagues could have misunderstood things so badly. This was no longer merely about the future of the Prime Minister — it was about the future of the country.

46. Out in the South China Sea...

Australian Defence Ministry, Cambera, 28 September

'What the... Bloody...!'

Vice-Admiral Edward Lloyd of the Royal Australian Navy was not one for swearing – something that had marked him out during his rise through the ranks.

But what he had just seen was enough to push even someone who had grown up in the respectable town of Glenbrook in the Blue Mountains west of Sydney to use bad language. In front of him was the latest intelligence report from Pine Gap, the joint Australian/American intelligence analysis and satellite ground station in the heart of the Australian outback.

At the top of the file 'Five Eyes Only' was printed in red, meaning it had been shared with and included information from Australia's 'Five Eyes' partners: the USA, the UK, Canada and New Zealand. That provided some comfort: at least he wasn't alone. Studying the endless analysis and boring satellite pictures of the South China Sea was normally something of a chore, but this time things were different. He phoned his secretary.

'Can you arrange a call with the Chief of the Defence Force; tell him it's urgent. Topic – The South China Sea.' A few minutes later his secretary called back. 'The CDF is on the line for you.'

'John, good to speak to you,' said Lloyd hurriedly. 'Have you seen the latest report from Pine Gap? The South China Sea?'

'I was just opening it as you called. The conclusion in the executive summary leaves little to the imagination.'

'No, it's even worse than our most pessimistic scenarios. We've been caught unawares with our bleeding pants down. We need to speak to the minister urgently, and the Americans.'

General John Spencer, the Chief of the Australian Defence Force (CDF) was, as you would expect for an army and special forces veteran, very calm in a crisis. He'd seen this sort of scare before. But this couldn't be ignored.

'I agree. In the meantime, we need to get to bottom of this. This is serious, but we don't want to start a panic.'

With that the pair agreed to reconvene later that day. Spencer asked his office to put a call through to the Australian Head of Analysis who'd compiled the report. He had many questions. Chinese exercises in the Taiwan Straits had become a regular occurrence; why did they think this one was any different? He was always impressed by the reports, but he wondered whether being stuck out in the desert, as they were, they were occasionally prone to a little bit of attention-seeking.

However, the specifics of Chinese logistics, naval fuel depots, field hospitals and the requisitioning of commercial shipping now visible in the harbours of southern China was enough to convince Spencer that, regrettably, the analysts were right. China was indeed planning a major operation in the South China Sea. But exactly what the operation was, nobody knew.

Spencer had never been a fan of politicians, but they occasionally had their uses and this was one of those rare times. He needed Australian Defence Minister Clive Morley to take this seriously.

Spencer, Vice-Admiral Lloyd and Morley arranged to meet shortly after lunch at the Australian Defence Ministry to discuss the latest report.

Spencer began, 'Something very disturbing is happening in the South China Sea. We believe the intelligence is credible and points to the planning of a major Chinese military operation within the next month.

'You see the harbours in southern China, the commercial vessels, the landing craft and the larger amphibious vessels. All similar to what we've seen in previous exercises.' Morley nodded, keen to show Spencer he was following.

'Now Minister, those pictures were taken at the end of last week. This one's from yesterday.'

Spencer handed over an image of Xiamen harbour. 'That's what concerns us.'

The Minister looked first at Lloyd, then at Spencer, before giving in. 'Sorry, I don't follow – what has happened?'

'The harbour's empty,' said Spencer. 'The large ships and landing craft have departed, along with much of the commercial shipping. But they're not heading for Taiwan and the straits. They're heading south.'

The Minister looked at the pictures intently, the Chinese positions in the South China Sea.

'Minister', continued Spencer, 'one group is heading for the Spratly islands, probably Fiery Cross Atoll; the other seems to be heading for Cambodia. This is disturbing and uncharacteristic. Of course they can change direction at will, but it may indicate that China has decided to widen its operations to intimidate a wider group of states in the region, or even strike elsewhere.'

Morley was still taking it in. 'Are you sure there's no other explanation for this? Do we have any other information in addition to the satellites?'

Spencer continued. 'Not much to go on as to their intentions. But there's more, I'm afraid. We've detected Chinese PLA movement in other areas. Troops have crossed into Myanmar in significant numbers. There's also uncharacteristic activity at their naval base in Djibouti; it seems their ships there are preparing to move; not a powerful force, but given the other movements, significant. There's also the force China sent to deal with the hijacking of its ship, which remains in Myanmar.'

As Morley began to understand the significance of all of this, he felt a weight descend on him. Spencer, registering his discomfort, continued.

'I'm afraid that's not all. We have another headache closer to home. A Chinese-owned supply ship to the east of the Philippines has been detected moving south, joining a PLA auxiliary ship and a destroyer. We don't know their destination, but I wouldn't be surprised if our fears about Chinese penetration of the Solomons or perhaps Vanuatu are about to be realised. A Chinese presence there right in the middle of one of our busiest shipping lanes during a period of tension in the South China Sea is a serious threat.

'Minister, I have some suggestions. Firstly, we need to do our best to wake up the Americans. We also need to find out as much as possible about China's intentions without creating too much panic. But above all we need to prepare our defences; we have very little time.

'And there is also the matter of our British cousins…'

47. AUKUS

Ministry of Defence Main Building, Whitehall, London, 28 September

In London, the Chief of the Defence Staff, Admiral Sir Andrew Bell was irritable. He'd just read a message from Vice-Admiral Edward Lloyd. He knew him well, having cooperated on the AUKUS submarine deal some years earlier. He liked Lloyd and as they were both Navy men, they understood each other. He did not believe Lloyd was one to panic, but this message exhibited all the hallmarks. The message was clear. The Australian Chief of the Defence Force wished to speak to the Chief of the Defence Staff immediately, in person, in Australia.

'The cheek of it,' he thought to himself, 'they could at least come here; but then if they really do believe what they're telling us, perhaps they don't feel they can.' He knew he had no choice but to believe them.

He called his assistant. 'We'll need a plane today to Australia for myself, the head of MI6 and the head of our China desk. If the Secretary of State asks, say it's "urgent defence diplomacy". No further details.'

The drive out to RAF Northolt that evening was uneventful; the grey RAF Airbus A330 was there and the head of MI6 had beaten them to it. The plane was soon in the air and heading south.

'Not like the Australians to panic over an intelligence report, is it?' said the MI6 chief. 'Demanding we drop everything and go to the other side of the world is quite something, even for our cousins.'

'Quite,' said Bell, 'but I know Lloyd and he's very sensible. But you have to understand that the whole rationale for AUKUS was predicated on China – that has always been their concern. They're a small country rich in natural resources in a tough neighbourhood with some very large neighbours. That's why we helped them with nuclear-powered attack submarines. It buys them time, gives them a fighting chance to resist a Chinese attack long enough for the cavalry to arrive. We, my dear sir, in the absence of the Americans, are the only cavalry available.'

The head of MI6 smiled. 'They beat us at cricket and every other game we invented, and then demand we cross half the globe to help defend them against a rogue superpower! Still, we will help, they know that. But why are they so insistent we go there in person?'

'I don't know, to be honest. They'd better have a good reason.'

It was getting dark now, the plane already over Italy, scheduled to cross the Indian Ocean, refuelling at the British/American Base on Diego Garcia, and from there a direct flight on to Canberra.

• • • •

A party from the Australian Ministry of Defence were awaiting their arrival. From there they were driven to the Ministry of Defence to meet with Vice-Admiral Lloyd, Chief of the Australian Defence Force General John Spencer and Defence Minister Clive Morley.

'Gentlemen, I am so sorry to have made you travel such a long distance,' said Morley, 'but under the circumstances I believe it was necessary. You will have seen the report from Pine Gap. The Australian Government is taking this extremely seriously. Our Prime Minister has spoken to the American President. However, for now we've decided to keep our concerns to ourselves. But if this is what we think it is, we have very little time.'

Admiral Bell replied, 'We are also extremely concerned. As you know, HMS *Prince of Wales* recently had an incident in the South China Sea close to one of China's artificial islands; the Carrier Group's still there with one of your ships. That would place it right in the middle of this PLA operation. But what this operation actually is remains a mystery. A show of force perhaps, to drive us out of their backyard, or something worse?'

Morley looked around the room, 'You know General Spencer, I believe?' Turning to Spencer he said, 'I think it's time you enlightened our British friends.'

Spencer said, handing out documents, 'This information comes to us via Five Eyes and Australian intelligence. We'd normally share it with our closest allies, but in this case, I must ask for an undertaking that the content doesn't leave this room.'

Bell and the head of MI6 glanced at each other, clearly agitated. 'So am I right in thinking we're not even allowed to share this information with our own ministers?' asked the British admiral.

'Yes,' replied Spencer firmly, before adding, as if attempting to defuse the tension, 'This is as much for your protection as ours, but I'm afraid I must insist.'

Bell replied, 'This puts us in a very difficult position. We represent the military and the security services of our Government. We cannot act without their authority.'

Spencer continued, 'I understand, we have the same system here. But for very specific reasons, may we proceed on this basis?'

They agreed, and Morley gestured for Spencer to continue.

'You're aware of the satellite photos from a day ago. Since then the picture has become a little clearer. We have a major PLA marine element heading for the Spratly Islands, including landing craft. The second major element is headed for Cambodia.

'The Spratly Islands have landing strips; we now have intelligence of troops forming up in airbases in southern China, likely about to join up with the forces in the Spratlys and Cambodia.

'So, two elements: perhaps it's merely an exercise, designed to intimidate the West and its regional partners. If so, it's succeeding.

'There's also the troops in Myanmar, the ships sailing from Djibouti and, of even greater concern, the threat to the Solomon Islands and Vanuatu.

'So the PLA's on the move. But we've heard little chatter, no propaganda, electronic intelligence; none of our contacts have any idea what's really happening.'

This was rapidly turning into a full-blown disaster.

Admiral Bell asked Spencer, 'You're painting a terrifying picture here. But may I ask, why have you called us here? What do you propose?'

'I'm afraid there's even more to it,' replied Spencer, looking to Clive Morley.

His face solemn, the Minister of Defence addressed the two British officials. 'A few weeks ago, one of our MPs Bob McDonald contacted our security services. He'd visited

Singapore earlier in the month where he was approached in a bar by a female Chinese spy. She spun him a tale about Australia being full of Chinese spies – well, it is – but we thought we knew who they were.

'He was having none of it, but she gave him a memory stick containing a list of all Chinese agents in Australia, which he then handed to our security services.

'She also claimed she was privy to certain Chinese military plans and wanted our help to prevent what she feared would be a disastrous Chinese military defeat.

'Well, it turns out her information was genuine. We've been working our way through it, but the sheer quantity's a major headache for our security services.

'Furthermore, the current PLA manoeuvres tie in exactly with what she told McDonald.'

Bell then asked, 'But why not share this with us in the usual way? We're losing valuable time.'

'Embarrassing as it is to admit, we just don't know the extent of Chinese penetration into Australian politics. But that's why we called you here without your political masters. The spy also contacted one of your MPs, Richard Reynolds.'

Admiral Bell had a dim view of politicians, and this news seemingly confirmed his opinion of them. 'What?!'

The head of MI6 added indignantly, 'Politicians, eh!'

Spencer replied, 'I wouldn't be too hard on him; you see, he also received a list of Chinese agents in Britain, and I'm afraid a number of your politicians feature on it. Mr Reynolds has entrusted a copy to us for safe keeping.

'Now, we have a problem, gentlemen. We now know the names of several of your politicians who've been compromised by China and therefore cannot be trusted. We also know that a Chinese fleet is on the move. What should we do?'

Admiral Bell looked agitated. 'Can you at least share the information you've received on the Chinese military plans?

'Yes, the invasion of Singapore and Malaya in three weeks' time, as a prelude to the annexation of Taiwan. We have no time to lose.'

48. Fiery Cross

South China Sea, 28 September

The harbour on Fiery Cross Atoll was beginning to fill up with ships and landing craft.

From a tower above his main headquarters, General Hu looked out over his armada. On the airstrip, transport planes continued to arrive, the troops disembarking and moving to the accommodation blocks, hangers ready to receive the vehicles on board the ferries.

The operation seemed unstoppable, yet Hu still clung to the hope that someone in Beijing would reconsider. All it would take would be a submarine or surface ship engaging his troops while they were underway, and there'd be a massacre.

His troops' departure for Singapore was to coincide with the Chinese forces sailing from Myanmar and Cambodia – a three-pronged attack on the straits. The element of surprise was of prime importance; they had to attack before local defence forces could be mobilised. Taken unawares, the Western nations would be powerless to act.

A diversionary operation would focus on a naval base the Chinese had been preparing on the Solomon Islands, diverting the Australians and Americans from the main point of attack.

Chinese intelligence had assured him there was no danger of a direct military confrontation with the West, but what if they were wrong?

49. Cambodia

South Coast of Cambodia, 28 September

The Royal Cambodian Naval Base at Ream, on the south coast 100 miles from the capital Phnom Penh, had received some unexpected guests. A Chinese PLA aircraft carrier had just entered the harbour, for this was now a joint facility shared with the PLA navy.

Further to the west the Chinese-owned Koh Kong Beachside Resort, a personal project sponsored by President Xi, had never been intended for tourists. In reality a military base, it now buzzed with activity. Chinese transport planes and civilian and military vessels had been landing all day, disgorging Chinese troops who were spirited away to their accommodation out of eyeshot of the few remaining residents. The nearby commercial harbour had also acquired some new residents overnight: Chinese landing craft and naval vessels.

It was over 700 miles to Singapore and the PLA commander in Cambodia, like General Hu, had been told of the importance of surprise. They would be at sea for a little under a day, protected by J-20 stealth bombers. It was vital they avoided detection.

50. The Solomon Islands

The Solomon Islands, 28 September

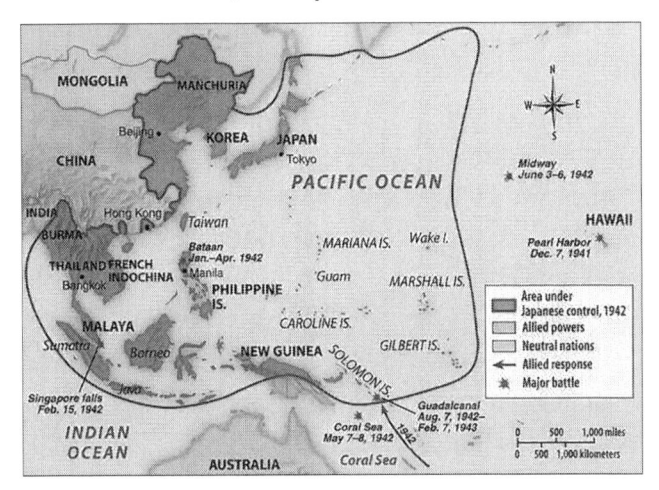

The Solomon Islands are a string of nearly 1,000 forest-covered islands in the south-west Pacific, fringed by coral reefs. Their beauty belies the fact they witnessed some of the hardest fought battles in the Second World War when Japanese forces attempted to cut off Australia's supply lines to the West and to the rest of the British Empire. They'd planned eventually to use the islands as a springboard to invade Australia itself.

The Solomon Islands had always been of key importance to the Australians, the gateway to the south-west Pacific and shipping lanes to the United States.

Early in the morning, just as the first PLA troops were arriving at Fiery Cross Atoll, Australian maritime radar observed a flotilla of five ships travelling south between the Philippines and Papua New Guinea.

This set off a frantic flurry of correspondence with the United

States. Requests for satellite pictures and information filled the airwaves between Canberra and Washington, as radars at the US bases in Guam and Palau were rolled into action.

By late morning a clearer picture was beginning to develop. This was a small Chinese PLA navy fleet consisting of a helicopter assault ship, a frigate, an auxiliary supply ship, a landing ship and a tanker. A force large enough to ring alarm bells in Canberra.

President Xi had studied the campaigns of the Second World War in great detail over many years, focusing in particular on Japanese strategy, how they came so close to achieving dominance in South East Asia behind a strong defensive line. Why they succeeded and why, ultimately, they failed. Xi realised that the key to all of this was Singapore in the west and the Solomon Islands in the east. If the Chinese could set up a naval base in the Solomons their foot would be placed firmly on Australia's windpipe.

The small print of a 2022 security pact, forced onto their unsuspecting Prime Minister, allowed China to send armed police and military personnel to the Solomons to 'help maintain public order and protect property'. This pact had in time widened. Chinese ships regularly stopped in the Solomons and Chinese economic dominance over the islands had solidified. The US and Australia realised too late what was happening and were unable to match the largesse flowing in from Beijing.

There was no need for China to forcibly occupy the Solomon Islands; their fleet could now dock at will and there was little the Australians could do about it.

51. Myanmar

South Coast of Myanmar, September

Myanmar is a vast jungle-clad state, run, as much as anyone runs it, by a military junta centred around the large cities of Yangon and Mandalay and the central belt along the Irrawaddy River. Beyond that, the military's control tails away in the hills and jungles of the interior, where opposition paramilitary forces hold sway.

That the military could continue their fight against the opposition was in large part due to the aid doled out by General Wenquing of the Chinese Ministry of State Security.

Weapons, training and money all crossed the heavily fortified frontier into Myanmar. In return went the dependence of a crumbling regime on the strength and money of China. This did not come cheap. Myanmar gave China what it needed – access to the Indian Ocean, and to oil – all of which went to China.

The Myanmar coastline stretches south for hundreds of miles from the Bay of Bengal down to the Andaman Sea, sharing a peninsula with Thailand until it fizzles out 400 miles north of Malaysia. The jungle-clad mountains drop sharply into the azure water of the Andaman Sea amongst a myriad of islands.

It was here, in this maze of inlets and estuaries overlooked by the mountainous interior that the Chinese navy was assembling an invasion force under the watchful eye of the local Burmese security forces.

General Min Aung Hlaing of Myanmar's State

Administration Council was an old-fashioned and unpleasant military ruler. Shunned by the world since the coup that brought him to power in 2021, he'd become gradually more dependent on Chinese money, manpower and diplomatic protection. This support did not come cheap, and Beijing was now demanding repayment. The price? To allow the transit of Chinese troops to Yangon for their embarkation on ships bound for…? Hlaing knew not to ask.

The operation was to be conducted in strict secrecy, and so he gave permission for the first PLA troops to cross the mountain passes. The Chinese troops were ordered not to talk to anyone and remain in their trucks.

On the coast the PLA had assembled a flotilla of small landing craft. Offshore, a powerful guided-missile frigate had arrived from Djibouti to provide air defence, and was joined by a general-purpose corvette that had been in the Bay of Bengal combatting piracy. More vessels were en route from East Africa and the Chinese air force based in Myanmar was to provide air cover during the crossing of the Andaman Sea.

52. The Conservative Party Conference

Manchester, 1 October

Richard picked up the Sunday papers at Euston before boarding a train to the Conservative Party's conference in Manchester. The headlines made for grim reading for the PM.

'PM on a knife-edge as she tries to rally the faithful,' declared the *Daily Mail*. 'Tommy Rosenfield, Robert Lacy and Nicholas Braithwaite neck and neck in race to replace Caroline Summers, as Sir William Mostyn loses steam,' was the verdict of the *Telegraph*, while the *Sun* went for a succinct front page: 'Is it Autumn for Summer in Manchester?'

Very droll, thought Richard. The opening of the conference was often a chance for leadership hopefuls to sound a discordant note, but this time there was a real leadership contest.

Conservative Party conferences were loved, loathed and feared by MPs and membership alike, and this year was to be no exception. At least there was the excitement of a leadership contest, although it was an excitement most of the MPs, including Richard, felt they could do without.

For the Party leadership little good ever came from a Party conference – too many politicians in close proximity to the media was a recipe for trouble – but it made a profit and helped pay the party staff's salaries, so the membership and their contributions could not be ignored.

This year the conference was to be held at the Midland

Hotel and the adjoining Conference Centre. Richard had booked to stay in a nearby hotel. As usual he caught the train up from London on Sunday, along with the assembled London-based media and lobbyists.

The frontrunner in the contest to succeed the Prime Minister was of course Scottish Secretary Robert Lacy. Having missed out earlier in the year he was the natural successor, but being the clear favourite wasn't always an advantage. He was also a government minister and therefore constrained in what he could say or do.

By contrast, Rosenfield and Braithwaite were free to campaign untrammelled by any need to feign loyalty to Summers. They wouldn't be speaking in the main hall, but that was never really the main focus of the conference. The real events would take place on the 'fringe'.

Leafing through the conference guide, Richard picked out the events where the leadership hopefuls would be pitching to the members and the press.

Firstly, the new and slightly shadowy 'China Group' – an alliance of back-bench MPs concerned about the spread of Chinese influence – were holding a discussion on China and the Far East at which Tommy Rosenfield was due to speak. Obviously, a chance for him to sound impressive and to galvanise his core team of MPs.

Likewise, former Defence Secretary Nicholas Braithwaite was due to speak at a 'Conservative Union Group' meeting to discuss the 'defence of the UK', a barely disguised attack on the proposed devolution legislation.

Richard met up with his agent for coffee and a chat in the convention hall on the Sunday afternoon. As old hands, they mostly spent their time at various fringe events, where the more interesting ideas and speakers could be found. They decided they'd attend the Rosenfield and Braithwaite talks the following day, plus a speech by Sir William Mostyn – no doubt aimed at rallying the more traditional members of the Party – to complete the picture.

That evening Richard attended a dinner and drinks reception organised by the Conservative Party's international office, organised for similar centre-right parties overseas, including the US Republicans and the Australian Conservatives. The party turned out to be about fifty strong, an eclectic mix, and Richard was asked to host a table at which sat a deputy Prime Minister from Ghana, a Finnish MP, an American Republican policy officer and, to his great surprise, an Australian MP – Bob McDonald.

Richard felt a flood of mixed emotions: shock at seeing him, fear that he might mention his predicament to the other guests, but also relief. The last few weeks had been increasingly stressful for him. Protecting Mei, the fear she'd be discovered, the death of John McVey and worries the killer might try again all added to the devolution debate and now a leadership campaign. Well, at least Bob knew what had really happened in Singapore and was trustworthy.

'Bob, great to see you, this is a surprise,' Richard said.

'Richard – good to see you too, let's have a beer later.'

The next day Richard was queuing up a long flight of stairs, waiting for the Conservative China Group's meeting to begin It seemed that virtually everyone, including the media, had decided that Rosenfield would officially launch his leadership bid there. They were not wrong.

Richard eventually got into the room and stood at the back; it was full to the gunwales, and the members hadn't come for the warm free wine at the back of the room or the fresh air; if they had, they would have been disappointed.

Rosenfield was sitting on a table at the far end flanked by a junior MP who acted as his supporter, and a retired general. He rose to his feet and began.

'Fellow Conservatives, this is a difficult time for our Party, our country and its place in the world. We are at a turning point and are therefore in need of leadership.' 'Here we go', thought Richard, 'not subtle in the slightest!' The room went silent, expecting a leadership pitch. But then:

'China is a clear and present danger, a danger that the Government needs to wake up to. On this we need leadership.'

Rosenfield went on to talk in a measured tone about the need to take China and its ideology seriously and stand up to it where necessary. Richard listened in amazement. He was used to the cynicism of his fellow politicians, but this was stunning even by those standards.

The discussion moved down the panel to the retired general, who dutifully reflected and amplified Rosenfield's speech, adding some anecdotes from his time in Kosovo before moving on. Next came the questions:

'Mr Rosenfield,' came a voice from near the front. 'Julian Bower, Mid Dorset Conservatives. Very good speech; could you comment on whether you think the Prime Minister is capable of the sort of leadership we need at the moment? And how would you do things differently, given the opportunity?'

'A planted question', thought Richard, 'but again, clever. Raise the leadership issue again, but through someone else.'

'I don't think any speculation over my future is helpful to the Party,' replied Rosenfield.

'And by not speculating he's written tomorrow's headlines,' thought Richard.

Having escaped the packed room Richard made his way back to the convention centre where Nicholas Braithwaite was about to speak. Again, a long queue snaked down from the function room above. Braithwaite began.

'In the past few weeks our Party has been divided on the question of how to meet the threat from Mr MacIntyre and his band of separatist Nationalists. This has been a painful discussion but one in which I know we all share the same goal – the unity of our country. We differ on how to counter this threat… We must reject those siren voices telling us to give in; we must rebuild our Union. We must not, for expediency's sake, do that which we know is wrong in the vain hope that it will come right.'

Braithwaite continued, rattling off the past successes of the UK, but none of it seemed to resonate with the audience. 'Not a great performance,' thought Richard, 'a difficult topic and he's absolutely right, but he lost the audience… Rosenfield will be pleased with that!'

The next morning the papers had their story. There were a few references to Braithwaite, but the day had been Rosenfield's.

'Well,' thought Richard, 'that's stolen a march on Lacy.' That at least was good news. The thought of going through the whole cycle to end up with Lacy was too much to bear.

The papers also ran an article around a poll commissioned by the Conservative China Group claiming that strong leadership over the China issue was far more important to the public than the Union, the economy and immigration.

It was no surprise to anyone that late on Wednesday, after

the Conference had closed, friends of Braithwaite let it be known that he was planning to pull out of the leadership race, having concluded he had no chance of winning. Speculation was rife that he'd done a deal with Rosenfield.

53. The High Commissioner

The Australian High Commisioner's Residence, Kensington, 8 October

The Monday after the conference Richard rang the doorbell of the Australian High Commissioner's Residence, a Victorian villa in a quiet side street near Hyde Park.

An attendant ushered him through to a drawing room at the back of the building overlooking a small garden. Bob McDonald got up from an armchair as he walked in.

'Good to see you again. This'll teach you what happens when you speak to strange women in bars, eh!'

Surprised by this jovial approach, Richard played along. 'Yes, more trouble than they're worth.'

'Well, as I explained in Manchester, we've found out some more information about this particular one. Come through and we can make a start, but let me first introduce Robert Smith, our High Commissioner.'

'Your Excellency,' Richard said to a man standing near Bob.

Bob went on to explain. Mei had also contacted him with a rather similar story. She'd warned him about various figures in the Australian Civil Service, and told him that China had something planned in the South China Sea. Bob had reported it all to the Australian intelligence services, who'd not taken it very seriously at first.

'And then you called,' Bob said to Richard, 'and that took it to a whole new level. So, what to do. We have a Chinese spy who may or may not be trying to stop World War Three, we have a list of agents in our respective countries and we don't know who to trust. It seems we're all in danger! I think we need to cooperate.'

'The UK in danger,' said Richard, not quite following.

'Well, isn't it obvious? The Chinese agents, the links to Scotland, weapons, you do realise what's going on? They plan to neutralise you, destabilise you, even put in one of their own as Prime Minister if they're lucky, and they may very well be. It's basically an attempted coup by China, and one that has every chance of success.'

Richard was shocked to hear this set out in such stark terms. He let Bob continue.

'They think that a destabilised UK with a compromised pro-China leader could disable the UK/Australian response to the invasion of Singapore.'

Richard replied, 'Our problem is, how do we present definitive proof to the people that matter... without being laughed at and dismissed as crazed conspiracy theorists?'

Bob replied rather brutally, 'Your problem – well, our problem – is that one of the figures China wants to install is a potential leadership contender. Added to the fact that the Chinese are up to their necks in Scottish Nationalism. It could get very nasty. The good news, however, is that we think we can help.'

'Now this brings me to a question,' said Richard. 'As you know, I had a visit from some American lobbyists who seemed to know about the spy in Singapore. I have no idea why they wanted to find out what she'd told me.'

High Commissioner Smith, who had remained silent up to now, responded. 'I think we have come up with an explanation. The Australian Secret Intelligence Service did some checks on Singer & McColl, and believe they're largely innocent of any direct wrongdoing. In fact, they've been quite cooperative: money talks and makes people talk, and money seems to have been at the root of it all.'

Smith paused and waited for the other two to catch up.

'Singer & McColl believed they were acting on behalf of the US Government, that they were sounding out British and Australian opinion that might help the US. But it appears they'd actually been employed by the Chinese Ministry of State Security. We've traced their payment back to a state-owned Chinese company.'

Bob said, 'Yes, they were working for the Chinese, but not the same Chinese that our dear spy Mei was working for, and that's where it gets even more intriguing. It seems Mei was also working for a hidden master within the MSS keen to prevent Chinese action in Taiwan and Singapore, someone who had access to the existence and extent of Chinese networks in the UK.'

'So, Mei is definitely on the good side, so to speak?' asked Richard.

'Yes, thankfully' replied Bob. 'She's cooperating fully with us., as are the Americans, who've confirmed exactly what information Singer & McColl sent back to their "client", which I'm afraid included your awareness of Mei's existence.'

Richard was finding it difficult to absorb all of this, but one question was troubling him in particular. Were the Chinese, or Mei in particular, involved in John McVey's death? He asked the High Commissioner.

After a brief silence, Smith replied: 'We'll need to find out. We've given this some thought and have a suggestion that may help us resolve our respective problems. Let me explain...'

54. An Unexpected Guest

Mandarin Oriental Hotel, Knightsbridge, 16 October

Michael Ashton, Chief Whip of the Conservative Party, looked, exactly how you'd expect a man charged with ensuring Party discipline to look – medium height but heavily built. He was good at his job and respected within the Party.

When that morning he'd taken a call from the Australian High Commissioner Robert Smith, he'd listened politely, but it had all sounded so preposterous he thought it was some sort of prank call. However, a return call to the Australian High Commission confirmed he'd actually been talking to Smith.

When Smith told him he needed to speak to him in private, Ashton was by equal measure intrigued, concerned and puzzled. He'd had little involvement with Australia and couldn't think of any MPs that might have got themselves caught up in something there. Nonetheless Smith had stressed the upmost importance of the matter, and as Australia was a close ally, he had to take it seriously.

So later in the day, as instructed, Ashton walked into the Mandarin Oriental Hotel and asked, as instructed, for a booking under the name 'Cathay Osmond'. He had little time even to grin to himself before he was asked to follow a staff member down a corridor and into a private dining room set for five.

As he entered, he was struck with amazement. In addition to Smith, the room already contained two MPs he knew: the Chairman of the 1922 Committee Sir Richard

McLean and a junior MP he only knew by sight as Richard Reynolds. There was another unfamiliar figure, but this did not seem the time or place to introduce himself. It was, in fact, the Australian MP Bob McDonald. Ashton struggled to hide the confusion on his face.

Smith beckoned Ashton to sit next to him. He felt anxious; what little he'd already heard from the Australian High Commissioner that morning had begun to sink in. If it were true it was undoubtedly the strangest and most sensitive issue he'd had to deal with during his five years in post, but he reminded himself he'd heard a great many stories that were never substantiated: rumours of Cabinet ministers having lurid affairs, enrichment from dodgy contracts. These stories often improved in the telling.

Ashton's instinctive reaction was to believe this was one of those, and he adopted his normal approach of listening with the straight poker face he'd perfected over many years for exactly these occasions. He began the proceedings in a light-hearted manner.

'Your Excellency, it's very kind of you to invite us all here to what I'm sure will be a first-class lunch. I am also grateful to everyone for making time at such short notice ...'

His comments were not met with the light-hearted reaction he'd expected. Smith glared at him and he realised he'd misjudged the occasion. He changed tack.

'Given we're all now here, would Your Excellency like to talk us through the reasoning for this meeting?'

Robert Smith lent forward and clenched his hands together in front of him on the table. There was no easy way to say it.

'Yes, thank you all for coming. I apologise for the amateur theatrics, but I'm afraid what I have to say to you must be done in person. It's a matter that has been raised separately with me both by Richard Reynolds and by our Secret Intelligence Service in Canberra.

'By way of background: in May, both Richard and Bob were staying at Raffles Hotel in Singapore, visiting Australian and British ships taking part in an exercise – you may remember the incident with the F-35. They were both contacted by a Singapore-based Chinese spy known to our Intelligence Agency.

'This on its own isn't unusual; we've regrettably had several MPs on foreign trips fall for… well, you can guess. But this was different.

'What appears to have happened here is that the Chinese agent who we know as "Mei Ling" was not acting on behalf of the Chinese state, but a faction trying to prevent war between China and Taiwan.

'She provided Bob and Richard with information regarding Chinese agents in the UK and Australia. We have examined it; it is genuine and of great value, but highly disturbing.'

Ashton found all of this fascinating, but couldn't see how it involved him. Perhaps an MP was on the Chinese payroll; that wouldn't surprise him and he could think of a few names that would fit the bill. He asked, 'Before you go on, Your Excellency, may I ask if British intelligence agencies are aware of this information?'

'No. Up to now this has been dealt with exclusively in Australia. We haven't shared the information with our partners yet, but will do so as soon as possible. You'll just have to trust us for now.'

Ashton was not at all reassured, but Smith continued. 'But what is truly astounding about all of this is the motive:

an attempt to forestall what they see as a doomed full-scale military operation in Taiwan and the Singapore Straits.

'Now, why would giving information to the UK and Australia prevent a Chinese operation in Taiwan? It's quite simple. We – Australia, the UK and New Zealand – are bound to a defence agreement with Malaysia and Singapore. Chinese planners have concluded that any operation against Taiwan would involve some form of retaliation, and China's weakest link is oil, 80 per cent of which is imported via the Straits of Singapore. Without it, China's economy would collapse and the country would be plunged into social and political unrest.

'To invade Taiwan they need open sea lanes to the Middle East. That means capturing Singapore, and denying the straits to Western powers. Their invasion is planned for three weeks' time and as things stand, our military commitments to Singapore and Malaysia hang in the balance because of internal UK politics.

'China wants a UK Prime Minister who can be guaranteed not to respond in the event of an invasion, and they're very close to achieving that.'

Ashton interjected, 'What do you mean? None of the leadership contenders are peaceniks.'

Smith continued: 'Now this a very delicate issue for me to raise as a representative of a foreign state, but I'm afraid there is a serious question mark hanging over one of them. The alarming truth is that the Chinese have penetrated far deeper into the UK political system than anyone had imagined. One of the leadership contenders has been seriously compromised.

'If China's candidate became Prime Minister, it would

grant them a free hand in the Far East, and keep their supply lines open to the Indian Ocean. Break the Durian Pact and weaken the Five Eyes Alliance... that would be worth its weight in Chinese gold.'

Ashton replied, 'If what you're telling me is true, and I have to tell you that is a big if, then we have to be 100 per cent certain before locking up a potential Prime Minister. I really can't see it myself. Personally, I have my doubts about Tommy Rosenfield in terms of Scotland, but he's a vocal critic of China.

Sir William Mostyn MP, eccentric and sometimes misguided, but a patriot, and honest as far as I know. I'd bet my life on him.

'There's Lacy, I guess. He'd be happy to betray any of his fellow MPs, but he's no China stooge. In any case, surely this is a matter for the security services and the police.'

Smith said, 'That is a very fair point, but I'm afraid my response is equally unsettling. Mei's list mentions a number of officials within the security services. Richard Reynolds was right to come to us; for the moment, MI5 cannot be trusted.

'You are of course perfectly entitled to demand proof. As they say, the bigger the claim, the more evidence is required. We've arranged for that.'

Ashton snapped back, 'Well let's see it then.'

Smith replied calmly, 'Yesterday, Mei Ling, at our request, requested an urgent meeting with the leadership contender in question. Something he could not, and has not, refused.

'When you arrived, you were requested to ask for "Cathay Osmond", an odd name. But there was a reason for that. That happens to be the name by which Mei Ling is known to a number of your politicians. The meeting was set for 3 p.m.

at the Mandarin Oriental hotel – we have fifteen minutes before he's due.'

Ashton exclaimed: 'Good Lord! And what happens then?'

Smith continued: 'When he arrives, and' – he looked down at his phone – 'I'm told he's en route, we'll be 100 per cent sure that he's in contact with Chinese intelligence. We have an agent in the foyer, but if he tries to run, well, he'd only be incriminating himself further. I believe he'll cooperate.'

The room fell into silence while they digested the news.

Sir Richard McLean, who had remained silent up to then, interjected, 'You're aware that the first round of voting on the Party leadership is due to take place tomorrow. The candidates' names are in the public domain. If we obtain this proof you've mentioned, I could ask for a withdrawal, but there'd be little I could do if it was refused.'

Smith replied, 'That's one of the reasons you're here. But I don't think we need be too concerned. The evidence will speak for itself. He'll have little option.'

McLean replied, 'If it were one of the small fry, I doubt it'd even be noticed. One of the three main contenders though…'

He looked to Ashton, who seemed deep in thought. 'Perhaps we could reduce it to one round of voting, followed by a coronation… That would leave only the small question of Scotland. That'll remain divisive whoever wins.'

Smith added, 'That brings me to the most fascinating aspect of this information. It appears that Mr MacIntyre is not all he claims to be. Would it shock you to know that the SNP has been funded by China?'

'Oh, now that is interesting,' said Ashton, forcing back a smile.

'Now, before our guest arrives, there's one more thing. Mei

Ling is next door; she'll greet the MP outside and show him in here. Everything will be recorded in case there's any dispute about it later. Now gentlemen, it's nearly 3 p.m. and I'm told our guest is about to arrive; if I may ask for silence.'

They obeyed, the only sound being McLean's nails nervously tapping on the tabletop. A few anguished moments went by, and then they heard talking outside, Mei and a man with a distinctive, authoritative voice. The voices came closer, then the door handle turned and Mei could be heard saying 'After you.'

And then in walked Tommy Rosenfield. He stopped for a moment, looked around and froze.

Ashton exclaimed, 'You? What?'

Rosenfield gasped for air and tried to gather his composure, before breathing deeply and stammering, 'What are you doing here? I think I must be the victim of some kind of prank; this woman here – she's tricked me.'

Ashton regained his composure from the initial shock and reasserted himself. This was the sort of situation he was familiar with and he felt quite at home again. An MP had been caught red-handed and he was going to get to the bottom of it.

'Sit down Mr Rosenfield; we want to have a chat with you.' He beckoned to an empty chair at the far end of the table.

'I might very well ask what *you* are doing here,' said Rosenfield.

Smith gestured to Mei and said, 'Ms Ling, would you please leave us?' She made her exit.

'Spare us the nonsense, Mr Rosenfield,' said Ashton. We know exactly why you came here and what you were planning to discuss with Mei Ling, an employee of the Chinese Ministry of State Security. We've received a full report on your activities.

You may be wondering why you're in our gentle hands rather than languishing in Belmarsh Prison. Well, there'll be time for that later, but we have more pressing business.

'Firstly, you will withdraw from the leadership contest. Secondly, you will cooperate with the security services and the police.'

Rosenfield slumped in his seat, a defeated man gasping for air. He nodded assent.

'Next,' continued Ashton, 'you will announce your withdrawal from the contest following this meeting. Pick your reason – ill health, family tragedy. It doesn't matter. Following that, you'll speak only to the relevant authorities, as directed by myself.'

McLean interjected, 'I'll take that as the formal withdrawal of your candidature. In addition, given the circumstances I'm banning you from voting in the contest.'

Rosenfield murmured approval.

Ashton then continued, 'We'll put out a statement at 6 p.m. saying you've informed us you're no longer a candidate. That'll be all for now, but don't believe this is the end of the matter. Unless anyone has any further questions, I think it would be best if Mr Rosenfield left us.'

Once he'd slunk out of the room, Ashton invited comment: 'Well, we've removed one potential booby trap, but what are we to do now? There's one remaining serious candidate for the leadership, but he's untested on China and given his close relations with Rosenfield, can we take the risk?'

With that, High Commissioner Smith took back control of proceedings. 'We're still left with an extremely serious situation: an imminent Chinese attack on Singapore, Malaysia and then Taiwan. China's plan was for Rosenfield to withdraw British support from Singapore, giving them a free hand. This needs to be reversed, and quickly.

'We have Australian troops and a frigate attached to the UK Carrier Strike Group. We have already been making preparations with your military, but we need to scale up our deterrence immediately and massively if we're to have any chance of forestalling the attack. I suggest you bring this into the open - update the Chairman of the Defence Committee, recall Parliament.'

McLean added, 'Oh, we can do better than that, we can ask him to rejoin the leadership contest, Mostyn was never a serious candidate and will stand aside; as for Lacy, given his relationship with Rosenfield, he'll just slink away before he is quietly sacked. Braithwaite will be the favourite.

'I'll announce a one-day delay to allow for a new nomination, something that, under the circumstances, shouldn't prove controversial. I could get an article into the papers tomorrow, with some senior figures backing him.'

• • • •

Back in his office Richard Reynolds turned on the news. The banner at the bottom of on the screen read:

> 'BREAKING NEWS: Leadership hopeful Tommy Rosenfield withdraws.'

He smiled to himself; half of the job was done. Then:

> 'BREAKING NEWS: Former Defence Secretary Nicholas Braithwaite to formally stand for the leadership.'

A clip showed Sir Bill Howard giving an impromptu interview backing Braithwaite.

'That was quick work,' Richard thought to himself.

The next day Sir Richard McLean called a meeting of the parliamentary Party. The first-floor committee room was packed and it took several minutes for McLean to call them to order. He spoke slowly and carefully.

'Good to see you all again. We shouldn't make a habit of meeting like this.' After a brief outburst of laughter, Sir Richard got down to business.

'I have a few pieces of news it is my duty to report to you. Firstly, as we know, there is a vacancy for the leadership of the Conservative Party. In the normal course of events we would seek nominations and we would hold an election.

'However, I've been taking extensive soundings of the Party. I have spoken to many of you here and to many of the potential leadership candidates.

'What with the developments in the South China Sea, I've decided this is not the time for another leadership contest; it would be seen as an indulgence by the public and a distraction by our allies.

'I've spoken to Mr Rosenfield,' – there was a murmur – 'and he has agreed to withdraw from the contest. I have also spoken to the Cabinet, who, including the Secretary of State for Scotland, have agreed that the best candidate at this moment is our former Defence Secretary Nicholas Braithwaite. I've now received a nomination paper for Mr Braithwaite signed, by Sir William Mostyn and Sir Bill Howard.

'So, with the withdrawal of Mr Rosenfield and Mr Lacy, unless there's any objection, given that there is a vacancy and only one candidate, it is my duty to declare that Nicholas

Braithwaite is the new leader of the Conservative Party.'

Cheers erupted as Braithwaite made his way over to McLean. The new leader raised a hand and silence fell in the room.

'Thank you colleagues, a week is a long time in politics and this week has been no exception… I was once told that Sir Richard did not partake in coronations… well, Archbishop, McLean will be a fine addition to the Church of Scotland.

'But seriously colleagues, this is a great honour. We've had a stormy few months and we're not yet in calm waters. There's work to be done rebuilding our great Kingdom, but also in the Far East. We have little time to waste, so without any further ado I'll get to work.

Even as the meeting was still going on, rolling twenty-four-hour news then showed a black limousine heading out of Downing Street onto Whitehall: 'It is believed that Prime Minister Caroline Summers is on her way to tender her resignation to His Majesty the King.'

Shortly afterwards a car came to pick up Nicholas Braithwaite from the Commons entrance by Westminster Hall, a car from Buckingham Palace. He was soon on the Mall, followed by the clattering of a helicopter.

55. Chinese Ship *PLAN Guangxi*

South West Pacific, 18 October

The Chinese helicopter assault ship *PLAN Guangxi* was sailing south in convoy with two smaller ships in the open expanse of ocean between Indonesia and the Philippines, avoiding the US-controlled island of Palau.

The captain had orders to travel directly to the Solomon Islands, where the new Prime Minister would allow his ships to berth and a Chinese marine detachment would secure the airfield for an incoming detachment of long-range bombers. They would be joined by an escorting detachment of nuclear-missile-equipped Chengdu J-20 Mighty Dragon long-range fighters, placing the entire east coast of Australia within range.

That a Chinese task force could exit the South China Sea undetected and head for the Solomon Islands was itself a testimony to how badly the US, the UK and Australia had neglected the area over the preceding decades. The Chinese had been heavily investing in the islands, constructing a new airport and sea port. For although still a member of the Commonwealth, with King Charles as the nominal head of state, the Solomon Islands had in effect quietly become a Chinese protectorate.

It was clear who was in charge from the fluttering red flags across the island nation, and it certainly wasn't the hapless Prime Minister, who was only now digesting the news that a Chinese naval force was on its way, intent on reducing his power and influence even further.

56. A New Broom....

10 Downing Street, 17 October

Braithwaite spent an hour inside Buckingham Palace before it was announced that he had been appointed as the new Prime Minister.

Richard was one of the first to receive a phone call. 'We have a lot on our hands and little or no time to act. You know all the background to this. Will you serve as my Minister for the Armed Forces under your old boss Alistair Murray?'

'That would be an honour, Prime Minister, but I feel I should tell you something first.'

'Oh yes, what's that?' Braithwaite sounded concerned.

'It's my grandfather. He was captured in Singapore in 1942 and like many others was imprisoned at Changi and then forced to work on the railways. So my interest in Singapore is personal, but there's more to it than that.

'My grandfather, Lieutenant-Colonel, then Major, Robert Buchan of the Gordon Highlanders, was part of the Singapore garrison protecting the island. He always felt he'd let the people down there, in addition to the shame and humiliation that Churchill heaped on those who surrendered.

'But it's worse than that, worse than the years he spent in prison and working on the railways, being starved almost to death.

'The thing is, he blamed himself. We've all seen the Chinese prison camps in Xinjiang, what they've done in Hong Kong. So, more than anyone, I know we have to succeed in Singapore.'

Braithwaite interjected, 'He was being too hard on himself;

I know the history. It wasn't an easy decision. But those who fail to learn lessons from history are condemned to relive it.'

Richard said: 'I know. I've thought about it so many times over the years. He was consumed by guilt. The thing is, he was actually there at Fort Canning on 15 February when Lieutenant-General Percival decided to surrender Singapore. At first he advocated fighting on, as any good Highlander would, but he eventually gave in and bit his tongue in the belief they'd be saving lives.

'Well, that turned out to be untrue. He'd feared at the time what the Japanese would do, but he kept quiet.

'Percival's actions were understandable at the time, but in hindsight it seems a counter-attack might well have succeeded because the Japanese lines were so over-extended. My grandfather blamed himself for keeping quiet. He wondered whether speaking up at the time might have changed things. He went over and over it, tormenting himself. It cast a long shadow over our family.

'Anyway, I'd just like you to know that I'm determined this will never happen again. I feel I owe Singapore a historic debt, one I'd love to repay in kind.'

Braithwaite replied: 'I think your grandfather would be very proud. No time to waste. Get down to the Ministry, they'll be waiting for you and we have much to do.'

• • • •

Arriving at the large Portland-stone building, Richard approached the large steel doors that presumably served as blast doors in time of war. He'd got there before Alistair so headed straight up to the Secretary of State's office. He called the Chiefs of the Defence Staff in.

'Gentlemen, time is of the essence. China, Singapore. We need to prevent a war. I want all the latest intelligence, what China is planning, what our allies are planning.

'I want to know what we have available in the area and what we can get there. What have the Singaporeans and Malaysians asked for? Whatever it is, if we have it we should start preparing to deliver it.'

Richard looked around at the three senior officers; he could see the hint of a smile on the face of the Air Marshal.

'Shall we reconvene in an hour?'

They left the room in a hurry and Richard, left on his own for a moment, glanced around. It was an impressive open-plan office on the top floor, with a large map of the world on one wall and a huge, highly polished conference table. Alistair arrived shortly afterwards.

'Well, we've ended up at the coal face!' he said. 'It's all kicking off in Number 10; lists of people to be sacked, arrested, imprisoned or deported – take your pick.'

'Yes, I have a copy here! Who would have thought it? I had my suspicions about some of them, but wow! There are some surprises. How low we've fallen. Anyway, we have a war to prevent; or, if we can't prevent it, we need to win it.. The Chiefs of Staff will be back in about thirty minutes with their proposals.'

When they'd reassembled, Richard took his place next to Alistair and the meeting began. Richard said: 'With your leave, Secretary of State, I think we should hear the latest intelligence from the Taiwan Straits and the South China Sea before moving on to other matters.'

Alistair signalled his consent and the Chief of the Defence Staff, Admiral Bell, said, opening a folder, 'I'll start with the

North, Taiwan and the straits area. As we know, the PLA began a major exercise in the Taiwan Straits a few days ago.

'The key military formations we are dealing with are the 73rd mechanised, based in Xiamen opposite Taiwan. Added to this we have detected formations moving to a series of ports along the coast. Most of the PLA's amphibious assets – landing ships, assault ships – are involved.

'We've also seen activity in the air, more than the normal probing of Taiwanese airspace. There are also signs they've redeployed fighter and transport squadrons from the North to airfields in the south.

'We estimate that about a million men are involved in one way or another. Adding to that, they've moved a range of missiles to within range of Taiwan and its outlying islands.

'So, what does that add up to? It could still be an exercise, but signs are emerging suggesting something more serious: fuel bunkering near Taiwan, the clearing of civilian hospitals in preparation for casualties.

'This is a credible force, one that has the potential to cross the Taiwan Straits. But apart from the info from our Chinese defector, we have little idea as to the intent and timing.'

Richard looked at Alistair, who was deep in thought. The military men looked agitated.

Bell continued, 'That's what we know about Taiwan. We have of course shared what we know with the Americans and our Five Eyes partners, who are understandably a bit wary of us at the moment. Their intelligence coincides with ours.

'Now, moving on, in the last few days we've seen a new development. China has built a chain of artificial islands in the South China Sea, some with airstrips and air-defence. We've detected a build-up of fighter planes and, more disturbingly, of strategic bombers. They have a huge range and a very large payload. There's little reason for them to come so far south.

'We've also seen landing ships diverted to the artificial harbour on Fiery Cross Atoll, probably associated with the recent movement of marines to the base.

'There's an increase in Chinese naval activity in the area and maritime patrol craft have been operating near the coasts of Malaysia and Vietnam.'

Alistair asked, 'CDS, where is the UK Carrier Strike Group at the moment?'

'Well, that's the really disturbing part. The naval activity I've mentioned coincides with the most recent location of the *Prince of Wales* group. We've withdrawn them towards the West where there's greater air cover.

'We also have reports of Chinese troops in Cambodia, ostensibly on exercise, but their deployment seems to be permanent.

'Two further elements are coming to light. Our Sentinel aircraft flying from Diego Garcia over the Andaman Sea have detected yet more naval activity in Myanmar: two frigates and what we believe to be an assortment of transport ships capable of landing PLA marines.

'To complete the picture, our cousins in Australia are deeply concerned by a small Chinese task force heading for the Solomon Islands. A helicopter carrier, escorts and, again, troops. They've detected activity at Honiara airport, which may be a prelude to the PLA air force moving assets there. That is being kept under review.

'Backing this all up, security police and paramilitary troops are being mobilised, the type that might be used after an invasion.

'To sum up, a three-pronged attack on Singapore is a distinct possibility, combined with the operation already planned for Taiwan and a probable diversionary attack on the Solomon Islands.'

Alistair said, 'I think we need to hear from the Navy.'

With that, the First Sea Lord, Sir Philip Cavendish, joined the conversation. 'Thank you, Secretary of State. I can add that the *Prince of Wales* group is now moving into safer waters, but we need to meet this threat head on. We're in constant touch with the Americans and the Australians.'

Alistair cut him off. 'I see. So, we have two Chinese threats, one to Taiwan, that is quite advanced, and another to Malaysia, Singapore and the straits. So, what are we going to do about it?'

The Admiral replied, 'Fortunately, due to advanced intelligence from the Australians, we have been able to use the last few weeks for planning. We're now ready to move. In front of you is the planning document for Exercise Mailfist.

'There are several elements to it. The Carrier Group will remain in the area for the foreseeable future; we have resupply plans in place. We've been working on some other plans based on two objectives.

'Firstly, force protection: we need to guard the Carrier Group from any surprise attack.

'Secondly, deterrence; we failed to deter the Russians in Ukraine and this would be many times worse; we need to demonstrate to China that they cannot succeed militarily. We need to show we are fully committed and act before it's too late.

'We must reinforce our garrisons in Singapore and Malaysia: we still have the cover of our own exercise to do so.

We need to move in air defence; plans for that are underway.

'We also need to work with the Singaporean defence forces to put on a show – something so bold that it makes the Chinese think twice. I have an idea for that.'

Alistair replied, 'Set the wheels in motion. This is a priority. I'll leave it to the Armed Forces Minister to determine the exact scope.'

Amongst all the noise, it was no surprise that a small announcement from the Ministry of Defence received little coverage. The current naval exercise in the Far East would be extended until further notice and would be joined by a number of other assets.

• • • •

While the Ministry of Defence whirled into action, at the other end of Whitehall a very different story was beginning to unfurl.

In Thames House a small group of MI5 officers were going through the lists of Chinese informants supplied by Mei, starting with the most senior.

One of the first to receive a phone call requesting his attendance at a meeting was a Permanent Secretary running a minor department. Confronted with the evidence, he immediately burst into tears. For him, as with many others, it had been a mixture of sex and money. Many years ago he'd been befriended by a female journalist in the pay of the Chinese, providing at first trivial, and then more and more important snippets of information, gradually being sucked into the Chinese net.

It was decided not to prosecute him immediately, but to remove him from the Civil Service and demand a detailed list of all his engagements with the Chinese. Dealing with a civil servant was one thing; a well-known politician was a different matter entirely. There was a full list of backbench MPs, one junior minister and a variety of Party officials and journalists.

The MPs were not prosecuted immediately but told not to attend Parliament and to stand down at the next election. The politician that remained elusive was Robert Lacy, despite many concerns and suspicions he was not on any of the lists, but accepted that he had lost the new Prime Minister's confidence and would stand back until there was time to replace him.

Richard took an interest in how the list was progressing. The one he was waiting for was not any MP from his own Party but the key prize – Malcolm MacIntyre. How would the security services deal with him? He didn't have to wait long to find out. The evening news carried images of counter-terrorist police raiding his house on the outskirts of Edinburgh. There would be no hiding for him: he was to be publicly exposed as an agent of the Chinese state and charged with offences linked to the transportation of weapons into Scotland.

The demise of the Nationalists was one thing, but Richard wanted to know who had killed John McVey. It had been consuming him for weeks. Was the murder somehow linked to Tommy Rosenfield?

57. Spilled Beans

HMP Belmarsh, 18 October

'Mr Rosenfield, when was the last time you spoke to John McVey?' said DI Holly Fenton in an interrogation room at Belmarsh Prison.

'After his garden party on Tuesday, 19 September,' Rosenfield replied coldly.

Rosenfield had been on suicide watch ever since he'd been brought in the day before. Between the self-pitying sobs, he'd promised his inquisitors he'd tell them everything, and so far he'd been true to his word.

'What did you discuss?'

'He rang to tell me that he'd just been given some information about a Chinese spy and potential UK informants, and wondered what he should do about it.'

'And did you tell anyone else about this?'

'Yes, I asked my contact with the Chinese – I was terrified my name might be on it.'

'Did you ask for the info to be retrieved, for John McVey to be killed? Do you know who killed him?'

Rosenfield broke down and sobbed. Only a few days ago he was on the cusp of becoming Prime Minister; now he was in Belmarsh Prison charged with offences that could lock him up for the rest of his days.

'Yes, I panicked, I thought I was about to be discovered. I told my contact where John had the list. I had no idea they'd kill him; I didn't want anything to happen to him. Just the files, they just needed to recover the files.'

'Perhaps it was already too late for you. Perhaps McVey had already read them. What then?'

Rosenfield sobbed. It had all been going so well. The money, the support and the network the Chinese had supplied him with. Like a drug, once he'd accepted the first dose he couldn't say no. Money for polling, donations to think-tanks, and the support the Chinese could provide in all sorts of unexpected ways. They'd managed to increase his profile, oil the wheels of his career. And now here he was, in prison.

The interrogation had been relentless, not just into John McVey's murder but also an anti-terror investigation handled by MI5. The moment one set of questioning stopped, another would begin. When DI Fenton left the cell, she was replaced by an MI5 officer.

'Mr Rosenfield. Your relationship with Robert Lacy, were you an ally of his? Were you aware he was also working for the Chinese Government?' Rosenfield replied.

'Lacy? No I don't think he was, I mean I wouldn't necessarily have known, but I don't believe it, we were competitors, the Chinese wanted me to beat him. Was I wrong?'

'We ask the questions Mr Rosenfield. Now. One last question for today.'

'Mr Rosenfield. Tell me everything you know about Operation Red Ocean.'

Rosenfield looked momentarily surprised.

'Taiwan, Mr Rosenfield,' the officer said slowly and menacingly. 'What do you know of Taiwan and China? What did they tell you? What did they want you to do when you became Prime Minister?'

58. Northwood

Northwood, 18 October

The United Kingdom's Joint Permanent Headquarters at Northwood is an unremarkable building situated in an unremarkable quiet suburb of north-west London. But it is from here that the UK's global naval and military operations are organised.

The nerve centre of the complex is the underground operations rooms, operating twenty-four hours a day. Richard thought it bore some resemblance to a Las Vegas casino, a place where time stood still. Entering, Richard noted the large screens, one now carrying a live satellite stream of what he recognised as Fiery Cross Atoll in the South China Sea.

'Minister, we're almost up and running,' said Lieutenant Commander Caroline De Lille of the Royal Navy, the duty operations controller. 'We have the Australian liaison party here; the commander of Exercise Mailfist is Commodore Fisher, formerly of the HMS *Prince of Wales* strike group, whom you know I believe. We have the latest intelligence on Chinese movements on the screens over there, and our assets are indicated here.'

'All very impressive,' said Richard. 'How much time do we have until the Chinese forces depart for Singapore and Malaysia?'

'We're in close cooperation with our command centre at RMA Butterworth in Malaysia, and of course the Carrier Strike Group, which for now is the main component of Exercise Mailfist. They believe we have five hours.

Commodore Fisher will see you now Minister, if you'll follow me.'

Richard followed De Lille through a maze of corridors before reaching another underground chamber, this one furnished like a board room.

Fisher was already there. 'Good to see you, Minister. I trust you're impressed with our speedy progress. Twelve hours into your new responsibilities and a major new operation – I mean exercise – is already underway.'

Richard asked, 'Could give me some idea as to how the opposing forces are deployed?'

'Certainly; we estimate about 20,000 troops are in place in the Spratly Islands, with strategic bombers and fighter aircraft covering the movements and landings.

'We've a detected a similar force in Cambodia, which we believe is intended for the east coast of the Malay Peninsula. The force in Myanmar is considerable, and could make its way down the west coast of the peninsula, perhaps landing in the Port Dixon area south of Kuala Lumpur, where we have elements of 16 Air Assault digging in.

'The Chinese are also threatening the Solomon Islands; our Australian friends are in the process of inviting themselves there; they have a Canberra-class landing ship with a force of Royal Australian marines on HMAS *Tobruk* escorted by a destroyer heading for the area – we'll see how they get on.'

Fisher looked intently at Richard. 'I appreciate you're only hours into your new job, but I'm duty bound lay out the risks.

'Firstly, we're planning to place our troops in the path of a potential attack by the world's second-largest military – a nuclear power with few scruples.

'We're unclear what we'd need to deter the Chinese. So

far they seem unaware of our plans and capabilities so they'll plough on regardless. The chance of a misjudgement on either side is extremely high.'

Fisher looked at Richard, judging his response. Not detecting any surprise or indecision, he continued. 'There is also a real possibility we may be too late; the delay in reaching a political decision in the UK has been… problematic to say the least. We've done our best to make our forces ready, but there's only so much we can do.'

Richard replied, 'I appreciate that. Can you run me through our deployments? I want everything we can use as a deterrent to be in the area and visible immediately.'

'Of course: our Carrier Group based around the *Prince of Wales* is approaching Singapore, having changed course last night. It will remain in the vicinity of the city as a visible 65,000-tonne deterrent.

'Next, we have 6,000 troops from 16 Air Assault Brigade, who are now ready to embark for a range of bases across Malaysia, including RMA Butterworth on the west coast from where air defence is run. They'll move out to protect key sites we think could be early PLA targets.

'We also have elements of the Royal Marines ready to go. They'll land in Singapore itself and at a Malaysian base in the south of the peninsula – Burkit Lunchu – a major air defence radar site.

'We're also in the process of setting up an air bridge between RAF Akrotiri in Cyprus and Diego Garcia in the Indian Ocean, which we'll use to deliver arms to Diego Garcia, ostensibly for the exercise: anti-ship, tank and air missiles with operators and trainers who will be mostly based at Butterworth.

'I've also managed to get a second carrier into the Mediterranean. HMS *Queen Elizabeth* is within days of the Suez Canal; at full speed she'll be approaching Singapore in about eight days, a rare piece of luck.

'The main deterrent is underwater, however; we now have three Astute submarines nearing the area; the Australians have a similar number split between Malacca and the Lombok Straits. That'll really upset the Chinese.

'Whether it's enough to deter them, I really don't know; we're talking to the Americans, pointing out the dire consequences for them of an accidental Australian/British engagement with the Chinese. We don't want to end up alone. Ideally Uncle Sam would show some stick, but knowing their President, that seems unlikely at the moment.

'However, I do have one more suggestion; it's high risk and you're not going to like it.'

Richard looked up, a concerned look on his face. 'Go on, what is it?'

59. Butterworth

RMA Butterworth, 19 October

Air Vice-Marshal Laurence Chichester, officer in charge at the Butterworth airbase, had had a busy few weeks overseeing the annual Five Powers exercise out in the South China Sea. But his day changed complexion completely when he received an urgent message from RAF Northwood on behalf of the joint commander of Exercise Mailfist. He was to expect the arrival from Diego Garcia of four RAF Globe Master transport planes each carrying 500 troops.

'What on earth is this?' Chichester shouted over to his subordinate. 'What have we done to deserve half the ruddy Pommy army bowling up on our doorstep?' But he was intrigued and a wave of excitement washed through him, something he hadn't felt since organising special operations for Australian troops in Iraq.

A second message from his Australian superiors and the Malaysians told him to expect more transport planes and troops within hours. This was only the beginning. Troops and equipment would be arriving every couple of hours, air defence equipment, missiles.

'A strange kind of exercise,' Chichester thought, but it wasn't his place to question it.

• • • •

In Singapore, the British Military Attaché at the High Commission had arranged an urgent visit to the Singaporean National Security Minister at 7 p.m. He was shown into his office and met with a mixture of surprise and alarm.

'So how may I help you at this hour?' asked the minister.

The attaché produced a folder, 'Five Powers Only' written in large red letters on the front cover.

'We've received some very troubling intelligence, Minister. A Chinese military operation in the Singapore Straits could be underway within hours. This file contains satellite imagery and our best analysis of the situation.'

Within a split second the minister's demeanour had changed completely. 'China? Why? Where are they coming from? Why have the Americans not warned us?'

'There are three main areas of operation. The Americans, I'm afraid to say, believe it's only an exercise, but there are too many elements in place: logistics, casualty-clearing stations etc.

'We're bound under the Durian Pact to consult and coordinate. I'm asking Singapore to accept our offer of an extension of the current military exercises, with some additional elements arriving shortly. We also suggest that Singapore declares a "practice" state of emergency, and calls up its reserves.'

'That's over 300,000 men! That will take some time, and cause massive disruption.'

'We're aware of that,' said the attaché, 'but we don't believe the final decision to invade has been taken just yet; anything that could persuade them otherwise is worth trying.'

'I'll have to speak to the Minister of Defence and the President.'

The next day, while the UK media continued to digest the fact that they had a new Prime Minister, it was quietly reported that the first of nearly 6,000 British troops from

16 Air Assault Brigade had been spotted arriving at Butterworth air base in the north and Bukit Lunchu in the south of Malaysia. Social media was soon awash with clips of British and Malaysian troops closing off beaches and preparing defences.

For Richard, Alistair and Admiral Bell, things had progressed as well as they could hope. The plan to rapidly reinforce the Malay Peninsula was swinging into action, and further reinforcements were on their way to Brunei. But this was only the beginning. For all the theatrics, the British force was small and the Malaysians and Singaporeans ill-equipped.

60. USA

Washington DC, 19 October

Bart Aldridge's China Desk in the United States State Department was in crisis mode. He'd received a constant stream of messages about the situation in the South China Sea from his British and Australian counterparts and had dutifully sent his own analysis to the Secretary of State.

When he received no acknowledgement, he'd tried to confirm his report had even been received. It had been. He'd be contacted if the Secretary of State needed any further information. Then, silence. Next, Bart had called an old contact of his from US Naval Intelligence to see if they knew anything else. Again – nothing. The British, he believed, were so embroiled in their internal politics they were unlikely to raise the matter directly at a higher level, while the Australians were too easy to ignore, having raised the prospect of Chinese expansionism one too many times.

Bart had a problem: how could he get the US politicians to take him seriously? He realised he needed to communicate with them in a manner they understood: via the newspapers. It was time the whole world knew. Not everything – that would be far too obvious – but enough to convince them they needed to pay attention.

He decided to contact a college friend who worked for the *Washington Post*.

Later that day, Bart left his office carrying printed photographs of Chinese landing craft on Fiery Cross Atoll. He'd been in the business long enough to know not to take an electronic copy. He would do this the old-fashioned way.

Crossing Constitution Avenue he entered the open space that stretches from the Lincoln Memorial to the Capitol building some miles to the east. He stopped to get an ice cream from a kiosk in Constitution Gardens and then continued his walk. In his many years working in the State Department he'd rarely been forced to break the rules, and he was apprehensive. Crossing the bridge onto Signers' Island, he spotted his college friend and waved to him.

After a brief conversation Bart handed him the envelope. 'Remember, these didn't come from me. You know the score.'

'Of course, we've done this before.' And with that, Bart changed the topic to mutual friends and finished off his ice cream.

The next day the *Washington Post* led with a satellite image of Fiery Cross Atoll under the headline '**CHINA WAR SCARE**'. Inside, maps showed the Chinese military build-up near Taiwan and Singapore.

Bart ignored the coverage, trying not to draw attention to himself, but he was gratified that the pictures were beginning to consume social media, and news channels were calling up a variety of experts to try to explain what they were seeing. Reactions varied from the professional to the hysterical and partisan. One Republican Senator blamed the build-up and inevitable invasion on the Democrat President.

'If this doesn't get the President's attention, nothing will,' Bart thought to himself.

61. Singapore

Singapore, 19 October

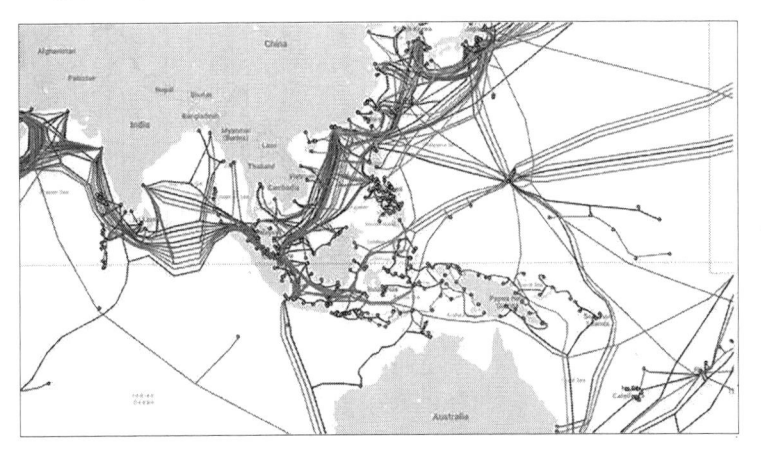

Back in Singapore the news filtering out of the US media that they were the intended target of a Chinese invasion was met with alarm, followed by a Chinese denial and a counter-claim from figures in Beijing blaming anti-Chinese Western scaremongering. By lunchtime everyone was talking about the photographs. The stock market was in free fall with hysterical conversations and media reporting fanning what was already a serious situation.

The President of Singapore attempted to reassure his citizens by addressing them directly. He claimed he had no direct knowledge of a Chinese attack; every defensive measure was being taken and they were talking to their allies in the Five Powers.

That evening, diners in the restaurants along Boat Quay were greeted with the shriek of a squadron of F-35 jets flying low over the city before turning to rise and head up the Singapore River. Startled office workers could make out the RAF roundels on the wings; these were British jets from HMS *Prince of Wales*.

The carrier's surprise return to Singaporean waters was greeted by a growing crowd in Straits View Park, who could make out the hulk of the ship in the dimming light.

That evening the President announced live on air that Singapore had requested help, and thanked the British and Australians for their quick reaction. He then went on to explain that they were seeking reassurances from Beijing, concluding by announcing a full call-up of the army reserves.

That night RAF and RAAF transport planes began to arrive in Changi with new equipment and a ground crew for the British Typhoon interceptor planes that had been based in Diego Garcia.

A little after midnight several of the main internet cables connecting Singapore to Hong Kong and India failed. Somewhere in the Andaman Sea divers working from a Chinese ship had identified and severed the main fibre optic cables, cutting off Singapore's internet from the outside world and shutting down their social media sites.

The following morning the Singaporeans woke up to formations of RAF Typhoon interceptors alongside Australian and British F-35 stealth fighters and Singaporean F-16s circling the city, doing their very best to be seen.

• • • •

Out in the Indian Ocean the nuclear-powered and armed Dreadnought-class submarine HMS *Victorious* was about to come into port, armed with its full complement of sixteen Trident ballistic missiles capable of carrying their 475-kilotonne nuclear warheads over a distance of 7,500 miles, easily bringing Beijing into range.

The crew were excited at their first landfall in many weeks. This was an unusual call for a nuclear submarine; usually they'd keep their whereabouts a closely guarded secret.

The captain signalled to the crew that they'd shortly be surfacing. The submarine made an impressive sight as it broke the tropical waterline, its immense black bulk against the cerulean water lit by a blazing sun. The boat sailed for about an hour on the surface in the direction of the atoll of Diego Garcia that served as a British and American base.

The captain received his first orders: a Royal Navy Coast Guard ship would join them, and they should be aware of a Chinese intelligence-gathering ship twenty miles to their stern. This was unusual and unfortunate; the Chinese usually took little interest in the base.

The captain said to himself, 'Oh well, the Chinese know we're here. But presumably London knew that was a risk when they sent us?'

62. Beijing Reacts

Beijing, 19 October

In Beijing the Central Military Commission was in a state of chaos. Operation Red Ocean had been compromised; it was all over the world's media.

This wasn't a complete disaster; it was expected that news would leak at some point as you can't hide millions of men indefinitely. However, they'd hoped to prevent the West reacting until it was too late for them to make any difference. What really concerned Beijing were reports of British and Australian military planes in Singapore and the announcement of the extension of Exercise Mailfist.

To compound matters, the news that Operation Sleeping Dragon in the UK and Australia had been compromised from within the Ministry of State Security itself had diminished the chances of a low-key response from the West. However, Operation Red Ocean was to continue; it was on time and going according to plan.

General Hu had recently returned from Fiery Cross Atoll to report on the build-up. The boarding of troops onto transport ships was going smoothly and air assets were in place to cover the South China Sea. Cambodia was also proceeding well, with ships rendezvousing as planned.

The operation in Myanmar was being conducted by a separate command and proving more challenging, but Hu felt reasonably optimistic it too was progressing well.

He was increasingly concerned, however, that the Malaysians and Singaporeans appeared to have advanced warning of their plans. The reports of British and Australian troops in Cyprus and Diego Garcia were evidence of this. He'd now received reports from Chinese intelligence that RAF planes had been seen landing on the Malaya Peninsula and that the *Prince of Wales* had changed course and was now in Singaporean waters. He'd been under the impression Exercise Mailfist was over.

Yet the planners were fairly sure Singaporean mobilisation was too late to be effective. The Chinese fleet would be upon them before they were anywhere near ready.

And then there was the question of the British and Australian nuclear-powered submarines. This was unfortunate, but unless they were prepared to use force, it was a risk that could be mitigated.

News from the Indian Ocean that the British had sent a nuclear-armed submarine to the area was something else. However, this was soon dismissed as another 'paper tiger'; everyone knew the British would never use a nuclear weapon to defend Singapore.

The discussion had not reassured General Hu, however, who plucked up courage to suggest they should re-evaluate the mission in light of the new information. No sooner had he spoken than his superior, General He Weidong exclaimed, 'These are mere details. Our orders are clear. We continue with Operation Red Ocean.'

A silence descended as both parties looked to the Vice Chair of the Commission, who was chairing the meeting. 'They are too late and too few; we continue,' he said slowly and deliberately, before adding, 'The General Secretary is adamant: this project must go ahead. Chinese unity is more important than these minor details.'

There was silence. Nobody was going to second guess the President of China.

63. Yangon

Andaman Sea, 19 October

Myanmar was a key ally and client state of China, under the rule of a military junta. A junta so devoid of friends that it could no longer say no to a Chinese request to move its army through its territory. Therefore, over three months, Chinese troops had moved across the border and been stationed in barracks close to Yangon, waiting for Chinese civilian ships to appear to take them on to their final (and secret) destination – the west coast of the Malay Peninsula.

Some were to embark directly from Yangon, while others had made their way down a highway that headed south down the peninsula towards Thailand.

It was here in the numerous inlets of southern Myanmar that a formidable force of PLA soldiers was now boarding a fleet of civilian and military craft, screened by the mountains and the secrecy of the Myanmar junta from prying eyes.

However, a fleet of ships cannot remain hidden forever. And on the same morning that HMS *Prince of Wales* re-entered Singaporean waters, an RAF Poseidon MRA1 maritime patrol aircraft on an urgent mission had flown directly from the UK to Diego Garcia, stopping only to refuel at the British base in Cyprus. Heading north from Diego Garcia the plane arrived off the west coast of Myanmar, its main task to hoover up as much information as it could.

It was not very long before the first Chinese vessels came into view, exiting the inlets off the southern tip of Myanmar, before heading south just outside Thailand's territorial waters and on towards the west coast of the Malay Peninsula and the Butterworth air base.

The RAF Poseidon along with two UAVs launched from Diego Garcia moved to the very edge of Myanmar airspace, feeding images back to Northwood. They were disturbing: Chinese frigates and a small armada of troop carriers, ferries and landing craft carrying light tanks and other vehicles.

Receiving a warning from an accompanying AWACS plane that Chinese fighters were in the area, the Poseidon turned away to the south, leaving the two UAVs to their fate.

Meanwhile another Poseidon landed at Butterworth to refuel, before heading out over the Malaysian jungle to the east and out over the South China Sea towards Cambodia. If China was on the move, Northwood wanted to know.

• • • •

Commander Bennett of the Royal Australia Naval frigate HMAS *Ballarat* had had an uneventful day. On a routine trip from Cairns to Fiji he'd just handed over the bridge and retired to his berth.

There was a knock at the door and his Command Duty Officer entered. 'Sir, we've received new orders: you'd better come and see. Direct from Canberra.'

'Okay, will be up in a second.' He felt a tingle of excitement. What could this be? 'What is it?'

'We've been told to head as fast as possible for Honiara in the Solomon Islands. No real explanation, but it must be serious: they've told us to bring the crew up to readiness.'

'Well, give the order. I'll be up in a moment.'

Moments later the captain was on the bridge. 'We'd better find out what this is all about. Can you signal Canberra? Tell them we've altered course, request further details.'

Shortly afterwards the deck began to tilt upwards as the ship began to change course and pick up speed.

Bennett took the ship-wide microphone. 'This is the captain speaking. As you can tell, we've changed course. We've been ordered to sail to the Solomon Islands. We'll also be conducting a series of exercises over the next few hours, so don't get too comfortable. I'll let you know more in due course.'

Further orders arrived from Canberra: 'Proceed to Honiara at your best speed. Once there proceed to the harbour and await HMAS *Tobruk* and her escort. A Chinese task force is en route to the Solomons, intentions unknown.'

'Well, that's not exactly clear' said Bennett to his Duty Officer. 'Are we going to war with China? With one frigate?'

If the rumours were true, it was time to bring his ship up to the appropriate state of readiness. He sounded the alarm, which rang out over the ship.

'General Quarters! General Quarters! All hands man your battle stations. Set material condition Zebra throughout the ship.'

• • • •

Richard arrived back very early at Northwood to receive the latest update, which painted a depressing picture.

The Chinese fleet sailing from Myanmar had nearly reached the Malay Peninsula. Malaysian forces under cover of Exercise Mailfist had taken up positions to the east and west of the peninsula, reinforced by British and Australian troops who were still arriving around the clock at various airbases via the air bridges.

The command centre at Butterworth now had considerable air assets at its disposal. The Singaporean and Malaysian air forces were active, and the carrier-based planes from HMS *Prince of Wales* were shortly to be met by RAF Typhoons arriving from Diego Garcia. The air bridge via Diego Garcia and Cyprus was now in full swing, bringing in equipment to service the new RAF squadrons.

Richard looked at all of this on the monitors, which showed a vast area of ocean. The Chinese vessels and the increasing number of strategic bombers and fighter escorts were difficult to see, but even to the untrained eye they were relentlessly moving in the same direction.

'This is it, I suppose,' he said to the operations officer. 'They're really going through with it.'

'It looks like that, but we don't know for sure. They haven't made any public statements. We can still hope it's just an exercise.'

'Indeed! But there is one more option we should probably revisit,' said Richard.

'What's that?'

'I was briefed about a new type of missile being carried by HMS *Prince of Wales* and the *Queen Elizabeth*. The CVS401 Perseus, if I remember correctly – the hypersonic anti-ship missile.'

'Yes, but we can't fire on the Chinese vessels. That could mean war, nuclear war.'

'No, not directly at their ships, but a demonstration. We need to put on a show for our Chinese friends – a sign of intent that will be seen around the world. A demonstration of what would happen to them if they continue on their current course. We should extend our exercise to the east of the peninsula. Close off some of the sea and sink a ship, a cargo ship, any ship really. But it should be filmed and broadcast. Something to make them think the Americans will be dragged in.'

64. MV *Penang*

South China Sea, 21 October

The MV *Penang*, a large Malaysian-flagged fishing vessel, was coming to the end of its working day, trawling about twenty miles off the east coast of Malaysia. The skipper had just heard over the emergency frequency that a large exclusion zone had been declared by the military off the Malaysian coast, and it was time to head for port.

They then heard a direct appeal over the radio from the Malaysian Coast Guard ordering them to stay where they were. The skipper slowed the engine and called his crew members to the bridge. 'What's this?!' he asked

The emergency frequency was demanding an acknowledgement, and informed the skipper they'd shortly be boarded for a fisheries inspection.

Half an hour later a Malaysian vessel came into sight, followed closely by the grey silhouette of a small warship. The skipper reduced his engine speed again and asked the crew to check their paperwork. This was unusual.

The coast guard and warship were soon alongside the *Penang*, throwing it into shadow.

'MV *Penang*! This is the Malaysian Coast Guard. You are to be evacuated to a safe distance. Please come up onto the deck and await orders. This area is now unsafe.' They did not sound like they were inviting discussion.

The skipper considered. It wasn't his boat but he was bound to get into trouble if he abandoned it. But what could he do? A small ribbed inflatable was heading for the *Penang* and would soon be alongside. He complied and told his crew to come up on deck and put on their life jackets.

A Malaysian Coastguard official climbed onboard from the inflatable. The skipper was immediately aware that as well as Malaysian Coast Guard officials a group of Europeans were also preparing to board.

'How many people are on board?' asked the senior Coastguard.

'Four,' answered the skipper.

'You'll have to abandon ship and join us. Just one bag per person please; we have very little time.'

The Europeans now boarded the *Penang*. 'Yes, I think this'll do; it'll have to. It's the only boat in the area,' one of them said in a Mancunian accent. 'Set up the camera, will you, and check below deck for anything that needs to be removed.'

The remaining Royal Marines were now on board, going about their work while the crew packed their belongings. Eventually they were beckoned down into the inflatable and taken out to the Royal Navy ship.

As soon as they'd finished, the Royal Marines also climbed down into the inflatable as fast as they could, leaving the *Penang* without a crew.

It was not long before an arc of white water appeared at the stern of the vessels as they pushed their engines to full speed to escape the area. Moments later the fishing vessel slipped out of sight.

'We have about ten minutes. Check the camera's up and running,' said the Marine commander.

'Aye, aye sir. We have one onboard and the drone is working.'

In Northolt the order had been sent out to the HMS *Prince*

of Wales Carrier Group to prepare to fire its new hypersonic Perseus missiles.

A live stream showed an aerial image of a large fishing vessel in the South China Sea. Another screen showed the view from the bridge looking out to sea, while a third showed the missile hatches on the destroyer escort ship attached to the Carrier Group.

'Perfect,' said Richard. 'This is exactly what we need.'

As soon as HMS *Prince of Wales* received its target information, the weapons officer got ready. The missile was to be fired from the Carrier Group now based in the Singapore Straits, all the way over the peninsula to its target within the exclusion zone.

The clock counted down. Then, a live feed from the *Prince of Wales* broke in shortly before the Perseus missile soared from the destroyer's tube and headed skywards. Another feed from a neighbouring ship pictured the missile's course upwards, trailing billows of white smoke behind its bright light. It then turned to the horizontal before speeding up and heading away from the ships, accelerating up to around 3,800 miles per hour on its nearly 200-mile journey to the east.

The feed from a Royal Navy ship to the east of Malaysia picked up the missile moments later as it came down towards the *Penang* at a maximum speed of six times the speed of sound.

The camera on board the *Penang* picked up its last moments before impact. Nobody would have seen it coming. All that was left was a plume of smoke and a few scattered bits of wreckage.

'Get that film out to the media as soon as you can,' said

Richard. 'The caption should read something like "Royal Navy carriers practise with state-of-the-art top-secret hypersonic anti-shipping missiles in South East Asia". That should put the fear of God into them. There's more where this one came from.

'And now for the final part of the plan…'

65. China Military Commission HQ

Beijing, 21 October

In the operations room of China's Central Military Commission in Beijing, the new Minister of State Security, Cai Qi, had just been handed a file containing some rather disturbing information – the result of their electronic intelligence unit's investigation into British political figures.

It was undoubtedly genuine and had taken considerable effort to obtain, a high-level vetting report by the UK Ministry of Defence into the Minister of the Armed Forces, Richard Reynolds MP. Much of the information was already in the public domain, but the Chinese analyst had highlighted a section written by Reynold's psychologist into his mental state. Some years earlier he'd undergone treatment for depression.

'Subject to episodes of depression and euphoria... Bears the hallmarks of an obsession, resulting from an early life episode... Impacted by his grandfather's depression.... The client explained how as a child he had listened to stories from his grandfather about torture and captivity in the Far East. The grandfather blamed himself for surrendering and was obsessed with the bombing of Hiroshima and Nagasaki, which he believed saved his life... the client seems to dwell on these episodes in an unhealthy manner...'

Cai Qi slammed the file down and shouted, 'Are you telling me that the British have a madman obsessed with nuclear weapons in charge of their armed forces?'

An officer replied, 'Comrade, it's perhaps worse than

that. We now know the British have stationed a nuclear-armed submarine within range of China. This Mr Reynolds seems obsessed by Singapore. We already knew he'd lived in Singapore, but his family history there is particularly... complicated. We think there's a danger he could become irrational once Operation Red Ocean is underway.'

Cai Qi thought for a while and then responded quietly, 'We should prepare a report for President Xi. The British appear to have a madman at the helm.'

At that moment a screen in the operations room cut to CNN, where an excited news anchor was rattling off a confused story about a British missile, followed by some footage of a British Dreadnought-class ballistic missile submarine in the Indian Ocean firing a missile in the Indian Ocean, combined with an incoming missile destroying a fishing boat in the South China Sea.

CNN were reporting that the British were furiously denying they'd tested a hypersonic missile capable of delivering a nuclear payload, while also putting out footage of said missile. Maps of the Trident missile's range were displayed, along with Chinese-controlled atolls in the South China Sea and archive footage of UK nuclear tests.

A UK news channel was quoted as saying the missile test had been personally authorised by the Armed Forces Minister, something that was again denied by the Ministry of Defence.

An image of Richard Reynolds then appeared on the screen, immediately recognisable from the file Cai Qi had just read.

With a glint in his eye and seemingly in complete control of the situation, Richard told the cameras, 'We of course have no intention of using nuclear weapons; the submarine deployment is entirely routine. There is no threat to Singapore that would trigger a UK response of this kind, but matters are constantly kept under review and, as usual, we do not comment on matters of the nuclear deterrent.'

The translation was slow to come through but Reynolds' meaning was clear. Cai Qi addressed the room. 'Comrades, either the British have a madman determined to use nuclear weapons against us or they have hypersonic anti-ship missiles in the area. Either way, this would appear to change our calculations.'

• • • •

In Washington the news of a potential Chinese invasion of Singapore followed by a hysterical report claiming the British and Australia planned to counter it with nuclear weapons finally started the gears grinding in the State Department and Department of Defense. Even the President now had little option but to take it seriously; instructions and requests for information rained down on the State Department.

Bart Aldridge was suddenly in great demand, drafting communiqués to the Chinese Government, warning against military action, summoning the Chinese Ambassador and arranging calls with the British to warn them against escalation. British officials were suddenly, to great American concern, very difficult to get hold of. Bart's advice was consistent: the only way to prevent the impending invasion was massive deterrence of a magnitude the British and Australians were struggling to pull off on their own.

By lunchtime the Secretary of State had taken Bart's advice: if the Chinese refused to back down and the British and Australians were determined to stand in their way, the USA was left with no choice. It would have to throw its weight behind deterrence. And with that, combined with media uproar and Congressional hysteria, the President was forced to concur.

Within an hour the US military had swung into action. Out in the Pacific, Carrier Strike Group 5, based in Yokosuka, Japan, was ordered into the South China Sea, while Carrier Strike Group 9 from San Diego was to head for the Solomon Islands to support HMAS *Tobruk*.

This activity was immediately picked up by Chinese intelligence and conveyed to the operations room of the Beijing Central Military Commission, which only added to the gloom. But Cai Qi was still arguing that nothing had really changed; the invasion was to continue and they were only hours from success. President Xi was still in control.

66. Turning Point?

Northwood, 22 October

In Northwood the location of the Chinese ships was being streamed into the operations room. It had been a sobering experience. The amphibious warfare vessels leaving Fiery Cross Atoll were accompanied by a screen of frigates, with a Fujian-class Chinese carrier providing air cover. There were also signs of an increased submarine presence, and a squadron of fighters and strategic bombers.

Satellite imagery of ports in southern China opposite Taiwan also showed a new military build-up, with the remaining amphibious warfare vessels putting out to sea. The invasion of Taiwan seemed imminent.

The force in the Andaman Sea had swung to the south-east upon entering the Malacca Straits and had by now mingled with prepositioned Chinese and other nations' commercial vessels.

• • • •

In the Pacific, HMAS *Ballarat* was now within an hour of Honiara and had been detected by Chinese and Solomon Islands authorities, who were now filling the emergency communications channel with requests for the ship to stop.

Commander Bennett, following instructions from Canberra, politely declined the requests, claiming his ship was undertaking a routine port visit and that he'd be arriving in the harbour. His ship was now at full readiness, its Harpoon anti-ship missiles poised. He had briefed his crew that they'd been ordered to prevent a powerful Chinese force from occupying the archipelago, or at least delay it long enough for the helicopter carrier HMAS *Hobart* and escorts to arrive.

As the Chinese force from Fiery Cross Atoll streamed westwards, it was clear there was very little to stop them. Only one Malaysian submarine was at sea, and the few patrol boats in the South China Sea had been ordered to move towards the coast for their own protection. That was all.

The HMS *Prince of Wales* Carrier Group had now moved into the Straits to better protect itself from long-range Chinese fighters armed with YJ-12 missiles with a range of nearly 350 miles. Commodore John Fisher had brought the group up to full readiness and was receiving detailed information as to Chinese fleet and air assets from an RAF AWACS early-warning craft high above the straits which had arrived from Diego Garcia earlier that day. He was confident that his fleet's radar and anti-aircraft missiles could cope with the multiple threats on the horizon, but he was taking nothing for granted.

As well as Northwood, the impending clash was now being closely monitored in the White House Presidential Emergency Operations Center (PEOC), where Bart had been asked to join the President, the Vice President and the US Chiefs of staff. They were now constantly firing messages to the UK demanding updates and requesting they should de-escalate and remove their ships from the straits pending a diplomatic settlement.

Richard, Alistair and Prime Minister Braithwaite formed part of a select team formulating responses to the Americans. They were grimly aware of the danger of giving the United

States false hope. Their latest response was characteristic:

'The United Kingdom is conducting defensive actions in line with its treaty commitments to defend the Malay Peninsula. Any attack on the Malay Peninsula or on Singapore will be regarded as an attack on the UK and will be met with appropriate and strategic force.'

'Does that include nuclear weapons?' President Harris exclaimed incredulously. 'They want to destroy themselves and us with them? Maybe this Reynolds guy really is mad. And it seems to be catching.'

Bart said, 'That's one explanation Madam President. We suspect it's all a bluff, but it's difficult to tell. Their reply wasn't sent to us on a particularly secure channel, probably on purpose. They wanted the Chinese to hear it.'

'That's one hell of a bluff!' she replied.

Bart continued, 'I suggest we reply on the same channel, explain that we understand the UK position and of course will regard any attack on British or Australian troops in Malaysia as an attack on the USA. We can make sure it's heard in Beijing.'

'So you want us to up the ante on this British bluff? Well, what choice do we have? One last attempt to tell Beijing to turn around. We can't stand by and watch China take over the whole of South East Asia and close the seas to US shipping.'

• • • •

In Northwood the Chinese fleet to the east of Malaysia was beginning to puzzle the operations room. Reports from the AWACS confirmed what had been picked up by the satellites: the fleet had slowed down and was possibly changing course. Shortly afterwards the Poseidon aircraft over the Andaman

Sea confirmed the fleet heading from Cambodia to the northeast of the Malay Peninsula was doing exactly the same.

Shortly afterwards HMAS *Ballarat* came in sight of Honiara and held a position a few miles off the coast blocking the harbour mouth, its radars sweeping the islands for Chinese planes and the approach of the Chinese fleet.

General Hu was in the operations room on an assault ship heading out from Fiery Cross Atoll when the message from Beijing came through. They were to terminate the exercise immediately. It had been a complete success and President Xi sent his personal congratulations to everyone taking part for their exceptional work.

'So that's it,' he thought. 'As if it never happened.'

How close Singapore came to invasion became the subject of huge speculation. The Chinese Government's insistence that it had been a exercise held merely to test military readiness conflicted with sources within the Singaporean Government claiming that it had been a genuine threat. Nobody really knew, and with the internet reconnected, the city soon got back to normal.

The Five Powers exercise continued for a few more months, gradually winding down as the British and Australian troops departed, but not before Richard Reynolds came out personally to congratulate them and thank the crew and captain of HMS *Prince of Wales* and the Royal Marines involved in the destruction of the *Penang*. For Richard, the episode was now at an end.

Postscript

Aberdeenshire, some years later

The stone was light-coloured granite and about four feet tall. It stood in a graveyard overlooking the North Sea north of Aberdeen. It read:

> Lt Col Robert Buchan
> of the Gordon Highlanders
> 2 July 1912 to 17 August 1995
> Rest in Peace

Richard looked down at it, then knelt and cleared away the grass that had grown up around the base.

'Well grandfather,' he said. 'I think you can sleep more easily now. Without you I'd never have visited Singapore and we'd never have discovered the Chinese plans. Indeed, without you the Chinese would never have believed our story. Singapore would probably now be part of Greater China. So, you did your duty then and you've done it again today. You can rest in peace.'

• • • •

The fallout from the aborted attack on Singapore reverberated for weeks. As details emerged of the depth of planning that had gone into the Chinese operation, the denials from Beijing became ever more strident. There had never been an attempt to attack the Straits of Singapore, just a minor exercise that the British were inflating to create negative propaganda against China.

In London however, the official report into Exercise Mailfist was undeniable. The Chinese had fully intended to land in Malaysia and Singapore.

A Singaporean report reached the same conclusion and concluded that British action had been crucial in deterring the Chinese attacks, singling out Richard Reynolds for a commendation. It came as no particular surprise when, six months later, Richard received an invitation to attend Singaporean National Day, on the anniversary of the fall of Singapore on 15 February 1942. This time the presence of a British minister had added poignancy.

Richard dictated his reply to the Singaporean High Commissioner. He would be delighted to attend, but made one particular request which, under the circumstances, he hoped the Government of Singapore could accommodate.

Some weeks later Richard arrived in Singapore and made his way to Raffles, again as a guest of the Singaporean Government, along with an assortment of Royal Navy and Royal Australian Navy personnel. He was now a minor celebrity in the city and had been asked to address the Foreign Affairs Committee of the Singaporean Parliament on the role the British played in the events of earlier that year.

The next day a Singaporean TV crew accompanied him on a walk from the hotel to Fort Canning. On the way he spoke to them about his grandfather, how he'd suffered in the Second World War, how he'd blamed himself for the surrender to the Japanese.

Reaching Fort Canning, they descended into the museum and the room where that meeting had taken place in 1942.

There, the TV crew set up their cameras next to a newly made likeness of Richard's grandfather.

'When I visited last year, I thought my grandfather didn't look quite right. I'm so grateful that the museum can now show him as he really was.'

THE END